W9-AZZ-273

BUNNY BLOOD

The cousins paused at the open door, contemplating the murder scene in somber silence. A noise which seemed to emanate from the men's room across the hall made both women jump. Then stealthy Norma Paine emerged with Wilbur's rabbit suit over her arm.

"Norma!" Judith cried. "What's the matter, is the ladies' room out of order?"

"Oh, no," Norma replied, forcing a laugh. "I was retrieving Wilbur's costume. It has to be back at Arlecchino's by nine o'clock or they charge double." With a fixed smile, she nodded at both cousins. "I must run, I've only got an hour." Lowering her head, she brushed past Judith and Renie, heading for the school hall.

"Arlecchino's is all of a mile away," Renie grumbled. "What's she going to do, put the suit on and hop over there?"

"Maybe she's going to take it to the dry cleaners first," Judith replied. "Didn't you notice, coz? A new color has been added to Wilbur's purple and green ensemble." She arched an eyebrow. "Dark crimson. Not at all an Easter shade."

Other Bed-and-Breakfast Mysteries by
Mary Daheim
from Avon Books

BANTAM OF THE OPERA
DUNE TO DEATH
FOWL PREY
JUST DESSERTS

Coming Soon

A FIT OF TEMPERA

Avon Books are available at special quantity discounts for bulk purchases for sales promotions, premiums, fund raising or educational use. Special books, or book excerpts, can also be created to fit specific needs.

For details write or telephone the office of the Director of Special Markets, Avon Books, Dept. FP, 1350 Avenue of the Americas, New York, NY 10019, 1-800-238-0658.

HOLY TERRORS

MARY DAHEIM

AVON BOOKS ◆ NEW YORK

If you purchased this book without a cover, you should be aware that this book is stolen property. It was reported as "unsold and destroyed" to the publisher, and neither the author nor the publisher has received any payment for this "stripped book."

HOLY TERRORS is an original publication of Avon Books. This work has never before appeared in book form. This work is a novel. Any similarity to actual persons or events is purely coincidental.

AVON BOOKS
A division of
The Hearst Corporation
1350 Avenue of the Americas
New York, New York 10019

Copyright © 1992 by Mary Daheim
Published by arrangement with the author
Library of Congress Catalog Card Number: 91-93029
ISBN: 0-380-76297-8

All rights reserved, which includes the right to reproduce this book or portions thereof in any form whatsoever except as provided by the U.S. Copyright Law. For information address Donald MacCampbell, Inc., 12 East 41st Street, New York, New York 10017.

First Avon Books Printing: April 1992

AVON TRADEMARK REG. U.S. PAT. OFF. AND IN OTHER COUNTRIES, MARCA REGISTRADA, HECHO EN CANADA.

Printed in Canada.

UNV 10 9 8 7 6 5 4 3

To Dale and Lorraine,
who make the Good Neighbor Policy work.

ONE

JUDITH GROVER MCMONIGLE put an ice pack on her head and sucked on a cough drop. She hated Lenten fast days. Self-denial was no problem; coercion was. Fasting wasn't voluntary, even in the contemporary Church. Not being able to eat between meals never failed to make Judith absolutely ravenous. Any other time of the year, she could go for the better part of a busy day and not so much as think about food. But come Lent, she always got a headache and a sore throat, and felt weak at the knees. It was illogical, and therefore out of character. Judith sucked the cough drop so hard that it stuck to the roof of her mouth.

Her headache wasn't helped by the sound of her mother, who had thumped her walker into the living room. "Why are you wearing a turban?" she demanded in a raspy voice. "You some kind of swami? It's Good Friday. Why aren't you in church?"

"I was," said Judith, with a glance at the grandfather clock in the corner of the room. "It's three-thirty. I just

1

got back from Stations of the Cross. We had it out on the playground."

"The playground? What did they do, use home plate for the Tomb?" growled Gertrude Grover, whose chartreuse and lavender housecoat was misbuttoned. "That knothead of a pastor at Star of the Sea has some of the daffiest ideas!"

Judith shifted the ice bag on her prematurely gray hair and kicked off her shoes. "It was arranged by the school kids. We formed a procession inside the church, then went outside. Prayerfully."

"Nuttily. That's the doing of that nitwit principal, Quinn McCaffrey, you can bet your butt on it. Whoever heard of a Catholic school being run by a man instead of a nun?" Gertrude was still looking for her cigarettes, but found only a couple of old garters. Disgusted, she tossed them onto the coffee table between the matching sofas that flanked the fireplace. "Imagine, *Mister* McCaffrey, instead of Sister Mary Joseph or Mother Immaculate! It's all over, two thousand years down the drain. Might as well be a Lutheran or a Baptist or a Hottentot. Being a Catholic meant something in *my* day. It's a good thing I'm too crippled to go to church any more."

"You still go to bingo, you old fraud," Judith murmured, stretching out her long legs on the coffee table and hoping that Gertrude was too deaf to hear her riposte.

"Bingo?" Gertrude's little eyes bulged. "Don't tell me they're having bingo during Holy Week! Did I miss it?"

"No, Mother." Judith sighed. "I said it was nice that the Ringos brought you Holy Communion every week."

"Hunh. Those old saps." Gertrude thumped the walker on the dark green Oriental rug. "That's another thing, phonies like the Ringos running around Heraldsgate Hill handing out Holy Communion like Girl Scout cookies! I remember when I was in the Mothers' Club with Clara Ringo and she was so lazy she went to Begelman's Bakery and *bought* cupcakes for the bake sales instead of making them herself like the rest of us. Then she'd lie about it.

Bragged about her frosting, too. And then her and that lunkhead of a husband practically put on halos when Father Hoyle slaps a title on them like eucalyptus ministers!"

"*Eucharistic* ministers," Judith corrected, wondering why her throbbing head didn't just fall off and roll out the French doors.

But Gertrude, already in full spate, paid no heed. "And another thing, it used to be that nobody stirred a stump from Holy Thursday until Easter morning. No cards, no radio, no moving pictures. Zip. Look at me, I'm giving up my afternoon of bridge for Good Friday!" She made it sound as if she'd cut off her ears and offered them up for the hearing impaired. "But with your so-called modern generation, it's business as usual, make a buck, bring on the paying guests! You didn't do that last year!"

Judith didn't bother to remind her mother that the previous Easter had fallen in late March and that her bed-and-breakfast hadn't yet been booked every weekend. It had been just two years since Judith had opened the doors of her old family home in its refurbished state as Hillside Manor. In a cul-de-sac halfway up the south slope of Heraldsgate Hill, the location was ideal, with its neighborhood atmosphere and proximity to the city's downtown area. But building up a clientele had taken time and energy. Rather than taint Gertrude's argument with facts that she'd dismiss out of hand, Judith opted to defend herself on different grounds.

"You know perfectly well the guests who are coming for the weekend aren't regular customers. We're helping the Rankers with the overflow from their family reunion." Judith's rebuttal merely diverted her mother into other channels, this time a diatribe on having an Easter vigil Mass Saturday night instead of waiting until Sunday morning. "How do they figure?" she ranted. "Christ rose from the dead so He could hide the Easter baskets? What a bunch of wackos!"

A persistent knock at the back door saved Judith from a fruitless attempt to explain Vatican II to her mother. Ice pack in place, she angled around Gertrude's walker and went out through the dining room and kitchen to the narrow rear entry hall. Arlene Rankers stood on the back porch, carrying a picnic hamper.

"I brought some snacks," she announced in her breezy, outgoing manner, then paused on the threshold, staring at Judith. "Goodness, why are you wearing a beret?"

"I've taken up painting," replied Judith, stepping aside to let Arlene get by. "Snacks for what?"

Arlene made room for the hamper on the cluttered dinette table. "For the relatives, should they get hungry. Tuna spread, crab balls, deviled shrimp, smoked oysters, salmon mousse, barbecued trout." She ran a hand through her red-gold curls. "Oh, and crackers, of course."

Judith eyed the labeled containers covetously. It was clear that the Rankers's relatives weren't fasting. "I thought they weren't going to eat here," remarked Judith, taking off the ice bag and tossing it into the sink. She and Arlene had struck a bargain the previous month: The eight cousins, nephews and nieces who couldn't fit into the Rankers's house next door would stay at Hillside Manor for the two nights of the family reunion. Arlene had offered to pay the going rate at Hillside Manor, but Judith had insisted that after all these years, any relatives of the Rankers were like family. She wouldn't dream of taking money. Arlene proved equally obdurate, but allowed that since the group would eat all their meals with the Rankers, they should compromise. Relenting, Judith suggested charging half price. Arlene countered with the suggestion that they pay for the first night and get the second one free. The women had finally agreed, and at least an hour had passed before Arlene's convoluted logic had dawned on Judith.

"They might want to nibble." Arlene shut the lid on the hamper and gave Judith her wide, winning smile. "Besides, most of this is left over from Emily Tresvant's funeral reception Wednesday. Wasn't it lovely?"

Judith wasn't sure if Arlene was referring to the food or

the funeral. But after over twenty years of friendship with her neighbor, she opted for the latter. "Very nice. I still don't think I paid you enough to help me cater the reception."

Arlene held up a hand. "Nonsense! Before you started catering events up at Star of the Sea this year, Eve Kramer and I did our bit for free. Don't ask me why she wouldn't pitch in for poor Emily—Eve may be a trial, but she's basically good-hearted. I don't think she and Kurt even went to the funeral."

Arlene's well-defined mouth puckered with disapproval. Kurt Kramer was the parish business manager; Eve owned an antiques and needlework shop on top of the Hill. Judith recalled that until his early retirement at age fifty the previous year, Kurt had been the comptroller for Tresvant Timber. At the time, there were no rumors of bad feelings between Kurt Kramer and Emily Tresvant. But it wasn't impossible; during the fifteen years the Kramers had put four children through Star of the Sea, the couple's lack of tact and critical natures had earned them the nickname of The Prickly Pair.

"As far as I'm concerned," continued Arlene, once more at her most benign, "it was the least I could do when Phyliss got sick."

Judith made a face at the mention of her ever-ailing cleaning-woman-cum-laundress. Phyliss Rackley's ailments, real or imagined, were acquiring legendary proportions. To be fair, when Phyliss worked, she was diligent and thorough. But somehow her "spells" always seemed to occur when Judith needed her most. "She's not keen on Catholic occasions," conceded Judith, "but at least she's stopped trying to convert me into a Pentecostal."

"Frankly," confided Arlene, "I thought she'd love Emily's funeral. She kept house for her years ago, until they had a falling out. But Emily was hard to please, rest her soul. I'm so glad for Sandy and John."

Once again, Judith was having trouble following Arlene's erratic train of thought. Or maybe the headache was dulling her wits. But she caught on to Arlene's meaning. "Yes, the inheritance will certainly come in handy," Judith said, hoping to strike some middle ground in the conversation. "But it's a shame Emily died so soon after they moved out from the East. Of course, she had been ill for a long time. But I gather the Frizzells' kids never got to meet their great-aunt."

"No." Arlene's face, still pretty in middle age, took on a mournful expression. "I'm sure it was a great sorrow to her. They're both in boarding school, somewhere in New England. No doubt Emily helped with their tuition. I expect they'll be out this summer. Money can't be an obstacle for John and Sandy now." Her raised russet eyebrows were fraught with meaning.

Judith inclined her head. John Frizzell's windfall was the talk of Heraldsgate Hill. He'd already given notice at Eve Kramer's Old As Eve Antiques where he'd worked as her assistant for the past few months. Emily Tresvant, a spinster and the sole surviving child of a timber baron, had left her enormous fortune to her late sister's only son. As far as anyone knew, the only other beneficiary was Our Lady, Star of the Sea Parish. Judith said as much.

"Oh, yes," agreed Arlene, oozing confidentiality, "Father Hoyle is just thrilled! Didn't you notice how he was all smiles at the funeral?"

Judith hadn't, and wondered at Arlene's powers of observation. Bad taste was not part of Francis Xavier Hoyle's repertoire. "We could do with some improvements at SOTS," Judith temporized, using the nickname that had been attached to the parish somewhere back in the mists of time. "The carpeting is pretty threadbare, and the statue of Our Lady over the entrance has lost its nose."

Arlene bristled. "Do you know that Sister Bridget blamed our Matthew for that? She accused him of taking potshots with a B.B. gun at the Blessed Virgin! Imagine!"

Involuntarily, Judith glance up at the kitchen window where she had finally replaced the B.B.-shattered pane. Although Matthew was now a college sophomore, in his younger days he'd shot up everything in the neighborhood, at least as far as Judith could tell. She didn't see why Our Lady should have been left out, but made no further comment.

"Of course boys will be boys," Arlene said with a little jut of her chin. "After all, you know what kind of stunts Mike used to pull."

Judith did, but the reference to her only son rankled. "The latest one is that he won't be here for Easter," she blurted. Seeing Arlene's blue eyes widen, Judith tried to speak more calmly. "He's going to be with his girlfriend's family. They live about forty miles from campus on a wheat ranch in the Palouse."

"Kristin?" Arlene watched Judith nod. "I remember her from Christmas. Big girl. Blond."

"Strong. Like ox," agreed Judith. "She's majoring in forestry, too. I think she wants to be a redwood." Noting Arlene's semi-shocked expression, Judith turned repentant. "Sorry, I really don't know her very well. Kristin's the strong, silent type, but I'm sure she's a terrific girl. At least Mike seems to think so."

"Well, that's all that matters," soothed Arlene, starting for the door and ignoring the fact that she had fought her own children tooth-and-toenail over their various romantic attachments. "Carl and I are off to the airport to pick up the contingent from Omaha. Meagan is driving up from Oregon. Mugs had a fight with her husband and came over this afternoon. C.J.'s car broke down, so he and Matt are taking the bus from State." In reeling off four of her five children's return to the nest, Arlene's awkward pause testified to her sympathy over Mike's absence. "Kevin's going to get the Fargo bunch on his way home from work. They should be over here around seven-thirty, but they'll eat with us if they didn't get dinner on the plane."

Judith was expressing agreement when the phone rang in the kitchen. She waved Arlene off and picked up the receiver. Arlene paused just long enough to let in Sweetums, Judith's reprehensible cat.

Speaking in her most professional manner, Judith ignored Sweetums, who was weaving in and out of her legs in an uncharacteristic display of affection. At the other end of the line, she heard Sandy Frizzell's husky voice with the East Coast accent that somehow grated on Judith's ear.

"John and I wanted to thank you again for putting on such a wonderful reception," said Sandy. "Everything was very nice. Aunt Emily would have approved."

Emily Tresvant's heavenly stamp was duly noted by Judith, who had the feeling the testy old girl would have found something to gripe about, even at her own funeral. "I'm glad," said Judith, wishing Sweetums would stop rubbing against her in that annoying manner. "I only started my catering business in February, you know."

"You're very good at it," said Sandy with that deep voice that made Judith wonder if she had been a heavy smoker. Like Gertrude. The mental comparison was jarring. "In fact," Sandy went on, "I understand you're doing the children's Easter egg hunt up at church tomorrow."

"That's right," said Judith, nudging the cat with her foot. Sweetums got the message and slunk off into the dining room. "But it's basically a potluck. The parents are bringing most of the lunch. I'm just supervising . . ." She stopped cold, aware that something soft and wet was clinging to her stockinged foot. "Aaaack!" she screamed, then clasped her hand over the mouthpiece. A dead mouse reposed on her toes. Judith kicked out, sending the furry corpse across the kitchen. Images of a parboiled Sweetums flashed before her aggravated eyes.

"Mrs. McMonigle?" Sandy's anxious voice called out from the receiver. "Are you there? Are you all right? Is this an inconvenient time?"

"No. Yes. I mean, I just hurt my foot." Judith emitted a weak laugh. "A tack, I guess. Now—what were we saying?"

There was a slight pause at the other end, presumably while Sandy Frizzell collected her interrupted thoughts. "About the egg hunt. I know we don't have children in the school, but everyone has been so nice to us since we got to Star of the Sea. Especially with the funeral and all, and I thought that we'd like to contribute something for tomorrow. A sheet cake, maybe? I could call Begelman's right now."

"Oh." Judith averted her eyes from the dead mouse and held her head. "That's very kind. Sure, that's a great idea. Thanks very much."

In something of a daze, she answered Sandy's queries about time of day and numbers of participants and appropriate decoration. At last, sounding pleased with herself, Sandy hung up. Judith gritted her teeth, tore off a paper towel, and scooped up the mouse. Still in her stockinged feet, she marched outside to the garbage can by the driveway and dumped the poor animal inside. A glance at the open toolshed door informed her where Sweetums had found his prey.

"Damn," breathed Judith, "I hoped that wretched cat didn't knock Dan over."

Keeping to the narrow path that led between house and toolshed, Judith didn't pause to admire the deep purple of the gnarled old lilac tree or the apple blossoms that were about to bud in what was left of the old Grover orchard. She'd already picked the best of the daffodils and tulips to put in the guest bedrooms and the living room. Next to the toolshed, a blush-pink rhododendron was opening up. Judith reached inside the door and switched on the single bare bulb.

There, on the top shelf between a container of weed killer and a carton of snail bait, stood the boot box that contained the ashes of her late husband. Judith sighed with relief. One of these days she'd have to find a more suitable resting place for Dan McMonigle.

Like the local unemployment office.

TWO

THE ONE SANCTUARY that Judith could seek where food wouldn't tempt her was the hair salon. As a hedge against temptation, she had called Chez Steve the previous Monday to make an appointment, preferably in the morning. But they were already booked solid on the eve of the upcoming holiday weekend. Only a phone call around noon reporting a last-minute cancellation had saved the day. Judith could get in with Steve himself at four-thirty. It was perfect: The timing would see her through the dinner hour, which meant she'd not only miss Gertrude's dreaded clam fritters, but be able instead to have a hearty snack before bedtime.

In the front entry hall, she paused at the oval mirror with its Della Robbia frame. As ever, she was dissatisfied with her image. The features were strong and straight, the dark eyes still sparkled, the skin tone was really quite good. But the premature gray hair added extra years. Dan had refused to let her use color when the first white strands had shown up over twenty years earlier, soon after their marriage. Maybe, just maybe, she should get a rinse . . .

In her mind, she visualized the date on the calendar: April 13. After more than a year, only two more weeks to wait. Was it really possible to get a second chance at happiness? She smiled to herself, then blinked at her reflection. Good Friday. Friday the thirteenth. Judith made a face. She really wasn't superstitious. Besides, what could go wrong this late in the day? Of course the Rankers's relatives hadn't arrived yet . . .

"What are you looking at?" Gertrude rasped, clumping into the entry hall. "Just standing there won't improve your looks, kiddo. You'd better get your butt in gear or you'll be late at that fancy beauty parlor of yours. I'll bet they charge by the minute, like a taxi. By the way, Sweetums puked on the rug."

"Oh, swell!" Judith mentally cursed the cat and hurried into the pantry to get some rags. She wished Sweetums had simply expired on the spot. But when she got to the living room to clean up the mess, the cat was curled up on the window seat in a halo of sunlight. Judith's urge to throttle the animal ebbed temporarily.

Ten minutes later and with no time to spare, she was parked on the street a half block from Chez Steve in the heart of the neighborhood's business district. Surrounded by half a million people, yet isolated from the bustle, Heraldsgate Hill was something of an anomaly, a small town inside a big city. Its residents thought of themselves as Hill dwellers first, urban citizens second. Their world was self-contained, and it was rumored that a least a dozen natives had never crossed the big bridge that separated the Hill from the rest of the metropolitan area.

Heraldsgate's main commerical section ran along the flat across the top of the Hill for about a half mile. Tucked away between a dental lab and an insurance office, Chez Steve overlooked a small bricked courtyard that had once been the bottom of a stairwell in a much larger building. But fire had gutted the place ten years earlier, and an ingenious architect had come up with the idea of building around, rather than over, the ruined core. The result was a charming but expensive little hideaway where neighborhood residents of both sexes could be cut and clipped in more ways than one.

For once, however, Judith was not going to carp about Chez Steve's exorbitant prices. Instead, she handed herself over to the owner/operator and let him study her closely in the mirror. "Jeez, Judith, you could use just about everything we've got," Steve said in the gravelly voice that had once served him as a carnival barker after he'd given up his pro wrestling career. "You look like bird crap."

Judith was used to his frank manner. "Thanks, Steve. I'm half starved, the cat threw up, and Mother's going to make clam fritters which will stink up the entire house just before guests arrive from Omaha."

"Omaha," mused Steve, tossing Judith's limp curls this way and that. "I wrestled there a couple of times. Once, it was a tag-team match with Awesome Baker. You know him, the guy who owns Scooter's Delivery Service?"

Judith did. "What do you think about a rinse? I want to look less like James Monroe, and more like Marilyn."

"I don't know why, they're both dead." Steve grabbed a color chart from the counter. "Here, have a look. What'll it be? Amber Passion? Russet Roses? Tequila Sunrise?"

Judith studied the chart. She was sure that everyone in the busy glass- and chrome-accented salon was watching her make this revolutionary decision. "Gee—they all look sort of . . . obvious. My own hair used to be more like this one." She tapped the color key for Earthy Ebony.

Steve glanced at the chart, then at Judith's image in the mirror. He twirled her around in the chair with one finger. "Could be a bit harsh on you. Natural's in. Not that I go by what a bunch of glitzy lamebrains say on the industry grapevine, but at least that's one fad that makes sense." Having disposed of the national competition, Steve pointed to a frost sample. "Here's a compromise you could live with—Silver Streak. We leave half of it natural and color the rest Sable Satin."

Judith considered. Maybe Steve was right: A complete change would be too radical. She could hear what Gertrude would say: "Hussy," "tart," and "floozy" sprang to mind. "Okay," she agreed, "let's go with the frost job."

Steve was still regarding her in the mirror. "It'll take another hour if you're going to get a perm, too. If I were you, I wouldn't do both at the same time. You'll end up looking like Norma Paine's wire-haired terrier, only taller."

Judith decided to go with Steve's advice and get just the frost job. The Rankers's relatives were due in around seven-thirty; she didn't want to miss their arrival. She still had another two weeks in which to get the permanent. Judith was sinking back into the chair, waiting to be trundled off to the shampoo bowl, when she realized that the woman on her left who had previously been covered by a towel was Kate Duffy. Kate, whose good works with Star of the Sea were legendary, was midway through a cut of her honey-colored curls. In charge of the shears was Ginger, Steve's buxom wife, who was rumored to have been a world-class tassel-twirler in her carnival days.

"Judith," exclaimed Kate in her breathless voice. "I don't have my glasses on. I wasn't sure it was you!"

"It almost wasn't," responded Judith, smiling at Kate in the mirror. "I got in only because somebody canceled."

"That was Sandy Frizzell," said Kate. "She called Steve and said she hadn't had her hair professionally cut in years. It's quite long, you know, and now that she and John have come into money, she really ought to treat herself, but at the last minute she begged off." Kate's sweet face clouded over. "Maybe she's grieving too much."

Recalling that Sandy looked not unlike a sheepdog with her heavy mane of blond locks, Judith kept her opinion to herself. "Well, Sandy's lack of nerve is my good luck. How have you been, Kate?"

Kate allowed Ginger to snip at her bangs before answering. "Oh, fine, wonderful. I've been praying for the

Frizzells," she said, her sweet face turning appropriately pious. "They're going to need a lot of intercession."

"For what?" Judith inquired, swinging around in the swivel chair so that she was talking to Kate instead of her reflection. "They've got everything now that Aunt Emily kicked the bucket."

Kate cringed at Judith's candor. "But that's it, don't you see? They need to be guided in the most beneficial way to use their inheritance. There's so much good they can do! Shelters for the homeless, aid to unwed mothers, a parish food bank, live-in help for the elderly—why, I can think of a dozen projects I've been trying to establish all these years, but never could get Father Hoyle or his predecessor to come up with the funding." She leaned forward as Ginger fluffed up the curls at her neck. "Think of it, Judith, all that money for social action! How would you spend it?"

"Well, I'd start by giving Steve cash instead of using my Visa card, then I'd pay off the plumber and the electrician. After that, maybe I'd buy a new Mix Master. If I had enough left."

"Oh, Judith!" Kate giggled, her dimples deep and even. "You're such a sketch! Really," she went on, lowering her breathless voice, "we're talking about big money here. *Very* big money. Mark says it's millions."

Judith shrugged. "Millions, billions, jillions—it doesn't mean anything to me when it's not mine. Maybe they'll match Emily's bequest and give some of their own to the church, too."

But Kate was dolefully shaking her head, much to the chagrin of Ginger, who was trying to arrange the curls at her client's temple. "Sandy is very homesick for New York, I hear. She wants to go back. And who can blame her? I thought it might help if she got more involved in the community, especially in the parish, but just the other day Mark told me that Father Tim had called to ask if Sandy would help decorate the sanctuary for Easter, and John answered and had the most awful fit of temper! Poor Father

Tim—he's going to get the wrong impression of our parishioners." Eluding Ginger's ministrations, Kate placed a hand at her breast and leaned toward Judith. Judith's sympathies lay not only with Ginger, but with Timothy Mills, Star of the Sea's new assistant pastor. She had no chance to say as much, for Kate kept right on talking: "We really must do our very best to make Tim feel welcome, what with so few priests around these days. I ask the Holy Spirit at least three times a day to inspire young people. As long as they have a true vocation, of course," she added hastily, then reverted to her original subject. "But Mark consoled Tim and told him he thought John was very protective of Sandy. You know my husband, he's the soul of tact." Kate's eyelashes fluttered as the frustrated Ginger wielded a tall can of hairspray with an expression that suggested she wished it were Mace.

If nothing else, it occurred to Judith, Kate was right about her spouse—Mark Duffy, who owned a film production company that specialized in TV commercials, was an eminently tactful—and charming—man. As for John Frizzell, Judith didn't know him well enough to comment. Instead, she steered the subject into slightly different channels: "Whatever became of John Frizzell's father?"

Kate took a hand mirror from Ginger and studied the finished product. "I'm not sure," she said. "He and Emily's sister, Lucille, were divorced early on, when John was a baby. I think his name was Edgar Frizzell, but I only met Lucille once, after she came back to the family home to live with Emily. Lucille died quite young, you know."

"I remember." Judith turned solemn. Lucille Tresvant Frizzell's death had occurred the same week Judith and Dan were married. In fact, Lucille's funeral had been scheduled around the Grover-McMonigle nuptials. The inconvenience had not set well with Emily Tresvant. Gertrude, however, had gloated. "I don't remember John, though. Did he come to his mother's funeral?"

"I'm not sure." Kate frowned into the mirror, then broke into a sunny smile and looked up at Ginger. "I like it. You do such a nice job, Ginger, dear. Mark will be pleased." Accepting Ginger's reciprocal words of appreciation, Kate turned back to Judith. "When Lucille died, Mark and I were back in Wisconsin, visiting his relatives. We hadn't been married very long. You know, we've asked Sandy and John over to dinner twice since they moved here, but both times they had to cancel. Sandy is delicate, I'm afraid. I suppose that's why he takes such good care of her."

Steve had returned, now ready to shampoo Judith's hair. "You two yapping about the Tresvant dough?" He saw Judith's little smirk and Kate's diffident nod. "They won't spend it here. The old broad had somebody come to the house to fix her hair, and that niece or whoever she is must cut hers with a meat cleaver. I've seen her old man go into Snuffy's Cut-Rate Cut-Rite next to Porco's Pizza at the bottom of the Hill." Steve frowned, his leathery face creasing like an old catcher's mitt. Judith gathered that he took the Tresvant-Frizzell rebuff as a personal affront.

"Sandy and John only got here this winter," said Judith, trying to get comfortable over the sink. "They came from New York."

"New York!" Steve all but spat in the stainless steel basin. "I wrestled there a few times, at the old Garden. Jeez, what a pit! There I was, walking along Forty-third Street one afternoon when . . ."

Judith allowed Steve's reminiscences to lull her into a semi-somnolent state. It was such a luxury to let someone else take care of her after all those years of ministering to Dan McMonigle, of being the sole wage earner, of trying to keep up with the housework, the cooking, the chores. When Dan died four winters ago at the age of forty-nine, Judith had been more relieved than grief-stricken. He'd been a good father to Mike, but he'd been a rotten husband to Judith. Moving back in with Gertrude had seemed like the only sensible solution at the time. After the first two weeks of listening to Gertrude's rasping comments, Judith realized it was the second worst idea she'd ever had—the first, of course, being her marriage to Dan McMonigle. But then she'd gotten the wild idea of turning the capacious old family home into a bed-and-breakfast. Gertrude told her she was cracked. Cousin Renie thought it was a stroke of genius. Between them, they had talked Gertrude, Renie's mother Deb, and their mutual uncle, Al Grover, into selling the house to Judith. To Judith's amazement and Gertrude's chagrin, Hillside Manor had become a success. In recent months, she had been elated to receive recommendations in three national travel guides. In her own, small way, Judith felt as if she'd finally hit the big time.

Yet Judith would have been the last person—except maybe for her mother—to give herself the credit she deserved. More than the gracious old house and its tasteful, yet eclectic appointments; more than the hearty, delicious breakfasts; more even than the excellent location with its splendid view of downtown, bay, and mountains; more than all these parts was the sum of Judith McMonigle. A warm, genuine human being, she had a knack with people that raised hospitality into an art form. But Judith persisted in attributing Hillside Manor's prosperity to hard work and good luck.

Only half watching Steve pull strands of hair through the cap on her head, Judith mulled over the changes in her life. She hadn't been able to afford anything but a home permanent in all her years of marriage. She'd worked two jobs, during the day in her chosen profession as a librarian and at night as bartender for the Meat & Mingle. Looking back, Judith knew it had been a rough life, but at the time, she'd been too caught up in just getting from one day to the next to feel sorry for herself. In the four years since Dan had died, she'd been frantically busy, but her emotional energies hadn't been so drained. She'd been able to reflect, and had come to the conclusion that enduring her unhappy marriage had given her strength. After all, hadn't somebody once said that anything that didn't kill you had to be good for you? Or words to that effect, mused Judith, her eyelids beginning to droop.

The reverie was broken by a waspish voice at Steve's elbow. Eve Kramer, her artfully tousled curls newly done in what Judith judged to be Earthy Ebony, had paused on her way out of the salon. "Do either of you know anybody who wants a job and has some knowledge of antiques? John Frizzell quit on me. He won't work past six p.m. today, and he's picking up his final check tomorrow. You'd think he could at least have offered to stay on until I found someone else," she complained, rummaging in her over-sized snakeskin shoulder bag for her car keys. As usual, Eve carried with her several skeins of thread, scissors, and her latest piece of stitchery. "I've never understood how acquiring money can wipe out consideration for others," she asserted, finally producing a set of keys on an enormous silver ring.

Steve didn't break stride in plastering something that looked like peach yogurt on Judith's strands of hair. "The idle rich, huh? Wish I had that problem."

"It's my problem that he's leaving," said Eve, a pout puckering her deceptively piquant face. "John was very good. His references from New York were excellent, and he'd worked for one really first-class antiques dealer. He won't be easy to replace. I need someone thoroughly familiar with old pieces."

"How about Mother?" suggested Judith, but noted that while Steve chuckled, Eve was not amused. "Actually, I can't think of anybody offhand, but I'll try to keep my ears open," Judith amended.

"Thanks, I'd appreciate it," Eve said in her abrasive manner. "He's an ingrate, in my opinion. Experience or not, he would have had a rough time getting a job in this town where every pampered dilettante thinks he or she is an expert if they can tell a Sèvres tea service from a Bozo the Clown cookie jar. The antiques business is inbred and just as decadent as European nobility." She adjusted the shoulder bag and flipped a Hermés scarf over the collar of her black trenchcoat. Eve, as always, was expensively groomed. After getting her children virtually raised, she had discovered that a degree in Renaissance art history was worthless outside of academia. Disinclined to teach, she had parlayed her elegant needlework into a business that embraced not only hand-stitched footstool covers and pillowcases and small tapestries, but the furnishings to accommodate them. After less than two years, she had become the Hill's authority on antiques. And, like Judith, she had proved that middle-aged women could become successful entrepreneurs. Judith wasn't overly fond of Eve, but she felt a certain kinship with her.

Eve was still muttering about John Frizzell's lack of consideration as she sailed out of the salon. Steve watched her exit and shook his shaggy head. "That's one tough broad. I wonder what kind of living hell she puts Kurt through? Whatever it is, the old grump deserves it."

Judith didn't know—didn't want to know, if it came to that. She knew what her own living hell had been like, and that was enough. Now she'd like to look forward to a little bit of heaven. Only two more weeks, she told herself, and sat back to see what wonders Steve could work with his beefy magic fingers.

"What's happened to your hair?" screeched Gertrude when Judith came in the back door just after seven p.m. "You look like a trollop!"

"Funny, I left 'trollop' out," Judith murmured, but stood her ground. "It's Silver Streak. Most of it's my own, Mother," Judith fibbed.

"Bull. All you need is rolled stockings and a beaded bag. Go ahead, stand under a lamppost and see what happens! I always knew you'd end up in the gutter!"

"It smells like I'm already there," remarked Judith, shucking off her jacket and sniffing at the overwhelming aroma of clam and grease. "How was supper?"

"Best fritters I ever made," Gertrude said smugly. "Sweetums ate your share."

"Serves him right," breathed Judith. "Did he puke again?"

Gertrude drew herself up as tall as she could, which wasn't an imposing sight, considering that she was short to begin with and had to lean on the walker besides. "Do you want me to make potato salad for your stupid egg hunt or not?" barked Gertrude.

Gertrude's potato salad and her clam fritters were at opposite ends of the food spectrum. "Of course I do," Judith said somewhat crossly as the euphoria from her new coiffure began to ebb. "Your potato salad is the stuff of which legends are made. Your clam fritters, on the other hand, are the stuff on which stomach pumps thrive."

Getrude harrumphed and delved into her housecoat pocket to pull out a roll of Tums, thought better of it considering the topic under discussion, and lighted a cigarette instead. "You got a call from Norma, that big Paine. She wanted to make sure you'd be up at church before eleven tomorrow."

Judith gaped at her mother in mock surprise. "You answered the phone? Who did you think it was, your bookie?"

"She called on the private line upstairs," Gertrude grumbled, exuding a cloud of smoke. "I thought maybe it was Mike."

"But it wasn't." Judith's euphoria all but evaporated.

"Nope." She paused, the cigarette dangling on her lower lip, blinking away the sympathy in her eyes as if she ought to be ashamed of such maternal nonsense. "I suppose Norma Paine is the high mucky-muck for the egg hunt?"

"Egg-zecutive-in-chief," said Judith, wincing at her own terrible pun. "Anybody else call?" she asked in a casual tone.

"Check your machine, dopey. That's what you got the damned thing for, isn't it? I've no time for 'em, beep-buzz, 'Sorry, we can't talk to you right now, we're getting drunk and naked.' That's what they *really* mean, isn't it?"

Gertrude's jaw stuck out, making her look like a grizzled bulldog.

"Could be," said Judith, opening the refrigerator door and taking inventory for the elaborate snack she planned on having about ten o'clock. "It could mean that I've gone to the beauty salon to get my hair done."

"In your case, that's just as bad," snapped Gertrude.

The squeal of tires, a sudden deafening crash, and several piercing shrieks put an abrupt end to the mother and daughter bickering. Judith dashed to the kitchen window. In the soft April dusk, she could see the glare of headlights and the movement of people. Large objects sailed through the air, blows were exchanged, bodies thudded against the parked cars as more screams shattered the evening calm.

"What's happening?" demanded Gertrude, thumping up behind Judith.

But Judith was already turning away from the window, suppressing a yawn. "Nothing. It's just the Rankers. Their relatives have arrived."

THREE

HOLY SATURDAY DAWNED cloudy and damp. The sun, which had flirted with the city off and on the previous day, seemed to have gone into hiding. It was typically April in the Pacific Northwest, turning the waters of the bay a dingy gray and casting a blight on the downtown high-rises Judith could see from her living room window. She wished the rain would hold off until after the Easter egg hunt.

Gathering up Arlene's picnic hamper and three plastic bags filled with juice and pop, Judith started out the back door. To her dismay, the phone rang. She paused, hoping Gertrude would answer it. But as usual, her mother was pretending to be deaf, or else had taken refuge in the family quarters on the third floor.

Dumping everything on the floor, Judith rushed to answer by the fourth ring. Cousin Renie's cheerful voice greeted her at the other end.

"Hey, coz, I just finished my big and brilliant graphic design project for the computer-whiz kids over at Mech

Tech. Want me to make my famous bean glop for dinner tomorrow?"

"Get lost," said Judith with a sigh. "It's a good thing you're better at the drawing board than you are with the stove. Why didn't you call on the private line? I was just heading for SOTS. No, I do not want your bean glop. Or your clam doodoo. Bring the hot cross buns and the relish tray. Mother and I are doing the rest."

"I blanked out on your other number. You like my clam doodoo," said Renie with feigned hurt. "Remember the Fourth of July Dan threw it out the back door and hit Mrs. Dooley right in the kisser?"

"She didn't speak to me for six months," said Judith in not-so-fond recollection of the incident involving her neighbor to the east. "Hey, I've got to go. Hundreds of eager children await me up at church. Dozens of good eggs are going bad. See you guys tomorrow around four?"

Renie assured her that they'd all be there—her husband, Bill; Aunt Deb; the three grown children, Anne, Tony, and Tom; plus Tony's latest girlfriend, Rich Beth. The last name was added with a disdainful sniff as Renie hung up.

Turning out of the cul-de-sac that snaked up the south side of Heraldsgate Hill, Judith drove her Japanese compact toward the steep main thoroughfare that led up to the Catholic church. Traffic was heavy on Heraldsgate Avenue, as befitted a holiday weekend. Gearing down, Judith climbed the Hill behind an out-of-state sedan. At the four-way stop, she turned left, driving along the flat toward the Gothic eminence of Our Lady, Star of the Sea.

Under the gloomy clouds and in the shadow of the surrounding buildings, the old church looked shabby. The red brick seemed faded; the brown stone was worn. Across the street, cherry blossoms drifted down like sad snowflakes. Only the spring garden that ran the length of the church lent a hint of life.

Out in the parking lot behind the school, Judith craned

her neck to stare up at the single spire with its naked cross. Somehow, it looked crooked. Passing a hand over her newly colored hair, Judith was suddenly overcome with pessimism. It was an uncharacteristic emotion, and utterly inappropriate for the hostess of the parish egg hunt. It must be the capricious April weather, she told herself. Or maybe she wasn't spiritually prepared for the joy of Easter. Two days of fasting and giving up gum did not constitute total Lenten reparation. Whatever the cause, Judith had better shake off her mood and put on a happy face.

Rallying, she began unloading the trunk. Eddie La Plante, the rheumatic gardener, tottered out from the cloisters by the convent. He gestured at Judith.

"Damned squirrels," he muttered, shuffling closer and holding out a hand with swollen joints. "What did they do with my hyacinth bulbs? See here? Peanuts!"

"Squirrels are pesky," Judith allowed, though she secretly blessed the furry little fellows for their relentless taunting of the gullible Sweetums.

"Wicked, I call it," grumbled Eddie, his gnomelike face as weathered as the peanuts he held. He used his free hand to hold his down vest together as a breeze blew sharply through the parking lot. "Lot of wickedness going on around here, if you ask me. Think of it, old Emily leaving all that money to Stella."

"Sandy," corrected Judith gently. "To John, actually, he's the nephew . . ."

"Wicked, that's what I said it is. What did John Frizzell ever do for Emily? Or anybody else, if it comes to that?" Eddie's smoky voice rumbled right over Judith's words. "And what do the rest of us get?" He stared at his open palm, which shook ever so slightly. "Peanuts!"

Other cars had pulled in, spilling out various fellow SOTS who had come early to help. Eddie's small dark eyes scanned the parking lot, his forehead under the baseball cap furrowed with disdain. "Here," he said, thrusting the nuts at a startled Judith. "At least you're not a jumped-up snob or a bigmouthed hypocrite like some of them."

"Thanks," said Judith, not sure if she referred to the peanuts or the compliment. Eddie shuffled off, hands stuffed in the pockets of his forest-green work pants, eyes fixed on the asphalt. Two parking slots down, Norma Paine emerged from her pearl-white luxury sedan in a floral jumpsuit that reminded Judith of the Hanging Gardens of Babylon. Hopping behind her was a large purple and green rabbit. Judith discreetly chucked the peanuts into a drain and gaped at the big bunny.

"Yoo-hoo," called Norma. "I've got the eggs." She gestured carefully with a large carton. "There's a gold one that will be first prize. Father Hoyle suggested a homework pass for next week."

Judith was still staring at the big rabbit. "Huh? Oh, fine." She grinned as the rabbit spoke and waved. "Hi, Wilbur! I didn't recognize you without your clothes." Slamming the trunk shut, Judith got into step with Norma and Wilbur Paine. "Wait a minute, the kids have next week off. There won't *be* any homework."

Norma's nostrils flared as she put a hand to her mouth and emitted a horselike guffaw. "Oh, that Father Hoyle! He's a kick!" She stopped to stare at Judith. "You have a new hairdo. Now what's different about it? Let me think—is it a wig?"

"I had it frosted," Judith said with a dour expression.

"Yes, of course!" Another guffaw issued from Norma's ample lungs. Judith had always been convinced that Norma's jutting bust arrived at least fifteen seconds before the rest of her. "It's very nice," Norma remarked. "Takes off years, I'd say. Not that you need to, you're a lot younger than I am." She uttered the last statement without her usual conviction, clearly hoping to be contradicted.

But Judith was smiling at Wilbur, who was apparently nodding approval of her rejuvenation. At least his ears were flapping faster. "Maybe Father Hoyle can come up with another prize," suggested Judith.

Norma's chins jiggled in agreement. "He's clever, that one. We're lucky to have him, though in my opinion," she confided in a lowered voice, "the jury's still out on his new assistant." Judith spared a pang for Father Tim Mills, who thus far had shown an appropriate amount of Christian zeal, despite such setbacks as the rebuff from John Frizzell. Tim had received an endorsement from Arlene, whose elder daughter, Mugs, had dated him in his preseminary days in Montana. "I suppose," Norma conceded as they walked and Wilbur flopped across the parking lot, "Father Hoyle can whip him into shape, if anybody can."

At the moment, Father Francis Xavier Hoyle was standing in the door of the parish hall, exuding pastoral warmth. In Judith's opinion, the tall, silver-haired priest exuded much more, but as a chaste widow, she rarely dwelled on exactly what that quality might be. In the eight years that Frank Hoyle had been at Star of the Sea, no shred of scandal had touched his name, though rumor had it that several female SOTS had tried to put his vow of celibacy to the test.

But now Father Hoyle was teasing Wilbur Paine about his rabbit suit while Tim Mills helped Kurt Kramer and Mark Duffy set up the folding tables and chairs. Judith headed straight for the kitchen with Norma. Leaning against the storage cabinets were Kate Duffy and Eve Kramer, obviously engaged in a confidential conversation.

"Judith! Norma! How are you?" Kate spoke too eagerly, her composure ruffled.

Judith merely smiled in greeting, but Norma Paine was not so easily put off. "Well? Is this a private meeting, or can we dish the dirt, too?" She looked down her long nose at the other women. "Who ran off with whose husband? Or which teenager is in drug rehab this week?"

Judith cringed at Norma's tactlessness: At least one of the Duffys' four children had had a problem with substance abuse, and Eve's reputation was not without blemish. Indeed, she was rumored to have—in Norma's own words—thrown herself at Father Hoyle before he'd unpacked his clerical collars.

"We're discussing the state of the parish," explained Eve with a toss of her dark curls. "What will we do with Emily Tresvant's bequest? Kurt says it comes to a cool million."

"Phew!" Judith rolled her black eyes. As the wife of the parish business manager, Eve ought to know. "That's a bundle!"

"And why not?" demanded Norma, opening up her box of eggs. "She left at least ten million to John and Sandy. All Emily had was money." For a woman who was known to be as fond of a dollar as the next one, the statement was unbecoming, but at least it was informed. Wilbur Paine had been Emily Tresvant's attorney.

"I wonder what they'll do with the house," put in Kate, busying herself with paper plates and plastic silverware. "It was always too big for Emily, and frankly, it's a bit of a white elephant. John and Sandy could sell it and get out of that rental they're in. They hardly brought a thing out from New York, just what they could pack into that old Peugeot. If Sandy changed her mind about going back East, they could treat themselves and buy something really special." Her sweet face glowed at the idea.

Norma slammed a sack of sugar onto the counter. "Go back East? Why would anyone do a thing like that?"

Eve smirked. "Because that's where their kids are, for one. Two, Sandy doesn't like the Pacific Northwest. It rains too much." Her eyes narrowed at Norma. "What's wrong? Are you afraid they'll take all the Tresvant legal business with them and pull Wilbur's big fat retainer out from under him?"

Obviously disconcerted, Norma Paine tried to hide the fact by ripping open the sugar bag and dipping into it with a measuring cup. "You don't know what you're talking about, Eve. As the Tresvant family attorney, Wilbur would be the first to know if John and Sandy planned to move away. Besides," she added, almost more to reassure herself than the others, "even if they did, they'd no doubt keep the firm on as their legal representatives here."

Eve was unmoved by Norma's bluster. "I've already told them I want to go over the Tresvant house with a fine-toothed comb," she said, tossing a lipstick into her open snakeskin shoulder bag. The big purse, which served as a repository for Eve's latest piece of stitchery, contained what Judith judged to be an exquisite Oriental butterfly design in silver and gold metallic thread. "I'm sure I could find a ton of treasures for my antiques shop," remarked Eve with a flip of her tousled tresses.

Norma, having regained her aplomb, made a wry face. "At incredibly low prices? At least John Frizzell won't be duped. Tell me, Eve, what makes a walrus tusk umbrella handle jump from fifteen dollars in somebody's basement to a hundred and fifty dollars in your store window?"

"Careful restoration and an added zero." Eve's hard-edged composure was unruffled. "Come now, Norma, you're still irked because I discovered that your great-grandmother's clock was gold leaf and not gilt paint. You'd never taken the trouble to have it appraised."

"It was only a matter of sentiment to me," huffed Norma, "not dollars and cents."

"But Norma," Kate said in her breathless voice, "you said yourself that clock was an eyesore."

Norma pursed her lips. "It clashed with our Louis XIV motif. Since when," she continued, rounding on Kate, "did you become an expert on decor? Your downstairs bathroom wallpaper has chimpanzees on it!"

Eve slammed her hand on the stainless steel counter. "Shut the hell up, Norma! It's Holy Saturday, for Chrissakes! Why don't you go suck eggs? Or at least hide them."

Norma's gray eyes snapped at Eve, but she knuckled under, as usual. The only member of the parish who had ever gotten the better of Eve Kramer was her comrade and rival, Arlene Rankers. The redoubtable Arlene had once ended a heated argument by dumping a kettle of soft taffy on Eve's head during the parish's Mardi Gras carnival. Neither Norma nor Kate seemed so inclined to violence.

A faintly bewildered Father Mills wandered into the kitchen, eyeing the women warily. "Dissension among the Marthas?" he inquired with a feeble attempt at humor. Somehow, his youth and naivete seemed at odds with his boxer's frame. Under a shock of fair hair, his blunt features retained an almost babylike quality. Judith didn't envy his task as peacemaker between the three warring members of his congregation.

Neither, apparently, did Mark Duffy, who had followed Father Tim as far as the kitchen door and then sensibly backed off. Mark was a tall man, with graying brown hair and warm hazel eyes. He exuded relentless good cheer, yet Judith had always sensed a hint of Midwestern reserve. "Let me guess." He grinned, helping Judith cart the food into the parish hall. "Norma's expounding, Eve's carping, and my wife's praying over both of them."

Judith grinned back at Mark. "Close. Kate ought to pray less and speak out more," she said, carefully removing the plastic wrap from Gertrude's potato salad. Noting the sudden tightening of Mark's mouth, Judith shot him a perceptive look. "Or isn't she as easily intimidated as she seems?"

Mark inclined his head. "Under that lace exterior lurks a spine of steel," he conceded. Judith noted the pride in his tone, but there was something else, too, which Judith couldn't quite identify.

But further revelations were prevented when Sandy Frizzell, barely visible behind two huge bakery boxes, tottered into the hall. "Oh, help, please!" she called out in that odd, husky voice. "I can't see!" Her maligned golden hair cascaded around her face as she struggled toward the nearest table. Judith and Mark rushed to meet the new arrival, taking the boxes one at a time.

"Easy does it," said Mark, as a grateful Sandy slumped onto the nearest chair.

"Oh, they're gorgeous!" Judith exclaimed, lifting each lid. One cake was done in white icing with a bunny carrying a basket of colored eggs. The other was frosted with chocolate, a spray of Easter lilies on the diagonal. Sandy—and Begelman's Bakery—had outdone themselves. Judith looked up at the big wall clock next to the stage. "It's almost eleven. In my opinion, Lent is history."

Father Hoyle came over to admire the cakes with Wilbur Paine hopping and flopping behind him. "Praise the Lord and pass the paper plates," said Father Hoyle. "Do we have to wait for the kiddies?"

"Yes," asserted Judith, planting herself in front of the table like a Beefeater guarding the Crown Jewels. "They'll be here any minute, and they have to find the eggs before we cut the cakes. Have a crab ball."

Father Hoyle scrutinized the hors d'oeuvres tray that Kate Duffy had just set out. "Haven't I seen these somewhere before?" he asked with a twinkle.

"Waste not, want not," retorted Judith, taking Sandy by the arm. "Ogle the cakes Sandy brought, Father. They're a thing of beauty and a joy for about an hour and a half. Then they'll turn not to dust, but to crumbs."

"Splendid specimens," agreed the pastor with a big smile for Sandy. "Your generosity is much appreciated."

Sandy's sallow complexion darkened under her heavy makeup. She was an atractive woman, Judith supposed, though her use of cosmetics seemed to conceal rather than enhance her features. Mid-forties was Judith's guess, with a complexion victimized by New York City's filthy air. Yet if her appearance gave her a hardened aspect, Sandy's manner was girlishly uncertain.

"I'm just glad to help," insisted Sandy, who now stood by the table, fidgeting with the ties of her camel-hair coat. "With no children in the school, we haven't been very active in the parish. Aunt Emily urged us to do more, to sort of take her place, you see."

Since Judith couldn't recall Emily Tresvant ever lifting so much as a Shrove Tuesday pancake, the counsel seemed strange. But Emily had certainly contributed financially to SOTS, both in life and in death. And if Father Hoyle was showing remarkable restraint in alluding to the fact, his assistant pastor was not.

"Mrs. Frizzell," said Timothy Mills with unfettered fervor, "I want to make sure you'll be at the Parish Council meeting Tuesday night. We're going to talk about how we can put Miss Tresvant's money to best use." The young priest blinked and paused, his enthusiasm visibly ebbing. "That is," he stammered, "Father Hoyle and I felt . . ." His index finger ran nervously inside his clerical collar. Tim Mills glanced at his superior. "Not the time or place, maybe. Excuse me," he said, with a series of ragged nods, "I forgot something in the sacristy."

Under the scrutiny of several pairs of curious eyes, Tim Mills beat a hasty retreat. Father Hoyle smoothed his silver hair back from his temples and twinkled at Sandy. "Our Timothy's youthful gusto carries him away sometimes. He will learn that the Mills of God grind slowly, yet they grind exceedingly small." Judith noted that the play on words diverted Hoyle's audience from Father Tim's precipitous departure. The pastor took up the original topic of discussion without missing another beat: "Kurt Kramer feels we ought to invest it and use only the interest. Personally, I'd like to call a meeting of the wizards at the chancery to see what they think."

"They think the moon is made of green cheese," declared a spare, balding man with a jaw like a bear trap. "Those chancery people are all alike—no sense of reality."

Judith, Father Hoyle, Mark Duffy, and Sandy Frizzell turned curious gazes on Kurt Kramer. Kurt was as opinionated as his wife, Eve, and just as abrasive. He was also extremely shrewd.

Wilbur, whose ears were drooping over his eyes, bumped into Judith and excused himself in a muffled voice before addressing Kurt. "Therd's a codzel, you bow," he said, whiskers twitching. "Emiwy spedifibed thurch onwee."

"Wilbur," admonished his wife, "take off your silly head. We can't understand a word you're saying."

Dutifully, Wilbur began to tug on his ears, but at that moment, the first contingent of children erupted into the hall. Fluffy tail abob, and hopping with all his might, Wilbur went to greet his squealing audience. Father Hoyle followed him with a welcoming smile, but Kurt Kramer was watching the scene with a distinct scowl.

"He's referring to a codicil." Kurt's sharp blue eyes rested on Sandy. "You know of it, I imagine. Your husband's aunt specified that her money should be used only for the church. Not the school or the gym or any other of what she considered frills." Kurt's mouth was still turned down, evidence of his disapproval.

Sandy nodded anxiously. "She loved the building. It was put up when she was a child. Her class was the first to prepare for Holy Communion here."

"Then you'd think she'd have remembered the school, too," Kurt said in his abrupt manner.

But Norma eyed him coldly. "Emily hated it when lay people began teaching at SOTS. She saw no point in Catholic education without nuns in charge."

Kurt snorted. "Where did she think she'd find nuns these days? Or priests. If you ask me, Emily Tresvant lived in a fantasy world."

"Don't we all," remarked Judith, trying to lighten the mood. "You were just talking to a rabbit."

But Kurt's ill humor wasn't so easily dispelled. He glared at Judith, even as Sandy responded with surprising equanimity. "Aunt Emily was like most older people. She didn't want to acknowledge that the world was changing and there was nothing she could do about it."

While pleasantly surprised by Sandy's outspokenness, Judith understood Emily's reaction all too well. Gertrude's image clumped through her mind's eye, but she thrust it aside and excused herself to assume her duties as general factotum. Father Hoyle and a subdued Father Mills had joined Mark Duffy in organizing the children by ages for the egg hunt. As they trooped outdoors, the youngsters' squeals and shrieks reverberated off the parish hall walls. More parents had arrived, too, sidling up to the buffet. Mark, whose experience with his film company automatically designated him as the official parish photographer, was hoisting a sleek black camcorder and capturing the Easter frenzy for posterity. Eddie La Plante circled the hall on stiff legs, making threats to would-be tramplers of his flower beds. Sandy had been pressed into service as nursery supervisor, watching over the children too young to participate in the hunt. During the next hour and a half, Judith was busy refilling platters, cutting cake, and consoling empty-handed egg seekers.

At last the din began to die down and the crowd trickled away. The serving plates were virtually empty, and the cakes had indeed been reduced to crumbs. The two punch bowls, one marked Tox and the other Detox, to distinguish which contained alcohol and which did not, were all but drained. Judith was thankful that only a minimal amount of rum had been used. She hadn't much liked the idea of her fellow SOTS driving around Heraldsgate Hill like a bunch of drunken bunnies.

Mark Duffy, Kurt Kramer, and the two priests cleared the tables while Eve bagged garbage. Norma manned the dishwasher, and Kate helped Judith clean up from the buffet. When she was done, Judith went to look for Sandy in the gaily decorated nursery room, located off the hall leading into the school.

"You survived," Judith said to a frazzled Sandy. "How are your eardrums?"

Sandy winced as she brushed bits of colored construction paper from her black slacks and matching turtleneck sweater. "It was incredible! The Paine grandson ate three pieces of chalk, the Kramers' niece bit the Dooley baby, then that crew of little savages I'd never seen before took all the stuffing out of Pooh Bear! Who are they, anyway?"

Having seen Arlene arrive with three toddlers and two older children, Judith could guess. "Visitors. A delegation from the Omaha Nation." Quickly, she changed the subject: "It was just as well that kids under three couldn't take part in the hunt, but they probably felt left out. Maybe next year Norma can arrange some special event for them, too."

Sandy shook her head, the shaggy golden hair spilling over her shoulders, nervous fingers still plucking at her slacks. "It was nerve-racking. I'm just not used to it."

Judith, in the process of putting Pooh's stuffing back, glanced at Sandy. "How old are your own kids, Sandy?"

"Oh—they're grown." Sandy's stone-gray eyes blinked dazedly at Judith. "It's been a long time since they were in the terrible twos category. You tend to forget."

"I figure you don't dare remember." Judith gave Pooh a final punch in the paunch and sat him on a tiny chair. "Here," she offered, amassing a pile of large plastic blocks, "let me help you pick all this stuff up."

"Oh, no," Sandy protested. "I'll do it. Just give me time to catch my breath. Chores always restore my equilibrium."

Judith didn't argue. She still had to go grocery shopping for the Easter dinner, stop at the liquor store, drop off some books at the library, and pick up Gertrude's prescription for crankiness, as Judith termed her mother's hormone medicine. Wishing Sandy well, Judith stopped at the women's room across the hall. On her way out, she paused for a critical look in the mirror. Steve's expert touch hadn't been matched by Judith that morning, but her new hairdo was definitely quite becoming. Her bangs, which she now wore swept to one side, accentuated her dark eyes and gave her face a more rounded look. The deep green eyeshadow Ginger had recommended, as well as the dark mascara, added a hint of drama. And there was no doubt about the Sable Satin—Judith looked ten years younger.

Again, she visualized the date on the calendar: April 14. Less than two weeks to wait. It occurred to her that Friday the thirteenth had passed without incident. Judith took a deep breath, smiled to herself, and walked out into the corridor. She called a greeting to the rabbit, who was just going into the men's room. Wilbur was definitely looking the worse for wear.

The parish hall was restored to order. Out of habit, Judith checked to make sure the stove and ovens were turned off and the freezer door was tightly shut. The kitchen crew was almost finished, and a grim Eddie La Plante was heading out the door, carrying a rake. He all but collided with John Frizzell, who was just coming in.

"Hi," Judith said, taking a quick inventory of what was left of her belongings. "You missed all the fun. Want a crab ball?"

John Frizzell shook his dark head. He was a good-looking man, tall and lean, with refined features and a reticent manner. "I'm here to pick up Sandy."

"Oh?" Judith glanced around the hall. The only people left were the Kramers and the Duffys, who were talking to each other in earnest tones at the edge of the stage. "She's in the nursery, just down the hall." Judith hoisted a shoulder, indicating the door at her back. "She's slightly bowed, but not quite bent."

John gave Judith a thin smile. "Sandy's high-strung sometimes. That's why she doesn't drive. Of course you don't need to when you live in Manhattan. A car is no asset."

"So I hear." Judith gave the hamper a boost with her knee. She was anxious to be off. "Thank you both for the beautiful cakes. And have a happy Easter." With a bright smile for John Frizzell, Judith headed for the door that led to the parking lot. Only a half-dozen cars remained, including John Frizzell's aging Peugeot, its black paint dappled with cherry petals, giving the car a polka-dot effect. In the next spot sat Father Hoyle's dark green BMW, the generous gift of a former parishioner who owned an East Side dealership. Norma was commandeering the steering wheel of their big sedan from Wilbur, who had finally shed the rabbit costume and somehow seemed to have shrunk in the process.

It was just beginning to rain. Judith scanned the dark clouds, found at least two promising patches of blue, and shrugged. Anything could happen with the weather by morning. Easter might bring sunshine and clear skies, which certainly would be fitting for the sake of symbolism. As she slid behind the wheel, Judith looked up once more at the tall church steeple.

It still looked crooked.

She was inside Falstaff's Market examining a crown roast of lamb when she heard the sirens on Heraldsgate Avenue. Stupid out-of-towners, she thought. Don't know how to drive on wet streets. She returned to making a decision on her entree, and opted for a Virginia ham.

The stop at the liquor store proved uneventful, though Judith had to wait in line, musing over the fact that far too many people seemed to associate even the most religious holidays with getting blotto. At Holiday's Drugstore, she chatted briefly with Mrs. Dooley, who was consulting with the pharmacist about the danger from human bites. Judith feigned ignorance.

Her visit to the library took longer than she'd planned: The temporary behind the desk turned out to be a fellow graduate of the university's school of librarianship whom Judith hadn't seen in years. She emerged with a stack of books and a flood of memories, humming to herself as she went back to the car.

She arrived home just as the Dooleys' eldest son came racing through the hedge that separated Hillside Manor from their neighbors to the south and east.

"Hey, Mrs. McMonigle!" shouted Dooley, whose given names of Aloysius Gonzaga had been dropped in kindergarten for obvious reasons. He waved his arms like a windmill. "Stop!"

"What's wrong, Dooley? Don't tell me you've got hydrophobia?" said Judith, referring to the act of cannibalism practiced by one of the Kramers' kin on Dooley's little sister. "Or are you giving up the paper route?"

Dooley shook his head vigorously, the fair hair sticking out like straw. At fifteen, he was shooting up in height, but not acquiring much width. For the first time, Judith realized he had gotten almost as tall as she was. With one hand clutching his Hard Rock Cafe–Hong Kong T-shirt, Dooley stopped to catch his breath. "What happened? Who did it? Did you see anything?"

Mystified, Judith stared at Dooley. "See what? Dooley, are you hallucinating? Here," she said, gesturing with the grocery bag that contained the drugstore parcel, "take some of Gertrude's hormones. They'll set puberty back about ten years."

But Dooley wasn't deterred by teasing. "Hey, Mrs. McMonigle, don't be so dense! Weren't you up at church this afternoon?"

Judith brushed the rain from her bare head. A typical native, she abjured the use of umbrellas as both unnatural and unnecessary. "Sure. And part of the morning." It finally dawned on Judith that Dooley was deadly earnest. She felt fear envelop her like a cold, clammy hand. "Why?"

"You know how I joined the Explorers police auxiliary for kids last year?" Dooley asked, speaking even more rapidly than usual. He saw Judith give a quick nod; Dooley had earned his spurs by nosing around during the fortune-teller investigation. "I got a CB, too. I heard it on the emergency band." His eyes darted up and over Judith's head, as if he could catch a glimpse of Our Lady, Star of the Sea from where they were standing halfway down Heraldsgate Hill. "There was a murder up there today, less than three hours ago."

Judith got an extra grip on her grocery sacks. "What? Who?" she demanded, her heart thumping like mad.

Dooley seemed to sway slightly before Judith's mesmerized eyes. "That new lady. Mrs. Frizzell. She was stabbed to death in the church nursery."

FOUR

JUDITH'S DUTY WAS to return to the church and assist in any way she could. After all, she'd had a similar ghastly experience under her very roof over a year ago when a fortune-teller had been poisoned. Then, on a brief vacation in the fall, she and Cousin Renie had managed to find a corpse in the elevator of their hotel. Judith knew something about police procedure, about homicide investigations, about casually interrogating suspects and drawing logical conclusions to goofy questions.

But Sandy Frizzell's murder hadn't occurred at Hillside Manor or outside the cousins' hotel suite. Now that she'd made it into some of the guidebooks, Judith was averse to potentially damaging publicity for the bed-and-breakfast. Though, in fact, the fortune-teller's demise had helped, not hindered, business. Cousin Renie had been right: Notoriety was an excellent marketing strategy.

But that was then, and this was now. Judith wanted no part of another murder investigation. She hadn't even been around when the body was discovered. If the police wanted to talk to her, they knew where to find her. At least, she thought with a sudden sense of something that bordered on panic, one of them did . . .

With Dooley's help, Judith unloaded the car, called a greeting to her mother, got no answer, and took a can of diet pop out of the refrigerator. "You want some, Dooley? I've got the real stuff in here."

"Sure." Dooley sank down on a chair next to the dinette table, but he was clearly on edge. "Hey, Mrs. McMonigle," he said, lanky legs sprawled out across the floor, "I think I'll volunteer to work on this case. I met Mrs. Frizzell once, and I know him, too."

"Volunteer?" Judith handed Dooley his pop, then began putting the rest of the groceries away. "To do what?"

"I don't know." Dooley frowned, then undid the black sweatshirt he had tied around his neck and pulled it over his head. "When you join the Explorers, you get certain privileges, though. So far, I've just helped with crowd control stuff, like a couple of rock concerts. But sometimes, like after you've proved you're reliable and stuff, you can help with serious crimes. What was that homicide detective's name? The guy with red hair and the pot belly?"

In spite of herself, Judith blushed. "That is not a pot! Joe's just spread out a bit. It comes with time." She gave Dooley a withering glance. "Frankly, you could use some meat on that frame of yours. Doesn't your mother feed you?"

"Sure. All the time." Dooley gave Judith a sheepish grin. "Did you say Joe? Lieutenant Joe Flynn, right?"

Judith turned her back on Dooley, ostensibly organizing the refrigerator. "Right." She pulled out what was left of the crab balls, sniffed, and emptied them in the garbage under the sink.

"What's the matter, Mrs. McMonigle? Don't you like him? I thought he was kind of a cool dude. I mean, for his age and all."

Judith didn't answer right away. Asking her if she liked

Joe Flynn was like asking a drought-ravaged region if it wanted rain. But Dooley was too young to understand. Deliberately, she turned around and eyed Dooley on the level. "Yes. I like Joe Flynn. He's a good cop. So is the guy who works with him, Woody Price. I don't suppose you could tell from the CB who was sent up to SOTS?"

"Naw." Dooley took a big drink from his pop can. "They just give unit numbers and stuff. I haven't memorized all those yet. Hey, what did you do to your hair? You spill paint on it or something?"

Judith shot Dooley a baleful look, then gave a start as she heard a noise above her head. The Rankers's relatives, maybe, or Gertrude. So far, she had seen little of her guests, who seemed to be mainly in the twenty-to-thirty age category, and married to each other. Their children, presumably the same crew that had butchered Pooh Bear, were staying in the Rankers's basement, which struck Judith as a good idea, as long as there was no reform school available.

But it was the butchering of Sandy Frizzell that stunned Judith. She finished restocking the liquor cupboard and sat down across from Dooley. "I still can't believe it. I must have talked to Sandy just a few minutes before she . . ." Judith swallowed hard, remembering the golden hair and the nervous mannerisms and the heavy makeup. Now Sandy was no more than a memory. "Delicate" was the word Kate Duffy had used in reference to her. Perhaps that was an accurate assessment, but John Frizzell's description of his wife as "high-strung" seemed nearer the mark. In any event, Sandy certainly hadn't died from natural causes.

Judith's thoughts were interrupted by the sound of Gertrude thumping down the back stairs. Dooley gulped his pop and announced that he'd better get home. Knowing that Gertrude and the paperboy had a rocky history, Judith wasn't surprised when Dooley opted to leave via the front entrance.

"I think I'll call that Flynn dude," Dooley said on his

way out. "Maybe he'll let me look for evidence. Explorers get to do that sometimes, at least in the woods."

Our Lady, Star of the Sea wasn't exactly in the woods, but Judith didn't say anything to squelch Dooley's enthusiasm. He was young, she wasn't, and youth should have its day. Judith would retire to the sidelines and let the Dooleys of the world take over. She was girding herself to relay the grisly news about Sandy Frizzell to her mother when the phone rang. It was Renie, aghast.

"Yeah, yeah, I blanked out again on your other phone number. Anyway, I can't get you on that line if you're downstairs all the time, can I?" she demanded, but didn't wait for an answer. "What's this I hear about Sandy Frizzell? I discovered my yeast was outdated for the buns and had to run up to Falstaff's to get more. Eve Kramer was there, and she was practically traumatized."

"Aren't we all?" said Judith, signaling for her mother to listen, but not to ask questions. Yet. "It's true, I guess." She turned so that Gertrude could also hear clearly. "Dooley heard it on his CB. Sandy was stabbed to death in the parish nursery, probably right after I left."

"Good God!" Renie lapsed into silence while Gertrude's eyes glazed over with shock. "Damn," Renie breathed at last. "And she and John just came into all that money! I can't believe it!"

"It's terrible," agreed Judith, motioning for her mother to sit down. A banging at the back door startled both women. "Hey, coz, I really don't know much about it, and there's somebody on the porch. Arlene, maybe. I'll call you back if I hear anything, okay?"

"Sure. I'll do the same." Renie clicked off.

Judith stopped just long enough on her way to the back door to help her mother into the chair. Gertrude was pale and unwontedly grim. The knock sounded again, this time with greater urgency.

"I'm coming!" Judith called. "Get a grip on it, Arlene," she added in a lower voice.

But it wasn't Arlene Rankers who stood on the back porch.

To Judith's astonishment, it was homicide detective Lieutenant Joe Flynn.

Joe's casual air masked his tenacious professionalism, just as the well-cut tweed sports coat camouflaged the spreading midriff Dooley had mentioned. His receding red hair was flecked with gray, yet his round face retained its freshness, despite over two decades observing the seamiest slices of life. At his side stood Woodrow Price, a uniformed officer on the verge of thirty and his next promotion. A stolid black man with a walrus moustache, Woody Price had displayed a hidden reservoir of talents during his previous adventure at Hillside Manor.

But it wasn't Woody Price's serious dark gaze which held Judith mesmerized at the back door. Rather, Joe Flynn's green eyes, with those magnetic flecks of gold, turned her faintly incoherent.

"You're early," she blurted. "It's still two weeks to go. But who's counting?" Judith giggled and mentally cursed herself for sounding like a half-baked teenager instead of a poised middle-aged widow.

Joe's mouth twitched slightly, showing the merest hint of his roguish smile. "This is business, not pleasure. I've yet to bring Woody along on a date." He put a highly buffed loafer over the threshold. "May we?"

Judith actually jumped. "Oh! I didn't mean . . . Sure, come in, I just heard about what happened up at church . . ."

Gertrude's rasping voice crackled from the kitchen: "Is that Joe Flynn?" She didn't wait for confirmation. "Where's he been for six months? One lousy cribbage board and a box of chocolates won't buy this old girl! There was a caramel in with the creams, and it wrecked my partial plate! Get that bastard out of my house!"

As always, it was useless for Judith to argue over the legal rights of ownership to Hillside Manor. "Mother," she pleaded over her shoulder, "you know why Joe hasn't called on us since Thanksgiving. That was the bargain. Now he's here about Sandy Frizzell's murder."

"Baloney!" snarled Gertrude, wrestling with her walker as she tried to get up from the dinette table. "Joe's here because you got your hair dyed like a two-bit hussy! Out!" Her thin arm flailed under cover of a baggy blue cardigan. "Beat it, and take your chauffeur with you!"

"Mother!" Judith was aghast. "Don't be so ornery!" Agitated, she rushed to Gertrude's side. "Settle down. Do you want to be arrested for impeding justice, you crazy old coot?"

While she was still seething, Gertrude's voiced dropped a notch. "Justice, my foot! If there were such a thing, Joe Flynn would have spent the last twenty-odd years in prison for breach of promise! But you, you gutless wonder," she raged on, wagging a bony finger in her daughter's face, "you just rolled over and married Dan McMonigle! Is that justice, I ask you?"

Judith had to admit that Gertrude had history on her side: Almost a quarter of a century earlier, Judith and Joe had planned to marry. Joe had followed through with the marriage, but took a different bride. The shock of learning that Joe had eloped with a blowsy thrice-divorced piano-bar entertainer ten years his senior had sent Judith rebounding into the arms of Dan McMonigle. It had never been clear whether Gertrude put more blame on Joe for dumping Judith or for consigning her to a life sentence as Dan's wife. Gertrude had never liked Joe much, but she had absolutely loathed Dan. Neither the death of the one nor the return of the other had changed her opinions.

It had been over a year since Joe Flynn had cruised back into Judith's life. His calling card had been his policeman's badge; his arrival had been in response to foul play at Hillside Manor. Judith had been astonished. Joe had been bemused. It was during the investigation of the fortune-teller's death that Joe had revealed that his marriage was over and he was seeking a church annulment, as well as a civil divorce. When he had insisted that his feelings for her hadn't faded any more than hers for him, Judith had reacted with skepticism. Such romantic notions were ridiculous for a woman of her age. Judith thought old dreams were too fragile to bring out into the bright light of middle age. But Joe was back in her life and Judith was happy for the first time in years, Gertrude notwithstanding.

Despite the blush that covered her cheeks, she fought to regain her usual aplomb. "I'm going outside and talk to the policemen," she told her mother in a firm tone. "You sit back down and smoke or something. If you want to get violent, take it out on Sweetums." Gently but firmly, she pushed Gertrude into the chair, then turned to face the two bemused detectives. "Come on," Judith said, leading the way outside. "As luck would have it, I got the lawn furniture out just this week."

On the other side of the driveway, a small patio bordered by the Ericsons' laurel hedge and the picket fence that marked the Dooley family's property line nestled in the shade of a pink dogwood tree. Judith's cherished birdbath with its statue of St. Francis rose from a bright border of ranunculus and creeping phlox. She offered the redwood chaise lounge and matching chairs to her visitors while she sat down on a small stone bench next to the portable barbecue.

The fitful rain had all but stopped, though the sky was still overcast. Yet the late afternoon April air was soft, and the dogwood gave them shelter. Like most natives, Judith, Joe, and Woody preferred drizzle to sizzle.

Judith looked over toward the back porch, momentarily fearful that Gertrude might charge out of the house and try to chase Joe and Woody off with Grandpa Grover's shotgun. "I'd apologize for Mother," Judith began, still faintly embarrassed, "but she's unrepentant. Joe understands," she said to Woody, "but I'm sorry she was rude to you."

Woody Price's grin was as dazzling as it was infrequent. "But I did used to be a chauffeur. That's how I got through college. The only bad part was prom night. I was just old enough to sneer and young enough to be envious."

Judith gave Woody a grateful smile. "Oh, yes, I remember when Mike ..." She caught herself and shook her head, then squared her shoulders. "Okay," she went on in a more businesslike manner, "how can I help?"

Joe and Woody also shifted gears. Woody produced a notebook, and Joe crossed his legs with the knifelike press in the tan flannel slacks. "You knew Sandy Frizzell, I gather?" Joe asked in the easy voice that had been known to lull suspects into unintended revelations.

Judith let out a little sigh. "Sort of. She and John hadn't been on the Hill for very long, you know. Since January, I think. I've seen them at church, talked to her at coffee and doughnuts after Mass, run into her at Falstaff's. But I really didn't know her." She gave a little shrug. "And John even less. They may have mixed with the SOTS or the rest of Heraldsgate Hill, but you know me, I don't have time to socialize much. Ask somebody like Eve Kramer or Kate Duffy."

"We did," said Joe dryly. "Kate was hysterical, and Eve's got a tongue like a laser. The Frizzells were pretty private people. Still, there's always gossip." The green eyes glinted. "Got any?"

Judith reflected. "No. Except that Sandy was supposedly delicate, and John was very protective of her."

"Does that translate as jealous?" inquired Joe.

"Jealous?" Judith frowned slightly. "It could, I guess. But that's idle speculation."

Joe gestured at Woody to ready his pen and notebook. "When did you last see Sandy?" Joe asked.

Judith thought back to the early part of the afternoon. "Just before I left the church hall. It must have been one-thirty or so. I think it was going on two when I got to Falstaff's." Idly, she glanced at her watch: It was now almost five p.m. The afternoon had flitted away as it so often did in a haze of errands, leaving Judith with a blurred sense of time.

"Where did you see her last?" Joe kept his voice free of emotion, but those keen green eyes never left Judith's face.

"In the nursery." Judith glanced down at the barbecue, subconsciously noting that one of the wheels was loose. She had the feeling that Joe knew all this, that he'd talked to John Frizzell, to Father Hoyle, in fact to anyone who had remained behind at the church hall. "I was with her for five minutes, maybe a bit more. I offered to help clean up, but she said she preferred doing it herself. Chores 're-stored her equilibrium', she said."

A slight frown creased Joe's high, wide forehead. "Which was upset by what?"

Judith spread her hands. "The kids. She had all the little ones. They were terrors." Her quick glance took in the Rankers's house, its solid outline looming over the apple trees and the lilac. "Sandy wasn't used to toddlers. Her own kids are older."

"Really." Joe passed a hand over his upper lip. "Was that the reason she was—what?—upset? Nervous? Anxious? Or was she afraid?"

Judith's dark eyes narrowed in the effort of concentration. "I wouldn't say she was afraid. John called her 'high-strung.' It was just the way she was. Neurotic, maybe. As I said, I didn't really know her."

Joe grimaced. "I wish you did. I could use a reliable witness. The fact is," he went on with a glance at Woody, "nobody knew the Frizzells that well. They didn't mix much."

"Typical New Yorkers," remarked Judith. "Suspicious. Stand-offish. And of course Emily was very ill. They probably spent a lot of time with her."

"Maybe." Joe paused, swinging one loafer-clad foot. A sparrow hopped onto the hedge, studied the birdbath, scrutinized the inhabitants of the patio, and took wing into the dogwood. "Did you see anyone else near the nursery when you left?"

"No," Judith replied. "Most of the people had gone by

then. I didn't see anybody until I got back into the church hall. Oh," she recalled as an afterthought, "except for Wilbur Paine, going into the men's room."

Joe leaned over Woody's notebook. "Wilbur Paine? What's the connection?"

Woody Price flipped through the looseleaf pages. "Attorney for Emily Tresvant, also for John and Sandy Frizzell. Hoover, Klontz, and Paine, old established firm in the Evergreen Tower Building. But not on retainer or otherwise connected with Tresvant Timber."

Joe nodded. "Emily Tresvant sold out to a Japanese firm about five years ago. They kept the name and the headquarters, but the power is in Tokyo." His gaze traveled skyward, where the sun was breaking through the clouds. "Wilbur played Easter Bunny, right?"

"Right. The kids loved him." Judith followed Joe's gaze. In the wake of Sandy's death, it didn't seem so important for the sun to shine. "Joe—who else was up at church? Don't tell me you're narrowing this investigation down to just us SOTS?"

Joe was on his feet, scraping an errant pebble off the sole of his right loafer. "You're not exactly coming up with a list of suspicious characters lurking in the rectory bushes. It would help a lot if you could remember more about Sandy than that small children made her nervous. Face it, Jude-girl, you were probably the last person to see her alive." The green eyes glittered. "Except for the killer, of course."

Wincing at the long-ago, much-despised nickname, Judith gnashed her teeth but kept her temper. "Come on, it was just a coincidence that I was there at all! I told you, I hardly knew the poor woman! I already did everything but solve that fortune-teller case for you two bozos. If you want to hire me, pay me. This one occurred off-premises. It's your murder, not mine."

Joe gave Judith his annoying, ingenuous expression before he turned to Woody. "Sounds like you've lost your sense of adventure. This one may not have happened in your dining room, but it *is* your parish, after all. Don't you feel a sense of proprietorship?"

Judith's gaze was even. "No. If somebody jumps out of a plane and lands on my roof, do I have to take over for the FAA?" She sounded emphatic but realized that she was already weakening.

Joe may have guessed as much. In any event, he stopped arguing. "Okay, Woody, let's strut our stuff. Who've we got on hand at the time of the murder?"

Woody Price again consulted his notebook. "Father Francis Xavier Hoyle, Father Timothy Mills, Eddie La Plante, Mr. and Mrs. Kurt Kramer—that's Eve—Mr. and Mrs. Mark Duffy—she's Kate—the aforementioned Wilbur Paine and his wife, Norma." He gave Judith an apologetic look from under his heavy eyebrows. "And Mrs. McMonigle, of course. But that's just for procedure's sake."

Judith groaned. "Swell. Why don't you throw procedure out the stained-glass window for once? And aren't you forgetting someone?" she inquired archly.

Joe turned wry. "I didn't think you cared." His green eyes were speculative as they rested on Judith's face. "Do you mean John Frizzell?" Joe saw Judith give a slight nod, but he shook his head. "No, we're not neglecting him. He was there, possibly before anyone saw him. A husband is always the primary suspect in the death of his wife. And vice versa." He gave Judith a needling glance. "Was Renie joking when she said Cousin Sue issued a notarized statement that she was with you all the time the week before Dan died?"

"Don't be crass!" But Judith flushed all the same. "Dan weighed four hundred pounds and had about seventeen pernicious diseases. He'd been bedridden for over two years. The whole family was amazed that he lived as long as he did."

Joe couldn't suppress a grin. "Who won the mortality pool, Uncle Al?"

An impish light danced in Judith's black eyes. "I did,"

she said, and then sobered again. "How was Sandy killed? I mean, what was she stabbed with?"

"A pair of scissors," Joe replied, adjusting his cream-and-gold-striped tie. "Unusually sharp to be left in a nursery. The killer may have brought them along, which would make it premeditated homicide. Did you notice any scissors?"

Judith tried to remember. "No." She suppressed a shudder as something tugged at her memory, then danced away. Judith saw the vision of a weary Sandy, a bedraggled Pooh Bear, and scattered colored blocks. It had seemed so innocent, the predictable finale to a children's holiday fete. "Why do I feel I should have, though?" Judith asked in a bleak voice.

Suddenly a message came crackling over the radio from the driveway where Joe and Woody's squad car was parked. Woody hurried over to listen in. On the far side of the yard, Judith could hear the Rankers assembling outside for what appeared to be a photo session. She stared in the direction of the neighbors' noisy gathering, deliberately avoiding Joe's eyes.

"I think it's going to be okay," he said suddenly in a low voice. "The canon lawyer told me I'd know by the first of May."

Slowly, Judith turned to look at Joe. Despite the long months of waiting, despite her feverish excitement, despite the newly discovered sense of anticipation, she had never really believed Joe Flynn would get an annulment from his wife after more than twenty years. Or that if he did, his freedom would affect her. But now here he was, two weeks short of the waiting period he had asked her to give him, announcing that he expected to be free. Judith realized that the prospect terrified her.

"Well." The word came out in a gulp. She was groping for something more eloquent when Arlene Rankers slipped between the houses and approached Judith and Joe.

"I *thought* the police were here!" she exclaimed, grabbing Joe by the hand and tugging his arm up and down as if it were a tire pump. "I just happened to be standing on top of our headboard upstairs when I saw the car! Is it about Sandy Frizzell? Who did it?"

Joe clutched at his sports coat and waited for Arlene to relinquish her grip. "The investigation has just begun," he said in a noncommittal voice. "We don't even have the medical examiner's report yet."

But Joe was mistaken. Woody Price, looking as shaken as Judith had ever seen him, virtually staggered from the squad car. "Lieutenant . . . You'd better come here. The M.E. has some startling conclusions."

Joe frowned, then excused himself and joined his subordinate. Arlene started after the two men, but Judith held her back. "They'll tell us if we need to know," Judith said with a hand on the other woman's sleeve.

But Arlene wasn't one to be dissuaded by discretion. "I can't wait forever! Carl's in the middle of taking pictures!" She smoothed the front of her yellow-and-white-polka-dot dinner dress. "The police are public servants, aren't they? As citizens, we pay their salaries. Don't we have a right to know?"

Judith had the feeling that the Rankers's tax dollars were pretty far down on the policemen's agenda, especially now, judging from the grim expressions on Joe and Woody's faces. Joe, in fact, was already getting into the squad car. Arlene wilted next to Judith, then bridled at the sound of her husband's summons from next door for his wife to get her fanny front and center. "Carl can't wait to capture the whole family on film. He's really thrilled over the reunion," she said in her most poignant manner. "Come over as soon as you find out what's happened. I just can't believe anyone would murder that poor sweet Sandy! She was such a doll!" Swiveling on her patent leather pumps, Arlene raised her fist—and her voice— toward the Rankers's house: "Shut your trap, you moron! You probably don't have any film in your camera anyway! As usual."

Still railing at her husband, Arlene disappeared behind

the rhododendrons. Carl's photography session reminded Judith of Mark Duffy and his camcorder. Was it possible he'd captured something important on film? She started for the police car, but Woody was now behind the wheel and already in reverse.

"Hey!" cried Judith, flailing with her arms. "Wait!"

But the siren was on and the lights were flashing as Joe and Woody screeched off down the street. Judith turned glum. The sight and sound of emergency vehicles were not new to Hillside Manor, but she still considered them incompatible with an image of gracious hospitality. As for Mark's movies, they'd been made some two hours before the murder. Overly excited school-age children tugging on Wilbur Paine's fluffy tail weren't apt to add much to a homicide investigation. Besides, Judith had sworn not to get involved. Joe and Woody could ferret out the facts for themselves. As Arlene pointed out, that's what they were getting paid for. Wearily, Judith headed for the house and hoped she'd remembered to put the ice bag back in the freezer.

FIVE

GERTRUDE WAS STILL fuming. "I'm warning you, Joe Flynn doesn't set foot in this house until the archbishop says he's a free man! Even then, I wouldn't trust that turkey an inch!" Leaning on the walker, Gertrude was making her stand by the open kitchen cupboard near the stove. Her color had returned, wrath apparently overcoming shock. Judith, weary from her long day, resisted further argument.

"It was strictly business," Judith said in as calm a voice as she could muster. "Joe had some questions about Sandy Frizzell's murder. Routine, that's all." Her mother didn't need to remind Judith that she'd spent the past year and more waiting for Joe to show up with an annulment in one hand and a bottle of champagne in the other. At least that was how Judith had pictured it. Now, seeing Joe again, and facing the reality, she was having unexpected qualms.

"Let's eat," Judith said, changing the subject. "How about lamb steaks and greenie noodles?"

"How about my blue bowl?" growled Gertrude.

"Where's my potato salad bowl? Don't tell me you got so addled under that striped hair of yours that you left it up at church?"

Judith's hands flew to her mouth. She had indeed forgotten the potato salad bowl. Running into John Frizzell must have distracted her. "I'll go get it after dinner," she promised. "The church is probably locked up right now." More likely, it was off limits for the police investigation, but Judith knew there would be access later on because there was a vigil mass scheduled for eight p.m.

Gertrude looked only partially appeased. Her little eyes were accusing. "You know I can't make potato salad unless I have my blue bowl."

As Judith knew, potato salad without the blue bowl was as impossible as pancakes without the cast-iron griddle. She sighed with resignation and took two lamb steaks out from the fridge along with half a head of cabbage. For the time being, Sandy Frizzell's murder and Joe Flynn's reappearance were put aside while Judith broiled meat, boiled noodles, and shredded cabbage. To her dismay, the appetite which had run so rampant the previous day now had diminished considerably. Watching her mother wolf down the noodles and cabbage fried together in butter, Judith toyed with her lamb steak. Soon the talk turned to the subject of Eve Kramer.

"She's very talented with embroidery, I'll give her that," said Judith, ignoring Sweetums, who had sidled up to the dinette table and was howling for his supper. "You know, Mother, you used to do some nice things yourself. The dining room chair covers, and that bench you finished for Aunt Deb."

Gertrude flexed her bony fingers. "I wasn't so crippled with arthritis then. I could see better, too. As for my sister-in-law, the only thing that moves fast with Deb is her mouth. It took her five years to do six inches of needlepoint on that bench cover, and I polished it off in a month. She should have stitched her lips together."

A smile hovered at Judith's own lips. Gertrude and Deborah Grover had married brothers, produced one daughter apiece, been widowed, and engaged in perpetual, if loving, rivalry for over half a century. The fruit of their wombs, Judith Anne and Serena Elizabeth, had grown up as close as sisters, but—as both were fond of saying—without the sibling rancor because each could always send the other home.

It was Serena Elizabeth Grover Jones who interrupted dessert, Judith's favorite homemade apple strudel. "Okay," said Renie into the phone, "I finally remembered your other number, but I knew you'd still be eating. Did you watch the news?"

"No," admitted Judith. "Since when did you and Bill stop relying on the print media?"

"Since Sandy Frizzell got skewered in our very own parish nursery, smart ass," retorted Renie. "Bill's put together a psychological profile of the killer. You want to hear it?"

"I sure don't," said Judith, trying vainly to reach the last of her strudel. Renie's husband was a respected clinical psychologist at the university, and while Judith was fond of her kinsman, there were times when his expertise drove her as crazy as most of his clients. And, Judith thought wistfully, gazing at the strudel, dessert was one of those times.

"Obsessive. Self-righteous. A keen sense of justice—or injustice, depending upon your point of view." Renie paused, obviously being cued by Bill in the background. "Passionate. But repressed. Basically opposed to violence. Spiritual. And . . . uh, hey, Bill, turn down that ball game! I can hear Larry Bird drooling on the Garden parquet floor all the way over here! What was that last thing you mentioned?"

Judith kicked Sweetums out of the way and lunged for the strudel dish. Gertrude made a swipe at the whipped cream on her upper lip, missed, and lighted a cigarette. Sweetums coiled into an orange ball of fur and snarled.

"Oh," continued Renie, "and at least subconsciously aware of symbolism. So who done it?"

"Bill," responded Judith, devouring the last bite of strudel. "Sounds just like him. Was Sandy a patient?"

"Come on, coz," Renie urged as Bill vented his own repressions on the Boston Celtics, "don't you know anything? I hear," she went on, dropping her voice to an insinuating whisper, "that Joe Flynn is in charge of the investigation. Now aren't you more interested?"

"I saw Joe this afternoon," Judith said casually. "He and your old chum, Woody Price, were here. Mother wore her party hat."

"You're kidding!" exclaimed Renie, though it was unclear to which of Judith's statements she alluded. "How was he?"

" 'He'?" Judith feigned misunderstanding. "You mean Woody, your culinary partner? He's terrific, moustache intact. Are you going to seduce him or adopt him?"

"Don't be a mutt," chided Renie as Bill's groan shook the receiver. "Hey, I've got to call 911. Bill's having a stroke and the Celtics just went up by twenty-four. I also have to drive Anne over to church—she's lectoring at the vigil Mass. Our daughter's turned traitor. Father Hoyle asked Bill first, but he said participating in a Saturday night service was one of the seven deadly sins, the other six being Principal McCaffrey's Sunday sermons on sensitivity and sharing in Catholic education."

Across the kitchen, Sweetums had sprung up onto the counter and found the rest of the whipped cream. Judith yanked off her shoe, threw it at the cat, missed, and swore. Renie mistook this as a reaction to the mention of the school principal's name.

"Whoa," she remonstrated, "take it easy! I didn't know you felt as strongly as Bill does about Quinn McCaffrey!"

"Never mind Bill," snapped Judith as a simpering Sweetums displayed cream-covered whiskers. "That was for the damned cat. And anyway, I don't think Quinn's such a bad guy. But a lot of people probably wish he'd been there today so he could be a suspect. Better yet, the victim. When are you going up to church?"

Renie hesitated, waiting out her husband's next unprintable onslaught on the Celtics. For a man who was erudite, articulate, sensitive, and urbane, Bill's filthy mouth still amazed Judith even after twenty-three years. "Huh? Oh, Anne has to be up there about seven-thirty, I guess. Tony needs our car to pick up Rich Beth. His isn't good enough for the gold-encrusted little snot."

Judith took umbrage with her cousin's venom. "Hey, you sound like Monster Mom. Since when did you get so overly protective?"

The sudden silence, punctuated by Bill's obscenities directed at the rampaging Celtics, indicated that Renie was no doubt dismayed. "You're right, I sound . . . jealous. But Beth and her family are a bunch of would-bes," explained Renie, resorting to Grandma Grover's description of people who would be better than they actually were. "You know how that sort gripes the hell out of me."

"And me," Judith acknowledged. Satisfied that Renie wasn't going off the deep end of motherhood, she switched back to their original topic: "I'm going up to church after a while to collect Mother's blue bowl. I forgot it." She made a face at Gertrude, who was grinding out her cigarette in Sweetums's cat dish. "Meet you there and go to Moonbeam's for coffee?"

"Sure. It'll make Tony late. Ha, ha." Renie rung off, chortling with wicked triumph.

Just before seven-thirty, Judith pulled into the SOTS parking lot. There were already at least two dozen cars, including the Duffys' red Volvo and two of the Rankers's assorted rolling stock. Judith parked next to Carl's van with the four-wheel drive he'd bought after the last big snowstorm in order to negotiate Heraldsgate's steep streets.

Outside the sunlight lingered, a pink and gold sky above the busy bay. Inside the church, Gothic arches soared into the vaulted ceiling, while sad-eyed saints stood in niches along the side aisles. Silken banners hung throughout the nave, proclaiming the Resurrection. In the north and south transepts, the stained-glass windows glowed with red and amber fire, luminous portraits of the life of Christ. Stately Easter lilies and clusters of lilac filled the sanctuary. The old wooden pews took on a soft glow in the evening light, and the communion rail was festooned with garlands of freesia and baby's breath. The shabbiness that Judith had noted earlier was not so apparent on the eve of Christianity's greatest feast day. Or perhaps, she reflected, as she paused to pray at the side altar with its statue of St. Thérèse of Lisieux, it was not so important.

Yet for all the venerable stone and polished wood, the gleaming marble and granite pillars, the external formality and the inherent tradition, the living, breathing present pulsated down the aisles, in the choir loft, and even on the altar. Next to the pulpit, Mark Duffy and Father Mills were making some last-minute adjustments with the microphones. At the far end of the church, the choir was assembling up in the loft amid much chatter and rustling of music sheets. Kate Duffy was leading three young girls and a boy about the same age into the vestry, apparently to suit them up as altar servers. Eddie La Plante was setting up the Easter candle, a composite melted down from the parishioners' left-over Advent wreath candles. Judith went out through the side door of the north transept and along the little cloister that led into the rectory.

Father Hoyle was on the phone in the office, his chiseled profile frowning into the receiver. He was still in his civilian clothes, a golf cardigan over a polo shirt and casual slacks. "This is entirely inappropriate. I'm getting ready for the vigil Mass. Call me back a week from Monday." With uncharacteristic vehemence, he slammed down the phone and gave Judith an apologetic look. "God should give some people good sense instead of good intentions. That's the fifth person to call today and ask what Star of the Sea will do with Emily Tresvant's money. And two of them don't even belong to the parish!" Father Hoyle flung his hands up into the air.

"Snoops," murmured Judith. "By the way, who notified John and Sandy's children about her death?"

Father Hoyle, who had picked up his breviary, set it back down on the desk. He gave Judith a blank stare. "I don't know. John, I suppose." His even silver brows came together. "The funeral will be in New York. John's flying Sandy's body back as soon as the authorities release it."

"Well, that makes sense. I suppose she has family there." Judith shivered a bit and hugged her jacket closer. "Whatever happened to John's father?"

"I'm not sure." Father Hoyle retrieved the breviary, checked to make sure he had his glasses, and started for the door. "Someone—maybe Emily—once said he'd remarried. I didn't know John's mother. That was before my time." He paused with his hand on the knob, giving Judith that winning smile. "Emily Tresvant didn't talk about her brother-in-law much. I gathered she thought he was a scoundrel. She had very strict moral standards, you know."

After leaving Father Hoyle, Judith went through the rectory into the corridor that led past the nursery. Sure enough, the yellow and black tape designating a police investigation area was in place. Judith paused; the door was open, but the lights were off. In the dusk, she could just make out the room and its contents, unchanged to the naked eye, except that the toys seemed to have been picked up. Apparently Sandy had finished her chores before she died. Pooh Bear still reclined in his little chair, as if he were waiting for a visit from Christopher Robin. The colored blocks reposed neatly in a carton. The only sign of child-induced chaos was the dusting of broken chalk on the serviceable carpet. But the grim outline of a body sprawled near the cloakroom door gave mute evidence of the tragedy that had taken place since Judith had left Sandy to regain her equilibrium—and lose her life.

With a little shiver, Judith hurried into the church hall.

She flipped on the lights and was relieved by the sight of ordinary things: the limp velvet curtains on the stage, the stacks of folding tables and chairs, the bingo caller's booth, the high ceiling with its old-fashioned opaque light fixtures. Surprisingly little had changed since her own tenure at SOTS parochial school. Judith remembered cavorting in a chorus line for a talent show that had been short on the former and long on the latter. The eighth-grade graduation potluck dinner had been memorable for a set of dentures Sister Bridget had found in the tomato aspic salad. Then there was the Christmas pageant the year Renie played the Angel Gabriel and her wings got caught on a cardboard palm tree, causing her to let out a very unholy four-letter word. One of the few regrets Judith allowed herself was that Mike had not gone to Star of the Sea but to a series of public schools in whichever neighborhoods offered the most lenient landlords. The nostalgic laughter that had bubbled up inside faded as Judith recalled that Mike wouldn't be with the family for Easter. And Sandy Frizzell was going home in a casket.

There was no sign of Renie. Judith went into the kitchen, where she found Gertrude's blue bowl on the stainless steel counter. It had been washed and set out along with a cookie tray, a lazy susan, and a baking dish left behind by other absentminded SOTS. The sound of a door opening in the school hall caught Judith's attention. Hurriedly, she made one last check of the kitchen, just in case she'd forgotten something other than Gertrude's precious blue bowl. If Judith hadn't been afraid of getting appointed to chair a committee, she would have suggested to Father Hoyle that he use some of Emily's money for renovating the parish kitchen. But having so recently finished her own remodeling, Judith was inclined to keep her mouth shut.

The door in the hall opened again. "Coz?" Renie's voice cut into the silence.

Clutching the bowl, Judith turned off the kitchen lights

and came back into the hall. "Did you come in twice?" asked Judith, noting that her cousin was wearing Bill's Gortex jacket.

"Huh? No. Why?" Renie's brown eyebrows shot up.

"I heard the door open just a few minutes ago. That wasn't you?"

"No, I just got here." Renie gaped at Judith. "Your hair! It looks terrific! Good grief, you look younger than I do!"

"I *am* younger, by two years, dopey." But Judith was smiling broadly. "Do you really like it?"

Renie went through the motions of a critical study as Judith whirled and twirled. "Yes, I think it's really a wonderful change. Not too drastic, either. I won't ask what your mother thought." She glanced at her sleeve and gave a start. "Hey, I put on Bill's jacket by mistake! He'll shoot me!"

Accustomed to her cousin's occasional dressing errors, Judith shrugged. "Maybe Bill will buy you one of your own. Let's head for Moonbeam's. Shall we take both cars?"

Renie's round face puckered with annoyance. "I don't have mine. Tony insisted on bringing Anne and me up so he wouldn't make Rich Beth wait. I told him she could while away the time alphabetizing her stock options. If she knows the alphabet, of course. He was pissed with Mommy, but that's tough."

Judith grinned at her cousin. "Count your blessings. At least Beth doesn't look like a Viking."

"She's got the horns," retorted Renie as they started for the door. "Hey, wait—let me have a peek at that nursery. I haven't seen it in years, not since the kids were small."

Judith backpedaled away from the entrance to the hall. "There's nothing to see. It's taped off."

"I always wanted to tape the kids when I worked there," remarked Renie, then fixed Judith with narrowed brown eyes. "What's with you? Are you scared of this case?"

Judith's eyebrows shot up. "Of a mere murderer? After

eighteen years with Dan, tea with Torquemada wouldn't faze me."

"I know that." Renie made a wry face. "You could do a snarl-off with Attila the Hun. I meant scared of . . . Joe."

Judith's black eyes avoided Renie. "Joe? *Joe*." She stared at the worn hardwood floor, trying to be honest with her cousin—and herself. "No. I'm scared of *me*."

Renie's expression was sympathetic. "Are we talking lust—or love?" she asked quietly.

Judith uttered a heartfelt sigh. "After all these years, I don't know. I loved Joe way back when. Then I tried to hate him. Next came indifference. And all the while, I was eaten up with jealousy of Herself. Sometimes I think it was all those negative feelings that kept me going." She gave Renie a shamefaced look.

"Jealousy is a pretty strong emotion," allowed Renie. "I wish you'd talked to me more about how you felt then. You usually do."

Judith lifted one shoulder in a diffident gesture. "Instead of telling you how I felt about Joe, I bitched about Dan. I couldn't admit—even to you—that I still cared about Joe." Her black eyes finally met Renie's brown gaze. "You wouldn't believe the lies I told myself. The trouble was, *I* didn't believe them. Last Thanksgiving, when my dirty rat of a mother admitted that Joe had called me from Vegas and she'd never told me about it, I felt crummy for cursing him all those years. But whether he phoned or not, he still ran off with Herself. And yet Joe never went out of my mind, not for a minute." She rubbed her hands against the bowl, as if it were a magic lamp. "Then, when he popped up a year ago, all I could think of was hopping into the sack with him. But now, after so many months, I'm not sure what I really want. I've been a widow for four years, but I haven't really dated. And he's not going to want to jump from one marriage into another. We need time. Two weeks turns out to be too soon, not too long. There are so many things I don't understand about him—heck, I don't even know why he dumped me for Herself." She shook her head twice, very slowly, still mystified after more than twenty years. "If I keep out of this mess with Sandy, I can buy some extra time to figure out how I feel."

"You've had plenty for that." Renie, who often gave the impression of being dizzy, if not a bit dense, was wearing what Judith called her boardroom face. "You want to get to know the man, not the myth. All you had a year ago was twenty-four hours under intense pressure. Sure, he came for Thanksgiving, but family gatherings aren't conducive to intimate discussions. The way to find the real Joe Flynn is by watching him work in the harsh light of day, not in a candlelit bar when you're both half swacked."

"Well." Judith cleared her throat and gave Renie a look that was both dubious and grateful. "So much for romance. Let's face it, murder is a sordid business."

Having delivered her lecture, the diminutive Renie seemed to shrink inside Bill's extra-large Gortex jacket. "Letting somebody get away with it is even more sordid," she noted.

Judith grinned at Renie. "What do I do, start dusting for prints?"

"No," replied Renie. "Just be helpful. You talked to Sandy shortly before she was killed. You were probably here when the murder took place. Who knows what you saw or heard without realizing it at the time? Face it, coz, you're good at this sort off thing. You have an ability to win people's confidence and worm information out of them. You think logically and can fit all the pieces together so they make sense. Why waste your talent?"

For a moment, Judith was silent. If she'd gained inner strength during eighteen years of marriage, she'd lost self-confidence. Dan had battered her spirit, if not her body. Certainly her success in solving two homicide cases had bolstered her self-esteem as much as the success of the B&B.

Judith's statuesque figure stiffened with resignation. "Okay, I'm in. Again. I'll show you the blasted nursery. But we can't go inside. It's off limits."

The cousins paused at the open door, contemplating the murder scene in somber silence. Renie's eyes were riveted on the outline of the body.

A noise which seemed to emanate from the men's room across the hall made both women jump. Judith recalled the unexplained sound she'd heard before her cousin's arrival, and put a finger to her lips. The church had its own rest rooms, off the vestibule of the south transept. It struck Judith as unlikely that anyone attending the vigil Mass would come all the way outside, through the rectory or back across the parking lot to use the bathroom. Still clutching the blue bowl, she tugged at Renie's overlong jacket sleeve, dragging her cousin into the women's room.

They left the door ajar, Judith peeking around the edge and wishing she'd turned off the lights in the school hall. Barely a minute had passed when the men's room door swung open. A stealthy Norma Paine emerged with Wilbur's rabbit suit over her arm.

"Norma!" cried Judith, springing into the corridor. "What's the matter, is the ladies' room out of order?"

Norma gaped at the cousins, who were now in the hallway. Her long face was very pale, except for two spots of bright color on each cheek. "Oh, no," she replied, forcing a laugh. "I was retrieving Wilbur's costume. He left it in the men's room by mistake yesterday, and it has to be back at Arlecchino's by nine o'clock or they charge double."

"I see." Judith's expression was pleasantly bland. "He was quite a success. Has he had prior experience as a bunny rabbit?"

Norma's customary biting riposte was not forthcoming. Instead, she shifted her imposing weight and scrunched the costume up into a mangled wad. "He's played Santa Claus up here for the past three Christmases, and he was the April Fool at a law firm party." With a fixed smile, she nodded at both cousins. "I must run, I've only got an hour to get to the rental shop." Lowering her head like a running back on fourth down and inches, Norma Paine brushed past Judith and Renie, heading for the school hall.

Renie's skeptical gaze followed the other woman down the corridor. "Arlecchino's is all of a mile away. What's she going to do, put the suit on and hop over there?"

Judith was regarding Renie with a cagey expression. "Maybe she's going to take it to the dry cleaner's first." She paused, waiting for a reaction, but Renie displayed only puzzlement. "Didn't you notice, coz? A new color has been added to Wilbur's purple and green ensemble." She arched an eyebrow. "Dark crimson. Not at all an Easter shade."

For several minutes, Judith and Renie debated what to do about the alleged bloodstains on Wilbur's rabbit suit. Chasing Norma across the parking lot didn't strike them as a likely option. Renie suggested contacting Joe Flynn; Judith demurred, saying it was only a guess, after all. They finally compromised on a phone call to Arlecchino's.

"We'll tell them to hold the costume, that it might be police evidence," said Judith.

"That's assuming Norma doesn't try to wash the stains out," countered Renie.

"Bloodstains are hard to remove, and the dry cleaner isn't open on Saturday night. Of course Norma could simply burn the thing." Judith was starting back down the corridor. "Jeez, I don't see Wilbur as a murderer! It doesn't make sense!"

Renie didn't hear her. She was lagging behind, and suddenly called out to Judith: "Look! Footprints!"

Judith turned and gave her cousin a look of bemused skepticism. "Aren't you getting carried away, Sherlock?"

But Renie was bending over, reminding Judith of a small tent in her husband's big all-weather jacket. "I'm serious. See here—faint white footprints coming in and out of the nursery. Several, in fact." Renie stood up with triumph etched on her face.

Judith could see footprints on the spilled chalk in the nursery, but the light was too dim to discern what kind.

"Feet?" queried Judith. "Or paws?"

"Feet," replied Renie, faintly subdued. "But they could be anybody's, even the police's. Yours, too. So where are the paws?"

"We're drawing too many conclusions about the rabbit suit," said Judith. "Joe's people will deal with that stuff," she remarked. "Let's call Arlecchino's from the rectory office."

Renie balked. "What about Joe?"

Judith kept walking, her long strides forcing Renie into a trot to keep up. "At the moment, my attitude toward Joe is, if he won't call me, I won't call him. I forgot to tell you," she said, glancing at Renie over her shoulder, "he and Woody got a hot flash from the medical examiner. They didn't say what it was. Now we've got something to barter with, okay?"

They had reached the rectory, which was deserted except for Father Hoyle's Siamese cat, Pope Urban IV. The elegant animal, which struck Judith as unlike Sweetums as two members of the same species could possibly be, was curled up in the pastor's swivel chair, eyeing the newcomers with blue-eyed suspicion. Riffling through the pages of the phone book, Judith searched for Arlecchino's number while Renie made a deferential attempt to pet the cat and grinned mischievously at her cousin.

"What's with you?" asked Judith, her finger on the push-button phone.

"I'm thinking of Bill's last steelhead trip when he caught that twelve-pounder after getting skunked for over two years. He swore that was the same fish he'd been try-

ing to catch all along." She tickled Pope Urban IV behind
the ears and was rewarded with a faint purr. "Bill swears
it's a question of using the right lure. You, too, dear coz,
are hooked—on crime."

SIX

THERE WAS NO answer at Arlecchino's Costume Shop. Judith checked the yellow pages again and noted that their Saturday hours were from eight a.m. to eight p.m. Norma Paine had lied.

"So where did Norma go?" asked Renie.

Judith was sitting on the edge of Father Hoyle's desk, trying to replace the bulky phone directory in a wire rack. "We should have followed her. Damn! I wonder where Wilbur is?"

"Out hiding Easter baskets?" Seeing Judith grimace, Renie turned serious. "What about those footprints? Where did that dust come from?"

"Chalk." Judith examined a small silver Pieta on the pastor's desk. The depiction of a sorrowful mother and her crucified son made her think of Mike. "Ungrateful brat," she muttered.

"What?"

"Never mind." Judith was concentrating on the parish layout. "There's another entrance to the nursery, through the cloakroom. It comes out in the little alcove by the supply closet. But nobody could have gotten into the church that way because the connecting door was locked."

"That's right—I remember one of the Rankers's kids defecting that way years ago. He went back out through the hall. Kevin, it was," said Renie, still trying to make friends with Pope Urban IV. "I couldn't find him, and he ended up on the altar during a visiting missionary's plea for the starving Ethiopians. The poor guy didn't see Kevin and couldn't figure out why everyone seemed to find famine so funny."

Judith was absorbed in thought, drawing an imaginary line with her finger across the desk blotter. "So the killer could have come into the nursery that way, or through the main door off the hall." She shivered a bit. "Maybe while I was in the ladies' room. Oh!"

"What?" Renie stopped wooing the Siamese cat.

"I saw Wilbur go into the men's room just as I was leaving the church. But then I saw him driving away with Norma as I pulled out of the parking lot." Judith swung her long legs onto the floor and stood up. "I may be nuts, but I can't see Wilbur Paine as a cold-blooded murderer."

Renie pondered the idea. "He doesn't quite fit Bill's psychological profile," she admitted. "At least not the passionate part. Can you imagine Wilbur in heat?"

"Yeah, you're right. No wonder he made such a lousy rabbit." Judith started for the door. "Come on, let's see if we can find Norma."

Five minutes later, the cousins were heading for the Bluff, with the highest elevation and steepest prices on Heraldsgate Hill. It was almost dark when Judith stopped her car across the street from Norma and Wilbur Paine's impeccable Cape Cod. The white house with its dark blue trim was set on a rise above a well-tended rockery. Pot-of-gold, alyssum, saxifraga, and candytuft spilled over graceful boulders. Just as Judith shut off the engine, another car careened around the corner and came to a screeching halt in front of the Paine house.

"The Kramers," said Renie. "That's their white Mercedes." The cousins sat motionless as Eve Kramer leaped out of the car and ran up the stone steps that zigzagged through the rockery.

Eve was leaning on the doorbell like an impatient customer waiting for the express elevator to take her to a clearance sale. At last the front door opened, and Wilbur appeared in his bathrobe. Judith pressed the automatic button to lower the car windows a couple of inches. So far, neither Eve nor Wilbur had paid any attention to the blue compact parked across the street.

Eve, wearing her dark trenchcoat and high-heeled boots, seemed agitated. Wilbur acted nonplussed. It was clear that he had no intention of inviting Eve inside. Judith strained to hear the exchange, but couldn't pick up a single word. At that moment, Norma's pearl-white sedan came down the street and turned up the incline that led to the double garage. She braked the car at the top of the drive, the door flew open, and her imposing figure emerged in wrathful majesty.

"What's going on?" she demanded, marching along the side path to the front porch. In one hand, Norma carried her purse; in the other, a small shopping bag. Despite the oncoming darkness, Judith recognized the distinctive Falstaff's Market emblem.

Wilbur's response could not be heard, but Eve Kramer had now raised her voice, which carried across the street: "Keep out of it, Norma! It's too damned bad your brain isn't as big as your boobs! This could be a conspiracy, maybe even fraud! I'll sue the firm, the estate, every mother-loving son of you cheating crooks!"

" . . . Monday, in my office," came Wilbur's weary voice. He had shrunk back into the hallway, a small candelabra illuminating his pudgy frame. "Please, Eve . . ." The rest of his words were lost in the night.

"My husband's exhausted!" declared Norma, looming over the much smaller Eve. To Judith, they looked like a pair of feisty dogs, a boxer and a Pekingese. "He's been hopping all over Heraldsgate Hill. Leave him be, and get your vile tongue off our property!" She swung the shopping bag in a menacing manner, but Eve stood her ground.

"Listen, you self-righteous old bat, nobody makes a chump out of Eve Kramer! If you think you can scare me, you're crazier than I thought you were!" She whirled around, practically bumping into Norma's bust. "I'll be down at Wilbur's office Monday, and nobody'd better try to stall me!" Eve descended the stone stairs like a soldier on dress parade. Norma watched her go, then stomped into the house and slammed the door.

"Well." Judith looked at Renie as Eve started up her car with the ferocity of an entrant in the Daytona 500. "What was that all about?"

"I don't know," replied Renie, "but I don't think this is the time to call on the Paines and expect tea and cookies."

"No," agreed Judith, turning on the ignition and rolling the windows back up. "She didn't have the rabbit suit in that shopping bag, either. It was too small. Of course it might be in the car." She paused with her foot on the brake. "Think we should have a look?"

But Norma was already charging back out of the house, heading for the big sedan. She glanced at Judith's compact but kept walking toward the driveway.

"Too late." Judith sighed. "She's putting the car in the garage. Let's go home."

"What about Moonbeam's?" asked Renie. "I could go for some dessert. Vanilla mousse with blackberry syrup, or maybe that chocolate number with the orange filling." Her voice had taken on a dreamy quality.

"Look," said Judith, negotiating the corner, "you talked me into this caper. We're going to my house. I've got some apple strudel left, and I'll fix us a drink. We don't need caffeine this late in the evening."

Renie didn't argue. A few blocks later, they were pulling into Judith's drive. Just ahead, a bicycle swerved, and Judith plied the brake. "Damn! Who's that fool?"

The fool was Dooley. He stopped at the edge of the

drive and waved. "Hey, Mrs. McMonigle! Hi, Mrs. Jones! Want to know what I got?"

"Almost killed," said Judith, getting out of the car. "You could use more lights on that bike of yours."

"I was just taking the shortcut to my house," said Dooley, grabbing a parcel out of the basket on his bike. He saw the cousins eyeing him with curiosity and suddenly turned coy. "Got any more real pop?"

"Sure." Judith led the way to the back entrance, dimly aware of a cacophony emanating from the Rankers. Obviously, not all the relatives had gone to the evening Mass, but were keeping their own vigil in the vicinity of Carl's liquor cabinet.

Inside, Gertrude was nowhere in evidence. Judith figured she was glued to the John Wayne Guts 'n Glory TV movie festival scheduled for that evening. Getting a can of pop for Dooley, a bourbon for Renie, and a scotch for herself, she went out into the living room. So far, she'd had time to put out only a few Easter decorations—a fake tree branch covered with egg ornaments and lights in the shape of rabbit heads, a ceramic mother hen with her chicks marching across the mantel, and Gertrude's pride and joy, a late Victorian painting of the Resurrection with Christ rising from the dead using nimble footwork more reminiscent of Fred Astaire than the risen Lord.

Renie was already settled on one sofa, with Bill's jacket draped across the back. With studied nonchalance, Dooley was sprawled on the other couch, leafing through a book on the *Titanic* which he'd picked up from the coffee table. Unlike most teenagers, he wasn't just scanning the pictures, but actually reading the text. From Judith's experience in her chosen profession as a librarian, she found Dooley's love of books not only endearing, but decidedly abnormal.

"Where's the strudel?" asked Renie, taking the bourbon from her cousin.

"Shoot. I forgot." Judith started back for the kitchen, but Renie called out for her to skip it.

"I'm thinking of making a BLT when I get home. Or maybe pastrami and Swiss on rye with . . ."

As ever, Judith was dismayed by her cousin's prodigious appetite. Envious, too, since Renie never seemed to gain an ounce. Lenten fasting for Renie meant giving up *meals* between meals. Judith gave her cousin a baleful glance and flopped down next to her on the sofa.

"Gee," exclaimed Dooley, setting the book aside and putting a proprietary hand on his parcel, "did you know the *Titanic* went down on this same night in 1912?"

"Spooky," murmured Judith.

"Creepy," agreed Renie.

"Makes you wonder," mused Dooley.

"About what?" inquired Judith.

Dooley squirmed a bit on the sofa. "Well—you know, Fate and stuff. The stars. The planets."

Judith made a wry face. "Sandy Frizzell wasn't killed by an iceberg. What's in that sack?"

Dooley's adolescent face took on an age-old cunning. His sense of drama had run its course. With hands that were too big for the rest of him, he shook out the crumpled paper bag to reveal Wilbur Paine's rabbit suit. "Well?" His smug expression invited accolades. "What do you think of the Explorers now?"

Judith and Renie gaped at the gaudy costume spread across the coffee table. "Where did you find it?" breathed Judith, unable to wrench her eyes away from the rust-red stains.

Dooley swung one long leg over the armrest of the sofa, almost upsetting a vase of daffodils in the process. "The dumpster at Falstaff's." Seeing the proper amount of surprise register on his audience's faces, he grew more earnest. "Earlier, I went up to the store to get some cream cheese for my mom. She's making cheesecake for tomorrow. I was coming out when Mrs. Paine pulled in. She's a suspect, since she was up at church this afternoon, right?" He paused, rearranging his unruly fair hair into different, even stranger directions. "Ever since my brother got his bike ripped off at Falstaff's, I leave mine out of sight by the loading dock behind the dumpster. I was just going to get it when Mrs. Paine came sneaking across the parking lot. She'd waited in her car until she thought nobody else was around. I guess she didn't see me. Anyway, she went up to the dumpster and hoisted the lid—she's one strong lady, you know—and threw a package inside. Then she headed on into the store. I looked in the dumpster and sure enough, here's what I found." Dooley was looking pleased again, a faint flush on his usually pale cheeks.

"Amazing, Dooley," remarked Judith. "We'd better not handle it anymore." She glanced at Renie. "Should we call Joe?"

Renie was sipping her bourbon and looking perplexed. "We don't have a choice. Good Lord, I can't see Wilbur hurting a fly! But," she added thoughtfully, "it might explain the ruckus with Eve Kramer."

"What about Mrs. K?" asked Dooley, obviously disconcerted at having missed a beat.

Renie related the incident at Norma and Wilbur's house while Judith went to the phone on the pedestal table and dialed the homicide division. A bloodless female voice informed her that Joe Flynn and Woody Price were both out of the office until morning.

"I'm Judith McMonigle. I worked with Lieutenant Flynn and Officer Price on the fortune-teller murder a year ago last January." Judith was at her most businesslike. "Some important evidence has turned up in the Frizzell case. I must get hold of the detectives as soon as possible."

"Why," drawled the bland voice at the other end of the line, "don't you give the information to me and I'll see that it's passed on."

Judith thought she could hear the woman's fingernails drumming on her desk. "I'd rather not," said Judith.

The other voice grew faintly testy. "Why don't you come down to headquarters then?"

"What for, if Flynn and Price aren't there?" Judith could be testy, too. "Can't you page them or whatever?"

There was a long pause and the sound of faster drumming. "I could give you Lieutenant Flynn's home number," said the woman with the air of a benevolent empress bestowing a favor on a lowly peasant.

It was Judith's turn to hesitate. "Well—okay. What is it?" Judith listened closely and jotted the number down on a little pad she kept by the phone. Ringing off, she flipped through the directory, aware that Renie and Dooley were watching her. "Damn!" she breathed. "It's his home phone number all right."

"Why shouldn't it be?" asked Renie innocently.

Feeling the old jealousy take hold of her, Judith glared at her cousin. "What's he doing at home? He's supposed to be separated. I'll be damned if I'm going to call there and talk to Herself!"

It was Dooley who made the next call, at Judith's urging, to prevent his mother from fretting over her son's whereabouts. Mrs. Dooley was adamant—her dessert took precedence over Dooley's efforts at detection, and she needed her cream cheese right now. Judith soothed Dooley by assuring him that, in Joe's absence, nothing would happen until morning. Meanwhile, she would lock the rabbit suit away in her upstairs safe. Sad experience had taught her that police evidence could mysteriously disappear, even at Hillside Manor.

Just after Dooley's reluctant departure, Bill called, wondering where his Gortex jacket had gone. And, as an afterthought, his wife. The Jones car situation was now resolved, so Bill said he'd collect Renie about ten, on his way to pick up Anne at church.

The Rankers's relatives were going to be out late, so Judith had instructed them to lock up when they got in. After Bill took Renie home, Judith spent a half hour with Gertrude watching John Wayne single-handedly mow down great hordes of Chinese-American actors disguised as Axis Powers. Gertrude insisted that John Wayne wouldn't have had to go through all that if General MacArthur hadn't been such a pigheaded jackass. Not inclined to argue the point, Judith just shut up and waited for the eleven o'clock news.

The story on Sandy Frizzell's murder came almost at the end of the local segment and contained nothing Judith didn't already know: A forty-four-year old Heraldsgate Hill woman had been stabbed to death at Our Lady, Star of the Sea Catholic Church following an Easter egg hunt. Police were baffled. The victim and her husband had recently inherited the bulk of the Tresvant Timber estate. Except for a stock shot of the church steeple, there was no other film coverage. Judith was just as well-pleased. Her home parish didn't need the notoriety.

Feeling more tired than she realized, Judith put off her shower until morning. In her bedroom, she glanced outside, noting that it had clouded over again and a few drops of rain had splattered the dormer window. Lights were still on all over the house at the Rankers, but the rest of the neighbors in the cul-de-sac and higher up on the Hill appeared to be settling in to await Easter morn.

Judith's quarters were located on the third floor of the old house in what had been a servants' dormitory in the palmier Edwardian era. When Judith had converted the family home into a B&B, she'd found the top floor in a deplorable state. Rotting rafters, falling plaster, and broken floorboards had all but sabotaged her enterprise. It took a retired Swedish carpenter with endless patience and sixty years of know-how to turn the dilapidated space under the eaves into three bedrooms, a small foyer, and an office for Judith. Even Gertrude was pleased, so much so that within two weeks, she had taken over the office as her TV inner sanctum.

Now, amid yellow chintz with the window open just enough to let in the soft damp air, Judith clicked off the light on the bedside table and luxuriated under the covers. It had been a taxing day, though Judith was no stranger to stress and strain. Just as she closed her eyes, the phone rang. It was Joe.

"I heard you were trying to track me down," he said, his voice a bit fuzzy with fatigue. "What's happening?"

Judith started to blurt out her response, then turned cagey. "I want some answers from you first."

"Like what?" Joe sounded wary.

Judith propped herself up on one elbow. All thoughts of evidence fled. "Like . . . where are you?"

There was silence on the other end of the line before Joe's voice turned faintly impatient. "At home. Where else would I be at midnight after a fourteen-hour day?"

"Oh." Judith slumped back against the pillows. "Your house, you mean."

"Yeah, my house. The one I bought twenty-three years ago and have been paying off ever since. Seven years to go. What about it?" He sounded annoyed, but not necessarily with Judith.

Judith gripped the receiver tight. "Where's Herself?"

"Florida." Joe paused again. "I think. Where are you?"

Relief flooded over Judith. "In bed. Where else would I be at midnight after a grueling sixteen-hour day?"

"Gee. Wish I were there."

Judith resisted the urge to say, "Me, too." Instead, she smiled into the phone. "Where are your kids?" She knew he had some, at least two Herself had brought from her earlier marriages.

"Doug's married, Terri's living with some guy in San Francisco, and Caitlin's got a job with a chemical company in Switzerland. She dropped out of school for a while."

Doug and Terri were Herself's kids by two of her three previous husbands; Joe had fathered Caitlin the year after his marriage. He was alone in his house with the thirty-year mortgage.

"Where are you going for Easter?" Judith asked.

"Woody and his wife invited me over. But I'll spend

some time at work." He uttered a half laugh. "Don't tell me your mother has had a change of heart?"

"Not a chance."

"I like your hair. I didn't get a chance to tell you that this afternoon, what with dead bodies and all. When did you have it done?"

"Oh—not too long ago." Judith shrugged off the fib.

"You look like you lost weight, too."

"No, I haven't. Well, a little, during Lent." She winced at the outright lie.

"How's Mike?"

"Great. He likes forestry."

There was another pause at Joe's end. "The semester will be over in a few weeks. Then he'll be home."

Joe always had a knack for observation, for piecing together fragments of information. No doubt it made him very good at his job in dealing with criminals. It made him even better at understanding ordinary people. "He'll be gone most of the summer, working for the Forest Service in Montana," Judith said with a touch of bitterness.

"Caitlin might get home for Christmas this year." Joe sounded quite tired now. "She didn't make it last year. She'd only been on the job three months."

"It's weird—you spend half your life raising them and worrying and agonizing and then—they're gone." Judith spoke with wonder, voicing thoughts she'd never even shared with Renie.

"That's all part of the job description," said Joe. "Everything we do is supposed to make them independent, responsible adults. When it works out right, we're disappointed. But I've seen too many of the other kind. They'd break your heart if you didn't learn to look straight through them."

"Can you do that?"

Joe's laugh was dry. "Sure. I have to. Then I ask myself if I've sold out."

The rain was coming down harder, bouncing off the windowsill; the April breeze stirred the chintz curtains.

Across the way, the lights were going out at the Rankers. Judith tugged the comforter over her breast. She hadn't talked like this to a man in years. Not since she'd talked to Joe, in fact. She had bared her body to Dan McMonigle, but not her soul.

"How much is our fault?" she asked.

Only Joe would have known what she meant. "More than we like to admit. We are our children's keepers. That's our job. If I had my way, I'd fire about half the mothers and fathers out there. They stink. They've screwed up posterity."

"I don't know—most people do the best they can with what they've got, given the circumstances. You're getting hard, Joe."

The dry laugh came over the line again. "Go to sleep, Jude-girl. It's late."

In the distance, she heard the Rankers clan exchanging raucous good nights. Footsteps tramped across the walk and onto the back porch.

"Joe . . ." Judith's voice was surprisingly small.

"What?"

"You've grown up."

"God, I hope not!" He spoke with fervor. "Have you?"

Judith thought. "In some ways. I've had to."

"I suppose." Joe didn't sound too pleased at the prospect. "Just don't grow old, okay?"

"Okay," said Judith.

"Good," said Joe, and hung up.

It was some time later when it dawned on Judith that they hadn't discussed the murder.

To Judith's amazement, most of Sunday passed with no further developments in the Frizzell murder. Our Lady, Star of the Sea was packed for the nine o'clock Mass, the aisles crammed with the usual C&Eers, as Judith referred to Catholics who came to church only at Christmas and Easter. Father Hoyle made a tasteful allusion to Sandy in his homily, using her death as the basis for the meaning of the Resurrection. As ever, he was eloquent, dramatic, and witty by turn, climaxing the sermon with a call to walk the path of life as if it were the road to Jerusalem where Christ would appear along the way in many guises. Such as, he concluded, the person next to you in the pew.

Since that happened to be Gertrude in Judith's case, mother and daughter exchanged faintly sheepish expressions. It had taken half an hour of arguing, the prompting of Arlene, and the assistance of Carl to convince Gertrude that she could make it up to Mass. Her clumping entrance on the walker had turned a few heads, but not as many as she'd have wished.

"Newcomers," she'd hissed to Judith as they squeezed into the end of a pew near the side door. "Who *are* all these people? Why aren't the women wearing hats?"

Gertrude was, a twenty-year-old purple straw with floppy pink roses held tight to her head with several hatpins and a thick elastic band. Judith had suggested her mother cut holes in it for her ears. Gertrude had told her to kiss off.

The family dinner went off in typical style. Not to be outdone by her sister-in-law, Aunt Deb had arrived in a wheelchair. Gertrude undid the brakes and tried to send her flying through the French doors onto the back porch, but Anne threw a timely block in front of her grandmother and prevented disaster. Auntie Vance stopped nagging Uncle Vince—who was asleep anyway—long enough to tell both her sisters-in-law to go soak their addled heads. Bill bet Uncle Al fifty dollars that the Lakers would beat the Pistons by ten. Bill lost. Uncle Al crowed. Rich Beth said she thought gambling was a nasty vice. Renie said that Rich Beth was nasty, period. Tony called his mother a reverse snob. Tom called Tony a dweeb. Mike called Judith just after the family left around eight o'clock.

"Happy Easter, Mom," said Mike over a bad connection. "I tried earlier, but the circuits were tied up."

Judith was beaming into the phone. "Are you having a

good time? What did you eat for dinner? How's the weather over there? Are Kristin's parents nice?"

"What? I can't hear you, Mom. Kristin and I are going horseback riding. It got up to eighty degrees today on this side of the mountains. Hey, who got killed on the Hill? Anybody we know?"

"Sort of," said Judith. "Horseback riding in the dark? Are you nuts?"

"Huh? Arunitz? I don't remember any Russians from church. Hey, got to go! Say hi to Grams! Kristin's saddling up!"

It occurred to Judith that Kristin was so big she could put on a saddle and carry about four farmhands around the wheat ranch without breaking a sweat. Sighing, she replaced the phone and returned to the task of cleaning up the kitchen. When the phone rang again, she hoped it was Mike, trying for a better connection. Instead it was Dooley.

"Guess what!" he burst into her ear. "I had my CB on, and something weird has happened!" He took a deep breath, his voice cracking. "Mark Duffy has been arrested!"

SEVEN

"MARK DUFFY?" JUDITH was incredulous. Mark's tall, dark, handsome image rose before her eyes, the perfect husband to the perfect wife. As a homicidal maniac, only Wilbur Paine was a less likely suspect. "On what grounds?" asked Judith in a breathless voice.

"Breaking and entering," came Dooley's reply. "John Frizzell caught him trying to climb in the basement window of their rental house."

Mark Duffy as a burglar was only slightly less hard to take in than Mark Duffy as a murderer. "There must be a mistake. Or does John have a grudge against Mark?"

"I don't know. Want to go down to headquarters and see what's happening?" Dooley sounded eager.

Taking in the chaos of her kitchen, Judith winced. "Gosh, Dooley, it's after eight . . . Can't we just call?"

"Awww . . ." Dooley's voice wound down with disappointment. "Come on, Mrs. McMonigle, you don't want to prevent me from doing my duty as an Explorer?"

Judith weighed domestic chores against civic responsibility. The Rankers's relatives were gone, for all intents and purposes. No one else was due at Hillside Manor until Tuesday afternoon. "Okay." Judith sighed. "I'll pick you up in ten minutes."

On their way downtown, Judith asked Dooley to point out the Frizzell rental. "It's on my paper route," he said, "but I never collected. They always paid by mail."

Judith slowed at the bottom of Crabtree Street. A modest white bungalow nestled between an older three-story apartment house and a brick duplex. Behind tightly drawn drapes, a single light glowed amber.

"Cozy, maybe," remarked Judith. "But a far cry from the Tresvant place up on the Bluff."

"That's a mansion," agreed Dooley. "My buddies and I used to sneak over the fence and play spies. Old Miss Tresvant threatened to call the cops on us once."

Judith pictured the Tresvant house, an imposing brick and stone turn-of-the century estate in a parklike setting. Its baronial splendor had been well-suited to a timber magnate, but was something of an anachronism in the last decade of the twentieth century. Judith wondered if John would return to New York now that both Sandy and his aunt were dead. Certainly there was nothing to hold him on the Hill. Assuming that Wilbur Paine wasn't a murderer, he and his law firm could handle John's local legal business.

Downtown was virtually deserted at nine o'clock on Easter night. The sun had come out in the morning, but a late afternoon rain had left the streets a shiny black. Judith had no trouble finding a parking place next to the Public Safety Building. She and Dooley went inside and asked directions to the homicide division. They were waiting for the elevator when Kate and Mark Duffy emerged, looking shaken to their shoes.

"Judith!" exclaimed Kate in her wispy voice. "How kind of you to come!"

"Ah . . . well, thanks, but . . ." Judith submitted to a hug from Kate and a pat on the back from Mark.

"I posted bail," he said, his chiseled features grim. "I don't understand why John is being such an ass about this. He wouldn't even look at us when he was pressing charges, then he high-tailed it out of here like a rocket without saying a word. I suppose it's because he's not himself."

"Of course he's not," agreed Kate, taking her husband's arm. "John's beside himself with grief. He wouldn't even come to the door when Mark rang the bell. Poor man, he must have been sitting alone in the dark, mourning." Her pale lashes fluttered up at Mark. "To be fair, how could he expect that you'd be looking for our wheelbarrow on Easter Sunday?"

Mark gave a little shrug of his broad shoulders. Over the years, his efforts on behalf of the parish and the school had been surpassed only by those of his wife. "I planned on taking tomorrow off. I usually do on Easter Monday. Kate's been nagging me to get some yard work done." He smiled down on his mate, whose sweet face glowed up at him in a mutual display of devotion.

"John borrowed the wheelbarrow a couple of months ago," put in Kate as what appeared to be a gang of murderous drug dealers were hustled into the elevator, "not long after they moved into their rental. He forgot to return it, and when he didn't answer the door, Mark decided not to bother him in his time of sorrow. Lord help John, he was so devastated that he didn't even go to church today."

"I see," said Judith, but wasn't sure she did. At her side, Dooley fidgeted, disinterested in the discussion of manners and mores. "So he called the cops on Mark for trying to reclaim the wheelbarrow?" inquired Judith, shifting her tote bag from one hand to the other.

Kate clung to her husband's arm, oblivious to the six-foot, six-inch screaming maniac with shoulder-length hair and a long, matted beard who was being hauled past them in handcuffs. "John thought Mark was a burglar! Imagine! Bless his heart, John wouldn't listen to reason. He called

911 and the police came right away, as I guess they were sort of watching the house, and John pressed charges. Hysteria, I suppose. Not in his right mind." Sadly, she shook her head. "But I'm sure when he realizes what he's done—after the shock of Sandy's death wears off—he'll come to his senses and apologize. At least Mark is free, and thank the Lord that all's well that ends well." She looked up again at Mark, smiling beatifically.

"That's good," said Judith, lacking her usual conviction. "Have a nice holiday." She nodded at Mark, who was caressing the hand that Kate was resting on his arm.

Kate's blond eyebrows lifted. "You're not coming home with us for coffee and cake? But I thought you were here to help."

Judith shuffled a bit awkwardly as three screeching, kicking, cussing prostitutes were herded into the elevator. "Actually ... I came down with Dooley because he's an Explorer. He needed a ride and his folks are ..."

"Drunk," said Dooley, saving Judith but not sparing his parents. "I mean, just enough so they shouldn't drive. They belong to MADD."

"Oh." Kate looked disappointed, though whether in Dooley's family or Judith's lack of support was impossible to tell. "Still," she brightened, "it gave us a lift, just seeing friendly faces in this place." A little shiver underscored her point. "Really, jail isn't at all nice."

"True," agreed Judith, willingly being dragged off by Dooley toward the next empty elevator, which was blessedly devoid of perpetrators. "Good night, now."

"Yuk!" exclaimed Dooley as the doors slid shut and he leaned against the rear of the car. "Mrs. Duffy is unreal! All that mushy stuff. And I can't believe she'd make Mr. Duffy go chasing a wheelbarrow on Easter Sunday."

Judith wrinkled her nose. "Neither can I."

The doors opened onto the fifth floor. Judith and Dooley stepped out, following an arrow pointing to the homicide division. "You mean you don't think he really was trying to get his wheelbarrow back?"

"I think," said Judith as they turned a corner and saw the office they were seeking at the end of a long hall, "that the only thing more farfetched than Mark Duffy breaking and entering is Mark Duffy looking for his wheelbarrow on Easter Sunday." She broke stride just long enough to ruffle Dooley's unkempt hair. "Come on, Dooley, the first thing you have to study in detective work is people. Consider their character and draw logical conclusions. Granted, people don't always do logical things. But they usually act in character. Besides, have you ever seen the Duffys' yard?"

"Sure. They're on my route, too."

"They've got a lovely house, but they're no gardeners. A few bulbs, perennials, half a dozen rose bushes, and about four shrubs. Mark Duffy needs a wheelbarrow like I need ten more pounds."

Judith paused at the open door. A stained mahogany desk ran along one wall. A chunky Japanese woman with glasses dangling on a chain eyed the newcomers quizzically. Before she could ask what they wanted, Joe Flynn ambled out from a side door, a paper cup of coffee in one hand, a sheaf of papers in the other.

"Well! Two of my favorite Crimestoppers," he greeted them with forced cheer. It struck Judith that he wasn't entirely pleased by their visit. "What's up?"

"Mark Duffy, on charges," replied Judith. "What's with him and John Frizzell?"

"Good question." Joe's eyes darted around the reception area, as if he was hoping someone would rescue him. He took a couple of quick swigs of coffee. "Mark's story is lame, but John's reaction was out of proportion. According to the patrolmen, he went off his head and pulled a gun on Mark."

"Wow!" exclaimed Dooley.

Judith's response was more circumspect. "I wondered. Mark's a big guy. John's fairly tall, but on the slim side. I couldn't imagine him subduing Mark unless he knew karate."

"What kind of gun?" asked a fascinated Dooley.

"A .38 Special, carry permit in order." He shrugged the weapon off and gestured toward the door with his coffee cup. "Listen, guys, I've got to run. I only came in tonight to wrap up that houseboat case on the lake. Tomorrow I'll be going full bore on this one. Call me then, okay?"

"Hold it." Judith planted herself in front of Joe. "First, we exchange Easter presents." She unzipped her tote bag to reveal a lumpy parcel. "You tell us what the M.E. said, we'll give you this. I promise you'll like it."

Joe scowled into the bag, then relented. "Okay, come on." He pushed open a waist-high swinging door in the counter. The woman at the desk peered at the trio over her glasses. Judith wondered if she was the nail drummer of the previous night.

Joe's office was as disorderly as his grooming was meticulous. File folders littered the desk, computer printouts unraveled onto the floor, the walls were covered with charts and maps, the in basket was so crammed that it pressed up against the almost-empty out basket on top, and the ashtray was full of half-smoked cigars. All but hidden among the clutter was a framed photograph which faced away from Judith. Taking in a breath of stale air, she resisted the urge to turn the picture around.

"Have a seat," invited Joe, despite the fact that both extra chairs were covered with yet more paperwork. "Here, we'll move this stuff onto the filing cabinet."

Judith looked askance at the double steel cabinet that was already loaded with strange objects, including a human skull. Her darker side wished it was Herself.

"Okay," said Joe, sitting down opposite his visitors and pitching the paper cup into a wastebasket so crammed that he had to put his foot in it to make room, "what have you got?"

"You first," insisted Judith.

Joe started to balk, saw the set of Judith's strong jaw, and leaned back in his chair. "Okay. The M.E. says that the fatal wound was inflicted by a sharp object about four inches long which pierced the skin an inch and a half to the left of the breastbone, puncturing the heart. Death was almost instantaneous." Joe was reciting from memory. "Said weapon was left in the body, and was described as a pair of Japanese-made embroidery scissors belonging to Eve Kramer, owner and operator of Old As Eve, an antiques and needlework shop located at 2774 Heraldsgate Avenue. Eve identified said scissors this morning."

Judith and Dooley exchanged startled glances. "You mean she did it?" Dooley asked.

Joe shook his head. "We aren't saying anything. Yet. Ms. Kramer says the scissors were in her shoulder bag which was left in the kitchen off the church hall. According to her, anyone could have taken them."

"That's weak," said Dooley.

"No," countered Judith, realizing that it was Eve's embroidery scissors she'd thought of when Joe had first mentioned the weapon that had killed Sandy. "It's true. Everybody knew Eve carried her stitchery things with her. And she often left that bag wide open. I don't consider Eve a trusting soul, but I've wondered if that was her one concession to the better side of human nature." She turned to Joe, who was flipping through the papers he'd carried into the office. The fluorescent lighting cast a jaundiced glow on everything, including Joe's usually rubicund complexion. "You know that's odd—I remember seeing Eve's stitchery in her handbag in the church kitchen, but not the scissors. And yet I saw them when I spoke to her Friday at Chez Steve."

"Maybe," suggested Joe, "they'd just slipped to the bottom of her bag."

"Maybe," said Judith, not entirely convinced. "What about fingerprints?"

"None," replied Joe. "I imagine the murderer wore gloves, though it wouldn't be impossible to wipe the scissors off even when they were still in the body."

Judith's face sagged. The image of Sandy Frizzell lying on the nursery floor with a pair of embroidery scissors sticking out of her breast was too gruesome to contemplate. "The chalk—were there footprints?" Judith asked hastily.

Joe's mouth twitched into a smile. "You've been detecting. Yes. All over the place, including one odd pair that led to the cloakroom, out into the hall, and back down to the men's room." He eyed Judith cagily. "Shall I tell you what kind of footprints?"

Judith took the package out of her tote bag and handed it not to Joe, but to Dooley. "Let's say I don't need a lucky rabbit's foot to take a guess."

Joe pulled out a single sheet of paper and put it on the desk. It looked like a form from where Judith was sitting. "Okay, Dooley," he said, "let's have it."

Joe whistled when he saw the green and purple costume. He stared hard at the dark stains, then shook his head. "I can't be sure, but it looks like blood." Judith and Dooley took turns relating their stories: Norma coming out of the men's room with the costume, her fabrication about returning it to Arlecchino's, Dooley's discovery in the dumpster, and last, but not least, the scene between the Paines and Eve Kramer.

"Why the hell," demanded Joe, "didn't you tell me all this last night?"

Judith let out a great sigh. "I don't know," she admitted. "I meant to. That's why I called in the first place." She gave him an appealing look. "We got to talking . . . about other things . . . and I . . ." Her voice trailed away as she felt a faint flush creep up her face. "It's Easter, after all. To everything there is a season, and last night wasn't it." Judith's tone had become sharper, her chin thrust out. She felt Dooley's eyes on her and swerved around on the chair to stare him down. "Don't you dare compare me to Kate Duffy!" she admonished, leaving the boy with a bewildered expression.

"Okay, okay," said Joe. "I'll get this outfit off to forensics. We'll see if this is blood, and if so, if it's Sandy Frizzell's. We'll run other tests, too, and maybe we'll come up with something that either will eliminate or implicate Wilbur Paine." Joe had gotten to his feet, hands at his hips. "Tell me again, when did you last see Wilbur wearing this suit?"

Judith didn't need to think. "Going into the men's room, on my way out. As near as I can recall, it was around one-thirty."

"What did Wilbur say?" Joe enunciated the question very clearly, as if he were speaking to a child.

Judith started to get huffy. "He said . . ." She stopped, a hand ruffling her new hairdo. "Actually, he didn't say anything. He just sort of waved."

Joe's green eyes held Judith prisoner. "Okay. Now concentrate. Are you sure it was Wilbur you saw go into the men's room?"

More mesmerized by Joe's electric gaze than the question, Judith faltered. "What? Oh!" Chewing on her lower lip, she tried to recall exactly what she *had* seen the previous afternoon. A rabbit. From the back. Purple and green, floppy ears, a fluffy tail, funny paws for feet, gloved hands. Looking tired. Or, in retrospect, furtive? Judith shook her head. "To be honest, it could have been anybody. I just assumed it was Wilbur because of the suit."

"Right." Joe gave Dooley a half smile. "You see, son, sometimes your eyes *can* deceive you. That's one of a detective's first rules. And remember, nobody sees the same thing the same way." He leaned down to pick up a pen and write something in a blank space on the form he'd set in front of him. "Here, Dooley," said Joe, handing over the single sheet of paper, "take this down the hall on your right to Officer Price's box. Mrs. Gorai will tell you where it is. Thanks." Dooley started off, but Joe had one last word: "You did good work. Finding this suit was a real smart bit of follow-through. I'll see that you get a commendation."

"Wow!" exclaimed Dooley, his fair hair seeming to spring to life. "Thanks!"

Judith had also gotten up. "I'd better go, too. I can't think of anything else I ought to tell you." She gave Joe a weary, almost diffident smile.

He'd come around the desk to take Judith's arm. "You probably can, but this isn't the time or place for it." He paused, the green eyes searching her face, then abruptly turned and picked up the framed photograph. "This is Caitlin. High school graduation three years ago. What do you think?"

Judith studied the smiling girl with the red curls, beguiling dimples, and merry green eyes. "I think she's lovely! She looks just like you!"

Joe laughed. "Nobody has ever called *me* 'lovely.' But thanks," he said, sobering. "She's quite a gal. Bright, too. A terrible temper, and stubborn as hell, but nobody'll ever get the best of her. I hope."

"Gee," mused Judith, "I wonder where she got all that?"

Joe held the photograph at arm's length and allowed himself a moment of paternal pride. "I have to admit, she's always been Daddy's little girl. But then," he added on a more somber note, "Herself has never been the motherly type."

Judith's memory of Herself was of a dyed blond with long legs, a high bosom, false eyelashes like bird wings, and dresses slit to the hip. She'd had something of a singing voice, a whiskey contralto that was usually drowned in gin. And she definitely had played a mean piano. Yet even after two decades, Judith still didn't understand the attraction. Or at least didn't want to.

Joe had set the photograph back down, pushing aside a stack of folders and a Rolodex to give Caitlin a little breathing room. "I'll walk you out," he said, again taking her arm. "There's something I should tell you, though."

Feeling his touch and aware of his gaze, Judith felt faintly breathless. Absurd, she lectured herself, but there it was ... "What?" she asked, and could have sworn her voice cracked like Dooley's.

"You'll know by morning anyway," said Joe, still somber. "I didn't tell you everything the M.E. said in his report. I held back because of Dooley." He frowned, and to Judith's puzzlement, gave a little incredulous shake of his head. "The medical examiner had a real shock when he started in on Sandy. It seems," he went on, his voice rising slightly, "that Alexandra Frizzell was Alexander. Sandy was really a man."

EIGHT

JUDITH DROVE DOOLEY home in a daze. She was exploding with the urge to tell somebody the astounding news she'd just learned, but since Joe had made a decision not to inform Dooley, Judith felt bound to silence. The department's delay had been based on several factors, Joe had explained: the Easter weekend, which left them shorthanded in terms of media relations; the need to consult with the police chief who had flown to California to be with his wife's family for the holiday; and most of all, Joe's determination to talk to John Frizzell and figure out what was really going on with such a bizarre charade. So far, John had refused to discuss the matter with Joe or anyone else. Succumbing to the Easter spirit, Joe had decided to wait until Monday before he became hard-nosed. Whether John had lost Alexandra or Alexander, he was still deeply bereaved.

But if Judith kept her counsel as far as Dooley was concerned, she was sorely tempted to call Renie. Or better yet, stop by the Jones house. But it was after ten when she dropped Dooley off, and Judith was tired.

There was still the kitchen to clean up. In the days of fore-closed mortgages and dumpy rentals, she had been an in-different housekeeper. But Hillside Manor had changed Judith's domestic habits. She never went to bed with a sinkful of dirty dishes.

She was putting the last load in the dishwasher an hour later when a knock sounded at the back door. Judith glanced out the window, saw that the Rankers's lights were still on, and went to let Arlene in.

"They've gone!" she exclaimed, collapsing onto one of the dinette chairs. "It was all just wonderful! We had the best time! I hope they never come back!"

It was vintage Arlene, full of earnest contradictions. Judith finished wiping off the counters and joined her neighbor at the dinette table. "They were certainly no trouble here. All they did was sleep."

"No wonder." Arlene lifted her red-gold eyebrows. "They wore themselves out having fun. I brought my checkbook. I want to pay you before I forget." She delved into the pocket of her red jacket.

"Oh, there's no hurry . . ." Judith began, but Arlene was already scribbling away.

"There," she said, handing the check over to Judith. "What a weekend! Did you hear about the Duffys getting broken into?"

Judith shook her head. "No, it was the other way around. Mark was accused of breaking into the Frizzells."

"No, no," countered Arlene. "I mean, yes, he was, but while Mark and Kate were down at police headquarters, someone broke into their house, too."

"What?" Judith shot back in her chair.

"Oh, yes," asserted Arlene. "Isn't it terrible? I don't know what this world is coming to. You're not safe in your own house these days. Why, you're not even safe at church! I still can't get over poor Sandy!"

Neither could Judith, but at this point not for precisely the same reason. "Back up," said Judith. "Tell me again, what happened at the Duffys?"

"That's all I know." Arlene didn't look very happy over her lack of information. "Kate called me about eleven o'clock and said they'd come back from police headquarters to find that someone had broken into the house. They called the police—who turned out to be the same patrolmen who'd arrested Mark—and filed a complaint."

Judith's head seemed to be spinning in rhythm with her dishwasher. "Was anything taken?"

"Of course." Arlene lifted her shoulders. "The usual—their VCR, the sterling, Kate's pearls, Mark's camcorder, stereo stuff, the TV the kids gave them for their anniversary. The house is a mess. I can't understand why burglars have to be so careless—they always know exactly what they're looking for." Arlene turned quite cross.

"Yes, they do," Judith agreed in an odd voice.

But Arlene took no notice. "I must run. I want to go over to the Frizzells tomorrow and see if I can help John with the arrangements. It's a shame they didn't have time to make friends. I honestly don't think anyone on the Hill felt very close to them."

Judith agreed—and thought she now knew why.

The sensation caused by the police department's announcement that Mrs. John Frizzell was actually Mr. John Doe sent Heraldsgate Hill reeling. The story had broken in a news bulletin on radio and TV shortly before nine a.m. Judith, who was in the shower at the time, didn't hear it, but Renie called about an hour later before going into a presentation she was making at the university.

"I had the radio on in the car," she said. "Honest to God, I just about ran over six people in a crosswalk! What's going on?"

"I don't know," Judith admitted. "Are you free for lunch?"

"Yeah," replied Renie, "until two when I meet with some old twit from the phone company. I ought to be done here just before noon. The usual?"

"Right. See you then." Judith hung up just as Dooley

sprang onto the back porch and Gertrude thumped into the kitchen. It was too late to stop either of them. Dooley was inside the house before Gertrude could get as far as the sink.

"Well, you little pervert," she rasped, "done any window peeking lately, or have your folks taken away your telescope?"

The incident involving Dooley's up-close and personal view of Gertrude, naked as a jaybird, was still a source of friction between the two. Dooley attempted to look abject, caught Judith holding up two wiggling fingers behind her mother's head, and almost lost control.

"I'm interested in astronomy," he explained. "You know, stars, planets, meteors, heavenly bodies."

"Which leaves *you* out, Mother," murmured Judith, still gesturing behind Gertrude's back.

Gertrude, however, was willing to suspend hostilities in the wake of the newest sensation about Sandy Frizzell.

"I know all about homosexuals and transvestites and stuff," said Dooley, "but this is *too* weird. Why would a man pretend to be a woman?"

"It's stupefying," agreed Judith, automatically pouring orange juice for Dooley and coffee for her mother and herself. "The charade had to be necessary. But why?"

Gertrude had taken her coffee mug over to the sink, where she was cutting up cabbage for cole slaw. "I can think of ten million dollars worth of reasons," she barked. "What if somebody's impersonating the real John?"

"Huh?" gasped Judith.

"Unreal," breathed Dooley.

"I don't get it," confessed Judith, as surprised by her mother's late entry into deduction as she was by the remark. Judith turned pensive, both hands curved around her coffee mug with its smiling but blurred picture of Queen Elizabeth II in her coronation regalia. Indeed, Judith thought as she gazed down at the mug, after going on forty years, the Queen looked like she could use a cup of coffee, too. "I've heard screwier ideas," she admitted to her mother and Dooley. "But Emily must have known John, or at least seen pictures. His mother—what was her name, Lucille?—lived with Emily for a time."

Gertrude ground away at some carrots. "I don't remember seeing John Frizzell. Ever. When Lucille came back to Heraldsgate Hill, John was in college someplace, California maybe, I forget. As far as I know, he never set foot in this town until old auntie was on her last legs and loaded for bear."

The more Judith listened, the more plausible Gertrude's theory became. As she headed down the Hill and into the city's metropolitan district, it struck Judith that John Frizzell and Sandy had shown up a bit too conveniently. The possibility of John being an impostor was the first topic of conversation between Judith and Renie when they met at their old haunt, Papaya Pete's, on the edge of downtown. Amid Polynesian decor and the aroma of curry, the cousins discussed the latest details in the Frizzell case. Renie insisted Joe must have a notion of what was going on; Judith insisted that he had seemed as genuinely baffled as the police were always supposed to be.

Savoring the Green Goddess salad dressing on her enormous crab louie, Judith did her best to peddle Gertrude's theory about John. Renie wasn't buying.

"No," she asserted. "Emily Tresvant was neither trusting nor gullible. She wouldn't accept an utter stranger as her sole relative and heir. Maybe she never met John until this winter, but I'll bet she'd seen pictures. Lucille must have had some, and he'd have been grown by the time she came back to live with Emily, so he wouldn't have changed that much. John and Sandy . . ." She stopped, fork poised over a slice of tenderloin beef slathered in curry sauce. "Good grief, I just can't take in that Sandy was a *man!*"

"Some Sandys are," said Judith dryly.

"One's a dog," agreed Renie, "if you count L'il Orphan Annie."

Judith savored a mouthful of Dungeness crab before she

responded. "No wonder Sandy wore so much makeup. I just thought she—he—had lousy skin. What about those kids?"

Renie snorted, causing the two businessmen at the next table to turn discreetly in the cousins' direction. Leaning closer to Judith and lowering her voice, Renie was oblivious to the damage she was doing to her fuji silk banana-yellow blouse. "Ten to one, they don't exist. Or they're some relation of Sandy's. If they were John's, they might stand to inherit, too."

Judith winced at the curry sauce stain on Renie's left breast. There was no point in mentioning it yet. Renie wasn't finished eating. "Joe will check on that, I'm sure." Judith picked through the romaine for more crab, but came up with a slice of avocado instead. "I wonder—what was Eve accusing Wilbur of? She mentioned an estate. Do you suppose it was Emily's?"

"Could be." Renie licked rice from her lower lip. "As for family pictures, who would have seen them at Emily's?"

Judith reflected. "Emily wasn't much for company. She was a virtual recluse in her later years. But Eve was in the house at some point. She knew there were a lot of valuable antiques there." Wearing a sly expression, Judith delved for the last crab leg. "Speaking of pictures, that reminds me, what if that wasn't a real burglar at the Duffys? I mean, I was thinking, what if it was someone going after Mark's videotape of the Easter egg hunt? The other stuff might have been taken just as a cover."

Renie's brown eyes widened. "Well! That's right, all you do with those things is take them out and slip them into your VCR, right?"

Judith went for the last piece of cracked whole wheat bread, but Renie had beaten her to it. The cousins exchanged mutual mock glares. The businessmen at the next table eyed them surreptitiously. "What was on that tape, I wonder?" mused Judith.

"The scissors snatcher?" suggested Renie with a grimace. "That would make it premeditated murder. Ugh." She glanced down at her front. "*Ugh!* I've practiced piggery. As usual."

"You don't need to practice, you're very good at it," replied Judith as Renie frantically dabbed at her blouse with a napkin soaked from her water glass. "We're assuming, of course, that Eve is *not* the murderer. She's got the nerve, I think she's a bit ruthless, but I don't see any motive. Yet."

Their waiter approached with coffee. The cousins paused, going through the ritual of accepting tall glasses encased in macrame holders, with sugar but no cream for Renie, black for Judith.

The waiter departed. Renie inspected her blouse. Judith noted that the garment was now wet enough to make her look like a nursing mother, and wondered, not for the first time, how Renie had survived so long in the corporate world. Obviously, neatness didn't count.

"When," inquired Renie, holding her coffee glass close to her bosom in an apparent effort to steam the blouse dry, "will Joe get back the lab report on the rabbit suit?"

"Late today," answered Judith. "Damn, I wish I'd paid more attention to the rabbit when I came out of the rest room."

"You think it might not have been Wilbur?"

Judith shrugged. "I don't know. I just *assumed* it was. And yet there was something about him . . . he looked . . . what?" She screwed up her face in an attempt at recollection. "He seemed all done in. Different, somehow. But at the time, I chalked it up to fatigue."

Renie stirred extra sugar into her coffee and stared down a furtive glance from one of the businessmen. "Wilbur Paine, homicidal maniac. It doesn't wash. None of the SOTS on Joe's suspect list strikes me as a killer. The only one I really don't know very well is old Eddie, the church gardener."

Judith brushed a few stray breadcrumbs from her orange linen skirt. "He hasn't been around too long. What was it, a year or so ago when Grandpa Dooley's kite got struck by lightning and he had to give up his gardening job?"

"He should have given up kites," said Renie. "Yeah, it was in the spring. March, I think. Father Hoyle was in a pickle about a replacement, and then Eddie came out of nowhere and volunteered." Renie blithely mopped up the last bit of curry sauce with the last bite of the last piece of the whole grain wheat bread.

Judith eyed her cousin in a speculative manner. "That's just it. Where was 'nowhere'? Sunday I asked Uncle Al if he knew Eddie, and he didn't, except for seeing him up at SOTS. And Uncle Al knows *everybody* on the Hill, especially everybody over sixty-five."

"Good point," conceded Renie. "But not hard to check out. We could start by asking Eddie."

"I suppose," said Judith. "Somehow, I've always felt that Eddie's switch isn't turned all the way on." She sipped at her coffee, nodding absently to the two businessmen who were now exiting from their table. "Meanwhile, I intend to find out what Eve Kramer was having such a fit about over at the Paines' house Saturday night."

"How?" Renie raised both eyebrows, never having mastered the art of lifting only one.

"I'm going to see Wilbur Paine on business as soon as we finish lunch. I've even made an appointment." She gave her cousin a crafty smile.

"You? For what? Getting a restraining order on Sweetums?"

Judith turned serious. "We really haven't had a family attorney since Ewart Gladstone Whiffel died right after Dan did. All this time I've been thinking about putting the money Dan left in a trust for Mike." Her dark gaze roamed the ceiling with its fishnets and glass balls.

"*What* money?" Renie demanded, then rolled her eyes. "Okay, okay, you're up to your old tricks telling monster fibs for a good cause. I get it, Wilbur doesn't need to know that not only was Dan flat broke, he ate the last warning notice he got from the IRS so you couldn't see it." She glanced over at Judith's watch. "Gosh, it's after one-thirty. I have to meet that phone company doofus at two. Want a ride down to Evergreen Tower? That way you won't have to park twice."

Judith accepted. Fifteen minutes later, she was in the mahogany and glass express elevator that carried her to the forty-first floor where Hoover, Klontz, and Paine practiced law in conservative splendor. The office suite showed no sign of Norma's more ostentatious hand, suggesting that the other senior partners had ganged up on Wilbur.

His desk, however, displayed a gilt-framed picture of his wife and their three children, taken before the little Paines had left the nest and Norma's bust, along with the rest of her, had expanded to dangerous proportions. In contrast to Joe's chaotic office, Wilbur Paine's was a model of order. A classic pen and pencil set in marble, a leather-bound day calendar, and a legal-sized folder were the only other items on the desk. Wilbur, however, looked frazzled, his white shirt rumpled under his dark gray suit jacket and his maroon tie askew.

"Extraordinary," said Wilbur, opening a drawer and pulling out a ballpoint pen. "I thought I was all booked up today. I'm afraid I can give you only about ten minutes. My secretary told me you were leaving for Albania tomorrow?"

Judith gave Wilbur her most innocent look. "Albania? Oh, no! I must have mentioned how I couldn't leave Uncle Al with his mania. For gambling," she added hastily. "He always goes wild on Tuesdays."

Wilbur's expression was, Judith noted gratefully, mystified. "Anyway," she went on in a brisker tone, "I've been remiss in straightening out my late husband's financial affairs." Judith proceeded to deliver a monologue on the nonexistent monies left by her late husband, mentally blocking out both the lie and the truth, the latter consisting of a debt-ridden debacle that she was sure had hastened Ewart Gladstone Whiffel's demise.

Laboriously, Wilbur made various proposals, all of

which Judith seemed to consider. "I like the joint tenant trust idea best," she finally said, "with provision that he becomes solely in charge when he reaches thirty." She paused, apparently mulling. "What if he marries in the meantime? Would his wife be entitled to half the trust because this is a community property state?"

Wilbur pursed his lips. "No. Not if it's set up properly. She would inherit if he, ah, passed away, of course. Unless the document were worded so that should your son predecease you, it would revert to you."

The topic had turned a bit more grim than Judith had intended. "In other words, you have all sorts of options." She tilted her head, watching the sunlight dance off Wilbur's glasses. "It's not a huge amount. Nothing like Emily Tresvant's wealth." Judith's laugh was intended to sound self-deprecating, but came out hollow. "I don't suppose," she went on guilelessly, "that poor Emily realized Sandy wasn't a woman?"

Wilbur's cheeks turned pink. "Shocking business. I'm just appalled. Emily must be turning over in her grave." He clicked the ballpoint pen several times in agitation. "Excuse me, I mustn't breach client confidentiality, of course. But facts are facts. It's quite clear that John Frizzell and Sandy ... whatever her ... *his* name was, were not husband and wife. Emily specified that John must be a respectable family man in order to inherit."

That, Judith realized, might explain Sandy's charade. But it hadn't dawned on Judith until now that Sandy's real identity was as much of a mystery as his murder. Hopefully, Joe was working on that angle. "That's true," agreed Judith, giving Wilbur a sympathetic look that invited his confidences. "I hope this tragedy doesn't complicate your role as the Tresvant attorney. Will Sandy's status change John's inheritance?"

Wilbur, clicking away at the pen, turned from pink to puce. "Well, um, the law isn't fond of surprises. This unfortunate matter raises, ah, *questions*. Emily was a great one for codicils." Purposefully, he put the pen back in the drawer and slid it shut. It was obvious that Wilbur wasn't going to say any more.

Judith's brain went into high gear, and she took an outside shot: "For the life of me, I can't see why Eve Kramer feels she should get involved in litigation. Her role seems quite obscure." At least, Judith told herself, the statement as worded was true enough. The insinuations were another matter.

The color drained from Wilbur's face. For a moment, his lower lip trembled, and Judith noticed that he kept his hands, which she presumed were shaking, under the desk. "Eve is acting foolishly," he said at last. "She hasn't a prayer of breaking the will."

The phone buzzed on Wilbur's sleek mahogany commode behind the desk. He turned on the speakerphone to hear his secretary announce the arrival of a client whose family prominence was as old as the city itself.

"My father, who helped found this firm, and his father played golf together," Wilbur said in tones of reverence. "God love the Borings, they've been faithful to us over the years. I can't bear to think what would happen if they took their business elsewhere." Wilbur's lower lip actually quivered.

Reluctantly, Judith realized it was her cue to leave. She stood up and proffered her hand. Wilbur took it in a limp clasp. "Thanks so much," she said, with her most winning smile. "I'll go home and think over what you've told me about Dan's money. Maybe I should discuss it with Mike when he comes home from college. By the way," she added at her most casual, "does John really have any children?"

Wilbur gave a little shake of his head. "I don't know. At this point, I don't even know who Stella is."

Judith's eyebrows shot up. "Stella?" The name struck a familiar note. Someone else had mentioned it earlier, but offhand, Judith couldn't recall the reference. "Stella who?"

"I have no idea. Luckily, I don't have to. If anything had happened to John, Emily's money would have gone to this Stella." The phone buzzed again. Wilbur jumped. "Excuse me, I really must see Mr. Boring. He's such a busy man."

Still smiling, Judith backed out of the office. "So are you, Wilbur," she said. And, she thought to herself, a nervous one. Judith wondered why. Unless, of course, he was about to lose the Boring business along with Tresvant Timber. That, she realized, would be enough to make any senior partner edgy.

And poor.

NINE

PHYLISS RACKLEY HAD recovered. The roar of the vacuum cleaner could be heard in the second-floor precincts as Judith entered Hillside Manor. Gertrude, who had fought Phyliss to a standoff over the years concerning housekeeping procedures, had retreated to the family quarters, no doubt smoking and sulking with a vengeance.

Judith decided not to interrupt Phyliss's work. She wanted to talk to her about Emily Tresvant, but once she started, the garrulous cleaning woman wouldn't shut up. With guests arriving the next day, Judith had to make sure that she had her house in order. She herself would tend to the kitchen. At least the fridge was stocked for breakfast, with enough sausage, eggs, bacon, and ham left over from her Saturday expedition to take care of the two couples who were coming up from Oregon for a three-night stay.

The phone rang, and Judith half expected it to be Cousin Renie, inquiring about the interview with Wilbur. Instead it was a prospective guest, asking if Ju-

dith had a room with a mirrored ceiling. Resisting the urge
to tell the gentleman caller that he could turn the dressing
table on its side and try crawling under the furniture for
the same effect, Judith merely answered no. Disappointed,
the man hung up.

Finally, Judith turned to her answering machine. Three
potential reservations, two for May, one for June, and an
inquiry about catering a wedding reception droned into her
ear. There was no message concerning Sandy's murder. Judith felt a sense of letdown. Maybe Renie was right—she
was indeed hooked on crime.

Sneaking upstairs to avoid both Phyliss and Gertrude,
Judith changed out of her orange linen shirtdress and
donned slacks and sweatshirt. Half an hour later, she was
thawing two chicken breasts in the microwave when
Phyliss Rackley came into the kitchen with a laundry bas-
ketful of dirty towels.

"Off gallivanting, your mother said," remarked Phyliss,
balancing the basket between her knee and hip. She was a
squat woman in her sixties with sluggish blue eyes and
gray sausage curls that squirted out all over her head. "I
hear you found another body." Her phlegmatic manner indicated that as usual, she took all manner of strange events
in stride.

"I didn't find it," protested Judith. "I wasn't even
there."

Phyliss didn't bother to look disappointed, but shifted
the laundry basket and started for the basement. "You're
out of bleach," she called over her shoulder.

"Wait up, Phyliss," Judith called after the other woman.
But Phyliss, the ties of her tennis shoes undone and a row
of ragged lace hanging out from under her striped housedress, had disappeared through the little passage that led to
the basement.

Judith started peeling potatoes, remembered the chicken
breasts were still in the microwave, removed them to a paper towel on the counter, and wondered if Joe had the lab
report on the rabbit suit back yet. Perhaps he would call

her. Then again, maybe not. She could call him. Her eyes roamed to the phone on the wall by the swinging door that led into the dining room. Judith didn't want to appear too aggressive in terms of their relationship. On the other hand, her inquiry was strictly business. In theory, the investigation was none of her business. Judith's brain went round and round, in rhythm with the potato peeler.

A scream from the basement brought her tumbling thoughts to a dead halt. Judith dropped a potato in the sink and ran to the stairwell. Another sound pierced her ears, this time more like a screech.

"Phyliss!" she shouted. "What's wrong?"

There was no answer, only another screech and several thuds. Judith started down the stairs.

Phyliss stood by the clothes dryer, holding a struggling, clawing Sweetums in her hands. "Your idiot cat tried to put himself on the spin cycle. Why don't you send this thing to the pound?"

"Damn," swore Judith, hurrying to Phyliss and taking the irate animal in her arms. Sweetums growled ferociously and went for Judith's face. "No, you don't, you horrible beast. Next time, try the washer. As usual, you're filthy."

Minutes later, when Sweetums had been subdued by a dish of cat tuna, Phyliss emerged from the basement, rubbing her arms. "That gruesome little devil better not have rabies," she said. "He got me real good. My nerves can't take it, my colitis is acting up something fierce. Can't you train him not to take naps in the dryer?"

"I'm trying to teach him to sleep in the microwave, but he won't go for it," replied Judith, taking the tea kettle off the stove and pouring boiling water into a blue ceramic pot. "Phyliss, do you remember when you worked for Emily Tresvant?"

Phyliss snorted. "I've been trying to forget for years. She was a real cranky old bat. Worse than your mother."

"Wow!" Judith got out a pair of mismatched mugs and set them on the dinette table. "Is that why you quit?"

Easing herself into a chair, Phyliss accepted the mug of tea and poured in what appeared to be half a cup of sugar. "Absolutely! She was too cranky. Fussy, too. Wanted everything perfect. Gave me migraines. I don't know why she cared, she never had company. She just sat there in that big old barn of a house and watched television. I don't think she knew what was on half the time."

"When was that?" Judith queried.

Phyliss ran a hand through the jumble of sausage curls. "Oh—about fifteen years ago. Maybe more. Not too long after her sister died, I guess. Lucille, that was her name. I went to work for old Emily just before Lucille came home to croak. I stayed on quite a while, which was more than most of her cleaning women did, I can tell you. I don't let things bother me like some do. One word of criticism and they're gone. I may not have the best of health, but praise the Lord, I can still put up with a lot. Nell Whitson quit the Paines because Mrs. P said she didn't dust the curlicues on her blasted broke mirror good enough."

"Baroque," corrected Judith softly, but knew that Phyliss didn't pay any attention. "Did you ever see John Frizzell?"

Phyliss looked askance at her employee. "John Frizzell! A queer, huh? What a stunt! He put one over on old Emily, eh? I say, good for him. I hope he goes through her money like poop through a pigeon. Now I don't hold with all this homosexual stuff, even though my youngest boy likes to wear women's undies now and then. Pastor Polhamus preaches that it's worse than playing cards, but I can't say as I mind if Emily got herself duped."

Carefully turning her Caesar's Palace mug around so that the logo didn't show, Judith made an attempt to get Phyliss back on track. "But did you ever meet John?"

Phyliss cast her eyes up to the nine-foot kitchen ceiling. "Can't say that I did. Lucille got letters from him, though. I think he was in California at the time. Los Angeles. Emily heard from him, too. In fact, he called once when I was there, that was after Lucille had passed on. He was in the movie business. I answered the phone, never mind that I had an ear infection at the time, and I asked him why he'd got himself into such an ungodly line of work. He just laughed. Depraved even then, I suppose."

"Movies?" Judith took a drink of tea. "I thought he was in antiques."

"Not then, he wasn't. Maybe he got saved." Phyliss slurped at her mug and then shook her head. "Nope, not if he was being queer. Did I ever tell you about my sister's boy, Randolph, in Sioux City?"

"Often," lied Judith. "Phyliss, do you remember anybody connected with Emily named Stella?"

Phyliss looked blank. "Stella? Not unless that was the woman who came to do her feet. One of them podium people."

"Podiatrist?" suggested Judith.

"Socialist. Held with radical ways. I've no time for any of it." Phyliss's forehead screwed up. "No, her name was Sophie. Probably Russian. If she'd had an accent, I'll bet she'd have been foreign. She looked the type."

Judith kept a tight rein on her patience. A sated Sweetums planted himself at her feet, his fur still ruffled from the brief bout with the dryer. "Did you ever hear anything about what happened to John's father?"

Draining her mug, Phyliss delved uninvited into the sheep-shaped cookie jar on the windowsill. "Snickerdoodles, my favorite." She munched away happily. "Kind of stale, though. Unless my bad wrist gives out, want me to bake you some gingersnaps?"

"Sure," Judith replied faintly. "What about John's father?"

But Phyliss shook her head, making the sausage curls sway. "Don't know much about him. He and Lucille were divorced early on. I think he remarried, some Jezebel, no doubt. Old Emily didn't speak of him much, and when she did, it wasn't fit to print. Edgar, that was his name. A rambling, gambling man, the very worst sort. Satan's tool. I figure he ended up in evil clutches." The vivid expression on Phyliss's usually impassive face conjured up images that would have made Dante wince.

Judith backed off the subject of Edgar, who was probably as dead as Emily and Lucille. In any event, he hadn't seemed to have surfaced for almost three decades. "Did Emily have any pictures of John?" Judith asked.

Phyliss took out a ratty handkerchief that looked to Judith as if it had been used to blow noses in several Western states. "Pictures! She had a ton of 'em, mostly old geezers in those fancy frames that are so hard to dust. Curlicues, like Norma Paine's broke mirror." Applying the crumpled handkerchief to her nose, Phyliss emitted a trumpetlike blast. Judith cringed. "She had a couple of John," Phyliss continued, punctuating her reply with several loud sniffs and snorts. "Plainer frames. In one, he's about seven or eight, wearing a white suit and holding a flower and a string of beads. With Lucille dressing him up like that, it's no wonder he turned out to be a queer."

Judith guessed it was John's First Communion photo, complete with rosary, but recognized the futility of trying to explain the ceremony to Phyliss. Indeed, Judith thought fleetingly, it would only confirm her belief in the family's decadent ways. "Did Emily have any of him when he was older?"

"She did. Formal like. Graduation, maybe, but none of those funny hats or long robes." Phyliss stuffed the loathsome hanky back in her pocket. "My sinuses are plugged up something awful. John was a nice-looking young fellow, I'll say that. I never ran into him after he moved here last winter. Or if I did, I didn't realize it was him. Too bad he got mixed up with moving pictures. Hollywood was probably the ruination of him."

Renie had been right, Judith reflected. Emily had indeed possessed photographs of John Frizzell. She would not have been fooled by an impostor. Gertrude's theory sailed out the window.

Heaving herself from the table, Phyliss got to her feet with a deep sigh. Squat and square, she reminded Judith of a fireplug. "No rest for the wicked," said Phyliss. "I've got time to do the windows in the front parlor before the wash gets out." She paused in the doorway, her homely face brightening. "Say, that's a beautiful picture of our Savior you got there in the living room. Almost as inspirational as the one upstairs."

Phyliss's reference to Gertrude's depiction of the Sacred Heart of Jesus which hung in the foyer of the family quarters caused Judith to wince. "Oh—yes. It's very . . . moving." Judith refrained from saying she'd been wanting to move it to the St. Vincent de Paul bag for years.

With Phyliss in the front parlor and Sweetums asleep in the sink, Judith sauteed the chicken breasts in a bit of butter. She wished she could do the same to Sweetums. It was exactly five p.m., according to the old schoolhouse clock above the refrigerator. Usually, Gertrude was at the kitchen table by now, never having given up on the idea that "supper," as she called it, should be served no later than five-oh-five. Judith managed to stall most evenings until at least five forty-five, and on one rare summer night the previous year, she had pushed mealtime all the way up to six-twenty. Gertrude had griped for a week.

Apparently Gertrude was delaying her entrance, in deference to Phyliss and her chores. The phone rang. It was Joe.

"You got any raw umber shoe polish?"

"What?" Judith held the phone out from her ear, certain that she wasn't hearing correctly.

"Shoeshine, in a raw umber shade," explained Joe patiently. "I scuffed my loafers on somebody's weapon of choice, which happened to be a rusty harpoon. I don't want my sartorial splendor marred when we go out to dinner tonight."

"We?" Judith sounded breathless.

"Sure. Why not?" responded Joe in his breezy manner. "Rummage around, see what you can find for my loafers. Is seven-thirty okay?"

"Joe, I've already got dinner started. Besides, you

agreed we ought to wait to see each other until the annulment was official." Judith heard the pleading note in her voice and was annoyed. "It's less than two weeks to go, right?"

"Probably." There was an almost imperceptible pause at Joe's end. "Look, Jude-girl, we're adults. We're not trying to set an endurance record for self-denial. What's the point of playing hide-and-seek at this stage of the game?" There was another faint pause, this time for Judith's answer. When she said nothing, Joe continued: "What about tomorrow night?"

"I can't. I've got guests, booked straight through for two weeks. I'm just getting into my busiest season. Come Memorial Day, I won't have any nights off until after Labor Day. I have some time to myself during the day, but evenings I stick around here. I feel I should, if only for insurance purposes." Judith was speaking faster and faster, as if trying to convince herself as well as Joe that she was a prisoner of her own success.

"You used to be more fun," he said, his light tone faintly forced. "Impulsive, even. What do you do these days for laughs, watch Gertrude take out her partial plate?"

Judith felt the sting in his rebuke. Joe was right: Before her marriage, she had been game for almost anything, at least where Joe Flynn was concerned. Hot-air ballooning over the university homecoming football game, showing up at the opera in matching panda suits, taking the city's newest fire engine for a joyride around Chinatown—Judith and Joe had done it all. But that had been almost a quarter of a century ago. A lot had changed since then, including, Judith realized with a pang, herself.

"Having your own business is a big responsibility," Judith asserted, now on the defensive. "If things keep going well, I can hire an assistant. But not yet. I'm still paying off the loan on this place and Dan's mound of debts."

This time the pause was lengthy. Judith was about to ask Joe if he was still on the line when she heard his voice

pour into her ear like warm honey: "The Manhattan Grill
... a small lamp glowing on white linen ... scotch aged
in an untamed Highland glen ... a steak so thick you have
to slice it on the horizontal ... happy voices all around
you, but the only one you hear is mine ... what do you
say, Jude-girl? We could ride the last ferry across the bay
and come home with the sunrise."

Judith's knees crumpled. She gripped the phone with
one hand and clutched at the sink counter with the other.
"Joe ... oh, dear, I don't know ... I suppose I could get
Mother fed and then ..."

The clump of Gertrude's walker brought Judith back to
reality. Her mother was coming into the kitchen, having
descended the back stairway. "Almost five-fifteen and no
supper? What's going on around here?" Gertrude growled.

Judith pulled the phone close and tried to sound business like. "We'll do it the first week of May. I'll put it on
the calendar. 'Bye." Sheepishly, she looked at her mother.
"Phyliss is just finishing up. Dinner will be ready in
twenty minutes."

"Twenty minutes!" Gertrude gave the walker an extra
thump. "Look at me, I'm weak from hunger!" She
stopped, fixing her daughter with a penetrating eye. "Look
at *you,* you're white as a sheet. Or as sheets used to be before they started putting tiger lilies and prancing pigs all
over 'em. What's the matter? Another stiff?"

"No. Just a ... reservation." It was actually true, Judith
thought, since she was the one with reservations about resuming an intimate relationship with Joe. She turned her
back on Gertrude and hauled Sweetums out of the sink.
Roused from his nap, he hissed and spat at Judith before
marching indignantly to the back door. Phyliss came into
the kitchen just then, immediately engaging Gertrude in
their ongoing feud. Judith tried to ignore them, busying
herself with potatoes and brussels sprouts while the
chicken baked in the oven. She was a fool to let her
mother intimidate her. Joe was right, it was ridiculous to
make such a to-do over a few days. It had probably been

absurd to keep away from each other all these months in the first place. And yet, when Judith looked deep into her own heart, she had to admit the truth: She was afraid. But she didn't know why.

As Gertrude and Phyliss got into a heated harangue over To Starch or Not To Starch, Judith realized that Joe had not relayed the information about the rabbit suit from the lab report. Maybe he hadn't gotten the data yet. Maybe he didn't intend to tell her. Maybe she should call him back.

But Sweetums was clawing at the back door and making ugly noises low in his throat. Judith turned down the potatoes, edged around the arguing women, and went to let the cat out. With her hand on the knob, she was startled to see a man coming up the back steps. It was Kurt Kramer, and he looked more disagreeable than usual.

"Carl Rankers said to use the back door," Kurt told Judith in his abrupt manner. "The front is reserved for paying guests, I take it."

"Well, sort of," replied Judith, booting Sweetums out and ushering Kurt in. The truth was that the back door was more convenient for neighbors such as the Rankers, the Dooleys, and the Ericsons. "Let's go into the front room," suggested Judith, stopping just long enough in the kitchen to introduce Kurt to Phyliss Rackley and to remind Gertrude that she'd met the Kramers at a parish picnic five years earlier.

"You the one who complained about my potato salad?" Gertrude inquired, with a bulldog thrust of her face at Kurt.

Kurt's rigid form twitched a bit. "What?"

"Never mind," said Judith, pushing open the swinging door that led into the dining room. "Have a seat," she called to Kurt over her shoulder as she led him into the big living room. "Would you like a drink, or a cup of tea?"

"Nothing." Kurt didn't take Judith up on her offer of sitting down, either, but assumed an intransigent position between the matching sofas and glared through his glasses.

"You've been meddling in my life," he declared without preamble. "Eve and I want you to stop. Now."

"Huh?" Judith was flabbergasted. "What are you talking about? Have you been listening to Arlene Rankers?" It occurred to Judith that his accusation could stem only from some wild piece of gossip inadvertently set loose by Arlene.

"I stopped to go over the lector list with Carl," said Kurt through tight lips. "I didn't even see Arlene. Eve found out you had an appointment with Wilbur Paine this afternoon. You were there an hour before she was. My wife gathered you made defamatory remarks about her. She's furious, and I don't blame her. Eve is a very sensitive woman."

Eve Kramer struck Judith as about as sensitive as a nuclear warhead, but she held her tongue. Still aghast, Judith tried to piece this little puzzle together. "Wilbur told Eve I was there?" Somehow, that didn't seem quite right, given Wilbur's natural discretion.

Kurt's square chin shot up. "Eve can read. She saw your name in Wilbur's appointment book. A last-minute scheduling, the secretary told her. Wilbur wasn't pleased."

The scenario unfolded in Judith's brain: Eve, sharp-eyed and nervy, forcing her way into the offices of Hoover, Klontz, and Paine as she had threatened to do, perhaps even barging in on Bob Boring, and provoking Wilbur to breaches of confidentiality. Judith wanted to sit down, but refused to give Kurt the advantage of direct eye contact.

"See here, Kurt," she said, trying to be firm but civil, "I went to see Wilbur on a personal matter. Eve's name—not yours in any way—happened to pop up in the conversation. All I said," Judith went on, taking a deep breath and a big chance, "was that I didn't see how she could possibly break Emily Tresvant's will."

Kurt Kramer's Adam's apple bobbed, and his pallid skin turned ashen. "What do you know about it?" His voice was an echo of its usually incisive tone.

Torn between a natural wish for candor and a practical

need for deception, Judith opted for the former, mainly because she couldn't think of a plausible fib to carry out the latter. "My cousin Serena and I came by the Paines' house Saturday night. Before we could get out of the car, Eve showed up. She made a scene. We overheard some of it." Judith lifted one wide shoulder in a self-deprecating gesture. "It puzzled me, that's all. I didn't understand your wife's connection with the Paines—or the Tresvants."

Kurt's color came back, and he started to pace the length of the living room, from the French doors to the telephone stand. His hands were clenched behind him, head bent, eyes riveted on the Turkish carpet. He seemed lost in thought, and Judith wondered how long it would take before Gertrude demanded her supper.

"You knew I worked for Tresvant Timber?" Kurt asked abruptly, stopping in front of the bay window with its sweeping view of downtown and the bay.

"Comptroller, as I recall," replied Judith. "You retired a while back, right?"

"Last year." Kurt's stern face clouded over. "It wasn't my choice. I was forced out by the Japanese owners. They wanted their own people." He avoided looking at Judith, his unseeing gaze on the eclectic collection of pillows that rimmed the window seat. "Understandable, I suppose. The only thing left of Tresvant Timber in this state are the trees."

And, Judith recalled, Emily's profits from the sale to the Japanese. Leaning on the back of the sofa, Judith studied Kurt Kramer's spare, tired figure. It occurred to her that his bark might be worse than his bite. She wasn't sure she could say the same for his wife.

"You're young enough to work somewhere else," she said kindly. "There must be half a dozen companies in this town that would be glad to get someone as competent and experienced as you are."

Kurt actually brightened, giving Judith the impression that he was unused to compliments. "I thought about it," he said. "But the settlement was generous, as was the pension. I'd been there twenty-six years. It seemed to me that it was time to give my talents—such as they are—to the Church."

"That was very charitable of you," Judith said, and meant it. "Did Eve agree?"

"Yes." He had stopped pacing altogether, and was now seemingly tempted to sit down in Grandma Grover's rocking chair. "Eve's a very understanding woman. In her way. She has always believed in me." He spoke with a trace of pride. Mark Duffy's image sprang to Judith's mind, with his comments on Kate. He, too, had been proud of his spouse, yet Judith had sensed something else under that thick veneer of mutual devotion. With Kurt, all emotions seemed honest, if raw. Judith didn't begin to like Mark less, but she definitely began to like Kurt more.

"So Eve thought Emily should have remembered you in her will?" It was a longshot, but the only logical guess.

Kurt's shrewd blue eyes zeroed in on Judith. "No. Well," he equivocated, "not as things stood. It was all very impersonal, you see."

Puzzled, Judith said nothing, but tipped her head to one side in an encouraging gesture. Kurt, flushing slightly, looked like a hunter who had walked into his own snare. "It's old news," he said, trying to extricate himself. "Originally, Emily had left everything to her sister, Lucille Frizzell. But when Lucille died, Emily remade her will. She left the bulk of her estate to all Tresvant Timber officer-level employees with twenty-five or more years of service. Naturally, at that time I was fairly new with the company and it meant nothing to me. But of course," he added, growing even redder, "by the time she died, I would have qualified, along with about a dozen others. Then John Frizzell came on the scene, and Emily changed the will again." The bear trap of a jaw clamped shut as Kurt Kramer made a vain attempt to hide his bitter disappointment.

The front door banged, signaling that Phyliss Rackley

was en route to the bus stop and her home across the ship canal in the Rutherford District. Judith half heard her cleaning woman's departure, but her brain was calculating the Tresvant millions divided by twelve. Whatever the amount, Kurt's share would have been hefty. She was surprised that he had told her about the previous will. But of course Wilbur knew, and so, probably, did Norma.

"Why," queried Judith, "did Emily wait so long to make John her heir?"

Kurt made an impatient gesture with his hand. "Don't you think John started writing and calling a lot? Emily might not have been sick then, but she *was* getting old."

Kurt's explanation made sense to Judith. Having sold her timber empire, Emily's interest in her ex-employees would have dwindled. In old age, she would have felt more kinship with whatever real family she had left, no matter how tenuous the connection. "Opportunism knocks," Judith said with a wry expression.

Kurt's thin smile was cynical. "You can't blame John, I suppose. Eve figures he'll buy up half of Europe and the Orient. He's a genuine collector. I'm afraid my wife has let John's good fortune upset her."

"*Huge* fortune," remarked Judith. "If he can keep it."

A muscle twitched along Kurt's steel jaw. "The court will have to define 'family man.' These days there may be a lot of latitude." He gave a sharp shake of his head. "I'd better go. Eve will have dinner on the table at six." For a brief moment, Judith thought Kurt was going to take her hand. Instead, he jammed his fists in the pockets of his brown leather jacket and allowed his facial muscles to relax a bit. "I was a bit boorish when I arrived," he said, sounding faintly gruff. "But Eve was having a temper tantrum. Maybe she exaggerated what was said in Wilbur's office."

"Maybe." Judith smiled. "It's been a rough weekend for all of us."

"So it has." Kurt frowned. "Especially for Sandy."

Judith's eye traveled unbidden to Gertrude's picture of the dancing Jesus. Somehow, it didn't seem so comical. "Yes," she agreed, "especially for Sandy."

TEN

IN A VIOLENT world, the murder of a Heraldsgate Hill housewife would have merited no more than one thirty-second story on the evening news. But because the housewife had turned out to be a househusband, Sandy's demise was once again worthy of TV attention.

Judith, attired in her favorite blue bathrobe and drinking a diet soda, watched the eleven o'clock news in her bedroom. Sandy, according to the toothsome anchorman, was in fact George Philip Sanderson, forty-four years old, and born in Paterson, New Jersey. Police had verified the weapon as a pair of embroidery scissors. Sanderson's roommate, John Frizzell, had no comment other than to confirm the victim's real identity. A shadowy John was shown in the doorway of the Frizzell bungalow. There was no mention of Wilbur's rabbit suit.

Judith stayed tuned for the weather, which was fifty percent chance of rain, fifty percent chance of sun, and possible thunderstorms. In other words, she thought, punching at the pillow with her fist, a typical Pacific

Northwest April forecast. Except for the possibility of an earthquake. Judith went to sleep.

Her dreams flashed by in neon, a testimonial to her mental unrest. Joe was parachuting out of a hot-air balloon over Paterson, New Jersey, while Gertrude chased a dancing pig that turned into Mark Duffy. A ten-foot rabbit menaced Judith, but revealed itself to be Cousin Renie, stuffing her face with brussels sprouts. Kurt Kramer announced his intention of marrying Phyliss Rackley, who announced her decision to have a lesbian affair with Norma Paine, who announced that she was really the Pope. Judith awoke at seven a.m. feeling very tired.

By eight o'clock, Gertrude was replete with scrambled eggs, bacon, and toast. Judith drank orange juice and coffee, but abstained from food, conscious of the two pounds she'd gained over the Easter weekend. She was also aware that her wardrobe needed replenishing, especially if she was going to dinner in less than two weeks at the Manhattan Grill. She vowed to call Kathy, her favorite saleswoman at Donner & Blitzen Department Store, at the crack of ten.

But just before eight-thirty, Arlene Rankers was banging at the back door. "Carl's saying Mass," she said, whipping in through the passageway with a blazing red azalea in her arms. "Here, this is a special thank-you for hosting the relatives. Weren't they great? I wish they'd been hijacked."

"Hold it," exclaimed Judith, set awhirl as usual by Arlene's blatant contradictions, but backing up to her first announcement. "Carl can't say Mass, he's not a priest. What are you talking about?"

Arlene had paused to hug Gertrude, who was still at the dinette table, drinking coffee and smoking like a steam engine. "You sweetie," Arlene cooed, "you look like a princess in that zebra-striped housecoat this morning! Carl could just eat you up!"

"How about replacing Carl with some lions and tigers and bears, oh my!" muttered Judith, setting the lavish azalea on the counter. "Arlene, explain yourself. About Carl and Mass, I mean."

"What?" Arlene's blue eyes danced from Gertrude to Judith and back again. "Isn't your daughter a regular *pest*? I already told her—Carl is doing a liturgy. We have no priest at SOTS this week. Father Hoyle went on vacation, and Father Tim is sick."

Like most Catholics in the archdiocese, Judith was well aware of the shortage of ordained clergy. Not only were priests sharing parish duties, but in some cases, the laity had been pressed into service. Men and women alike, they were not able to offer up the Mass, but they could—and often did—conduct a prayer service that was at least a meaningful substitute.

"What's wrong with Tim?" asked Judith. "Flu?"

Arlene gave the smug Gertrude a last pat and sat down in one of the four matching dinette captain's chairs. "No. I'm not really sure what it is, but he hasn't been well since Easter. In fact, he was barely able to concelebrate the services over the weekend. He won't come out of his room at the rectory."

Judith poured coffee for Arlene and refilled Gertrude's mug. "Why not? Is he too weak?"

Arlene poured milk from a pitcher into her coffee. "I don't know. Carl talked to Mrs. Katzenheimer, the housekeeper, and she said he's been in there since Sunday afternoon."

Alarmed, Judith stared at Arlene. "Is he . . . alive?"

"Of course he's alive," Arlene replied with a touch of impatience, as if the mere suggestion of death at SOTS was absurd. "He told Mrs. Katzenheimer he didn't feel well and he wanted to meditate." Arlene took a drink of coffee and gave an offhand shrug. "All that meditating is well and good, as long as you don't do it alone. It just gets too *quiet*."

Judith didn't bother to dissect Arlene's last statement. Instead, she told herself that Tim Mills was probably responding to the violence in—and violation of—the church.

He was, after all, a sensitive young man on his first parish assignment. Judith said as much.

"Tim?" Arlene scoffed at the suggestion. "Our Mugs dated him, remember? He's a pretty tough customer. Mugs could only deck him once in the six months they went together."

"I don't mean tough physically," Judith countered. "Emotionally. It wouldn't be easy for any priest to have a murder take place in the parish precincts. Tim's only been here about a month."

"No spunk," asserted Gertrude. "Not like the priests in *my* day. I remember old Father Houlihan at St. Mary's-in-the-Pines, he used to wear fur underwear."

Judith raised an eyebrow. "Do you mean a hair shirt?"

Gertrude shrugged under her baggy cardigan. "Whatever. Made him itch like crazy. We all thought he had fleas. Smelled bad, too. But he was *tough*." She gave a little shudder to underscore the point.

Arlene took another swallow of coffee and announced her departure. "I'm taking a chicken casserole over to John Frizzell's for his dinner tonight. Kate fixed her beef noodle bake for him, but he wouldn't accept it. I guess he's still upset about Mark trying to recover his wheelbarrow. People can be very strange."

Being upset over an alleged attempt at reclaiming a wheelbarrow was the very least of the oddities that circled around John Frizzell. Or so it seemed to Judith. "I'll come with you, Arlene," she said. "I can pick up something for his dessert at Begelman's."

Arlene left to get her casserole while Judith cleaned up the kitchen. In less than fifteen minutes, several things happened: Arlene's car wouldn't start, Arlene locked herself out of the house, Arlene got a jump-start from Gabe Porter across the street, Arlene backed out over her casserole, Arlene got a flat tire from the broken oven-proof glass.

Arlene was fit to be tied. She was forced to stay at home and wait for her son Kevin to come by with a house key and an assist with the tire. Judith tried to soothe her. "I've got a crab quiche in the freezer that I can take over to John's. We'll dispense with dessert."

Arlene, however, was not appeased. Disconsolately, she lifted a limp hand to wave Judith off.

The Frizzell bungalow looked bleak in the uncertain April sunlight. The drapes were drawn, and the morning paper still reposed on the small front porch. The lawn needed mowing, and the narrow flower beds that ringed the front of the house were choked with weeds. The forlorn old Peugeot stood in the driveway, washed clean, if not fresh, by the weekend rain. Judith parked at the curb just as Renie pulled in behind her.

"Coz!" Renie sprang out of the Jones sedan, a covered dish cradled against her breast. "Are you being a do-gooder, too?"

Judith hauled out the chilly crab quiche. "Why didn't you tell me you were coming over here?"

"I called, but your mother said you were outside with Arlene, backing her car over a chicken. I figured Aunt Gertrude had finally gotten into the soothing syrup. Where's Arlene?"

Judith sighed. "Never mind. What did you bring?"

"Swedish meatballs." Renie gave Judith a sidelong glance. "I thought you'd phone last night to tell me about your meeting with Wilbur."

Judith kept facing straight ahead as they mounted the three steps up to the porch. "I intended to, but I got busy. Guests are coming this afternoon." The truth was that she'd refrained from calling Renie because she didn't want to confess her cowardly refusal of Joe's invitation.

"Joe called, right?" Renie shot Judith a sharp look and saw that she'd hit home. "We'll talk later," she said, stooping to pick up the newspaper while Judith rang the bell.

It took quite a while before John Frizzell opened the door. Judith and Renie both knew he'd probably been watching them through the spy hole, deciding whether to let them in.

"Hi," said Judith, trying to strike a note between Christian optimism and secular sorrow. "We thought you might like to have some food on hand."

"Thanks." John Frizzell stood uncertainly in the doorway, unshaven and half dressed. His refined features had taken on a murky quality, as if the recent tragedy had already begun to erode his good looks. He wore thongs, a pair of dark slacks with his white undershirt, and a towel slung round his neck. Behind him, in the narrow hall, Judith could see several large packing crates. John followed her gaze and ran a hand over the stubble on his chin. "I'm moving back to New York. There's no point in staying. Now."

"No, I suppose not," Judith said somewhat vaguely. The still-frozen quiche was turning her fingers numb. "Could we put these in the kitchen for you? Mine should be thawed first."

John blinked. "Oh. Of course." The response was polite, but without enthusiasm. "Follow me," said John, threading his way between the packing crates. At the end of the hall was a small, outmoded kitchen, at least a generation behind the times. The sole concession to the modern age was a gleaming white espresso machine.

Judith set the quiche on the worn Formica counter while Renie deposited the meatballs and the morning paper on the round kitchen table. John shifted uneasily, tugging at the towel around his neck.

"Look," said Judith, turning to face him, "this is all terribly awkward for you. I don't understand what your reasons were for Sandy's impersonation, it's none of my business, but I want you to know that you have our genuine sympathy in your loss."

Slowly, John's haunted brown eyes veered in Judith's direction. "Thank you." He cleared his throat and carefully placed the towel on the back of a chair. "I can't help but think that most of the parish must despise me."

"I can't speak for most of the parish," said Judith evenly. "Your way of life is a matter of personal choice. I certainly don't despise you. Neither, I'm sure, does my cousin."

"Live and let live," chimed in Renie. "My Uncle Fred in Denver is a warlock."

Since Uncle Fred was also a cosmonaut, a pirate, and a giraffe, depending upon what medication he took at the Rocky Mountain High Rest Home, Judith couldn't quite figure out the aptness of Renie's remark. She concentrated instead on John's sad face and gave him a kindly smile.

"I assume you'd been with Sandy a long time?"

"Twenty-three years," replied John in a pained voice. "To us, it *was* a marriage. But I don't expect you to understand that." His tone had taken on a defensive edge.

"I don't in the way you do," Judith admitted. Certainly she would be the last to criticize anyone else's living arrangements. Friends and relations alike had thought she was hurtling down the road toward self-destruction during her eighteen years with Dan McMonigle. "But I do understand that it must have been a deep commitment, based on real feelings." She saw John relax a bit, and continued: "Love, after all, is love."

"Yes, it is," John agreed. He ran a hand through his uncombed hair. "Aunt Emily would never even have tried to understand any of it," he said bitterly. "That's why Sandy had to pretend."

Judith nodded. "I thought so. Had Emily known about Sandy all these years?"

"Yes—and no." John sighed, moving to the sink with its little window that looked out at the rear of a two-story frame house much in need of paint. "She always assumed Sandy was a woman. And my wife. I never corrected the impression."

"What about the children?" Renie blurted.

John didn't turn to look at her. His narrow shoulders sagged. "There aren't any, of course. Not even nieces and nephews. Sandy had no family. He ran away from the orphanage in New Jersey when he was fourteen. I met him in L.A." John's thin hands fumbled with a steelwool pot scrubber.

"I gather," said Judith, carefully phrasing her next question, "that you'd been afraid to try to visit Emily until she got sick?"

John put back the scrubber and picked up a potted African violet with foliage that was turning black around the edges. "I suppose everybody on the Hill is accusing me of being a rank opportunist," he said in a low voice. "I wanted to come—Aunt Emily was my only surviving relative. But to be frank, you're right, I was afraid. I could have left Sandy back East, but I didn't want him to think I was ashamed of our . . . arrangement. Then," he went on, setting the plant back down on the counter, "when Emily got sick, I knew I had to be with her. Sandy's . . . deception was to spare Emily's feelings. What would have been the point of devastating a dying woman?"

Judith suppressed an urge to say what popped into her mind, which was that Sandy Frizzell's presence as George Sanderson would have also upset the will. On the other hand, John had a point. Judith accepted it in good faith. "I'm sure Emily was pleased to have you with her at the end," she said in a kindly voice.

John inclined his head. "She was. Thank God, there wasn't much pain." He looked away briefly, then straightened his shoulders. "Excuse me, I must get back to my packing. Thanks again."

The cousins let themselves out. Judith glimpsed the living room off the hallway, a Spartan affair with tired furniture of the same vintage as the kitchen. Clearly, John and Sandy had rented the house already furnished. Only a seventeenth-century Italian planter with cherubs spoke of John's expertise in the antiques world.

As the cousins reached their cars, Dooley came pedaling up like mad on his bike. "Hey, Mrs. McMonigle! Mrs. Jones!" he called out in surprise. "What are you doing here? Sleuthing?" He braked to a halt next to Renie's car, then pitched a morning paper onto the porch of a gray stucco house across the street. Dooley grinned. "I forgot the Dowzaks. Again."

"We're just being neighborly," Judith said, keeping her voice down, lest John be listening through an open window. "Enjoying your vacation?"

"Sure," said Dooley, "except for getting up to deliver the papers. But I get to go back to bed." Following Judith's lead, he, too, lowered his voice. "I've been all over the parish grounds, looking for clues. No luck. Old Eddie chased me off with a hoe. I spied on Mrs. Paine, but all she did was go into Holiday's and buy flea powder for that ugly little dog of hers. Then I followed Mrs. Duffy, but she was picking up old ladies to take them to an Altar Society meeting. Finally, I stopped by the Kramers to collect for last month. I always wait until she's home because Mr. Kramer doesn't tip. Mrs. Kramer was there, but I didn't see her. Mr. Kramer came to the door, but he never says much." Dooley looked disappointed, as much with himself as with his suspects.

"Gosh, Dooley," said Judith, "you've been busy! Is this part of your official Explorers duties?"

Dooley wore a serious expression under his wayward hair. "No, I'm doing it on my own."

The trio paused as a UPS truck lumbered past. Across the street, Mrs. Dowzak, stocky and stern, emerged through her front door. She began to rail at Dooley for his chronic missed deliveries.

"Cow," muttered Dooley, but gave his nemesis an innocent smile. "Hey, Mrs. D, I've only missed three times since February. And you haven't paid me since New Year's!"

Mrs. Dowzak glared, then tramped back into the house, banging the door. The UPS truck had turned around at the corner and was pulling up behind Judith's car, apparently headed for John Frizzell's bungalow. Dooley grinned at the cousins and released the brake. "You meet some really weird people in this business. Like, I think Mrs. Dowzak is nuts. That reminds me," he said, leaning on the handlebars, "a couple of times when I was delivering papers I'd forgotten over on Quince Street by those old duplexes, I've seen Mrs. Kramer's car parked there. Do you suppose she's meeting some guy? A blackmailer, maybe."

Judith blinked at Dooley. She knew the location he was referring to: During World War II, a dozen frame duplexes had been thrown up to house defense workers at the nearby naval station. As a small child, she had found them quaint and cozy. But forty years later, the ravages of time and careless tenants had eroded their charm, along with the woodwork. "I doubt it's a blackmailer," she murmured. A lover, however, didn't sound as unlikely. It was hard for Judith to picture the fastidious Eve Kramer carrying on an affair with any of the Quince Street crew. The small enclave, just on the edge of downtown, was made up primarily of the elderly, single parents, and other low-income renters. Judith was puzzled.

Dooley's mind was still going a mile a minute. "Drug dealers? An escaped convict, hiding out? Antiques smugglers?" His tufts of fair hair stood up like question marks.

"Hold it," said Judith. Dooley's imagination was making her head spin. "I haven't any idea," she admitted, baffled by Eve Kramer's visits to such a down-at-the-heels area. Dooley, no doubt conjuring up fresh images of evildoers, pedaled off down Crabtree Street. Judith and Renie waved goodbye.

"Moonbeam's?" said Renie as they hit the sidewalk.

"What?" Judith was brought out of her reverie by Renie's suggestion. "Oh, sure, why not? It's not even nine-thirty yet. Are you working today?"

"Later. If I feel creative." Catching Judith's mood, Renie was suddenly subdued.

Moonbeam's, complete with its neon crescent over the door, stood at one corner of Heraldsgate Hill's busiest intersection. Indeed, it had become so busy in recent years that a traffic light had finally been installed, causing much confusion and more accidents than it sought to prevent. Accustomed to the four-way stop signs that had cautioned local residents for two generations, the Hill dwellers either braked on red and then kept going despite oncoming traffic from the other direction, or stopped on green and risked getting rear-ended. Judith herself had done both at least twice, but fortunately without incident.

Moonbeam's, as always, was crowded with the citizenry taking a break from their daily routine to drain heavy white mugs of at least two dozen types of coffee and twice as many various teas. Joggers recuperated from their workouts, mothers dragged in their baby strollers, and retirees whiled away their leisure time. The shop smelled of fresh-ground coffee, hot muffins, and orange spice. Judith and Renie squeezed in at the counter between a mailman and the local bank president.

Keeping her voice as low as possible, Judith replayed the scene in Wilbur's office, the chat with Phyliss Rackley, and the visit from Kurt Kramer. Renie listened attentively, somehow not spilling a drop of chocolate mint mocha on her person.

"So we still don't know why Eve was so angry," Renie said when Judith had concluded her recital.

"It's odd," remarked Judith over her Ethiopian blend. "Either you're mentioned in a will or you're not. Kurt says Emily wouldn't have left him anything, and I believe him. Tresvant Timber must have had hundreds of employees over the years. Why single out Kurt?"

"So why does Eve single out Wilbur?" queried Renie. "And who is this Stella he mentioned?"

"That's a funny thing—somebody else mentioned that name recently. I just can't remember who." Judith concentrated on the shining stainless steel coffee urn behind the counter. "I'd guess that Stella might be some neighbor or family friend who called on Emily. Except that it seems hardly anyone ever did, and I certainly don't know anybody by that name around here. Neither does Mother. I asked her at breakfast."

Renie was as puzzled as Judith. "Gee," she said, changing mental gears, "if John goes back to New York, do you think he'll take his legal business with him and leave Wilbur high and dry?"

"Probably." Judith gave Renie an ironic look. "That's almost motive enough to do in John. But not Sandy. It's odd," she went on, signaling to the freckled waitress to re-fill her mug. "There are several motives to knock off most of the alleged suspects—but none that I know of for the victim. Who benefits from Sandy's death?"

Renie's brown eyes widened. "John?"

"Only in the sense that he gets all the money. But he would have anyway. He's under no legal obligation to share it." Out of the corner of her vision, she caught Mark and Kate Duffy entering Moonbeam's. Mark espied the cousins, waved, and came over to sit on the stools vacated by the mailman and the produce manager from Falstaff's.

"You're still on vacation," Judith commented to Mark. "Any news on your burglary?"

Mark pulled a face. "The one at our house, or the one I committed?"

On the far stool, Kate leaned around her husband. "The police haven't had a chance to do much. They're so busy with Sandy's murder and all sorts of other really dreadful crimes that our burglary seems kind of minor. God bless our law enforcement people, they do the best they can. It's not very often they catch these burglars anyway."

"Unless it's me," put in Mark dryly.

"Don't you have a Neighborhood Block Watch?" inquired Renie. "Bill organized one on our street a couple of years ago after Tom's car was broken into four times in two weeks."

"Yes, we've got one," replied Mark.

"Mark's the captain," said Kate, putting a fond hand on her husband's arm. "We've had very few instances of crime since we organized. Maybe we got complacent. I think the Good Lord just wanted to show us we shouldn't be smug. He picked a time when we were all caught up in other things and not being vigilant. I mean, it happened on

Easter Sunday, you see, and it's just like God to show us that we should put our trust in Him and not mere mortals like ourselves."

Mystified as to how Kate could read God's mind, Judith asked if the Duffys had inscribed their belongings so that they might turn up later at a pawn shop and be recovered. They had, answered Kate, her pretty face very serious. At least the items that lent themselves to identification had been marked.

"I could describe my pearls and the silverware," she went on, smiling sweetly at the freckled waitress who was placing two steaming lattes on the counter. "I just wish John would come to his senses and drop the charges against Mark." She patted her husband's arm, giving him a look of heartfelt sympathy. "John really wasn't very nice when I took my beef noodle bake to his house. But I realize he's still in mourning. Though it's not as if he really lost a spouse. I mean, I just don't understand about gays. It all seems very sordid to me."

Renie, inexplicably turning pugnacious, leaned around Judith. "John was quite grateful when we brought our dishes over this morning. Maybe he's allergic to noodles." To Judith's surprise, Renie pulled a five-dollar bill out of her wallet, slapped it on the counter, and swiveled around on the stool. "I've got a meeting at eleven. Come on, coz, let's hit the road." Renie all but bolted out of Moonbeam's.

"Since when did you start telling tall tales?" Judith demanded when she'd caught up with Renie on the sidewalk.

"Since I discovered that Kate Duffy gives me a world-class pain in the butt," snapped Renie, whose temper was as quickly ignited as it was swiftly doused. "If she believes half that drivel she peddles, she's an idiot. If she doesn't, she's a fraud. I feel sorry for Mark."

"Maybe." Judith wasn't in wholehearted agreement with her cousin, but she had to concede that Kate's simpering manner could be irritating. "You really don't have a meeting, do you?" Judith asked as they reached their cars parked side by side next to the liquor store.

"No," admitted Renie, "but I should get home. I'm expecting a call from an ad agency before lunch, and Scooter's Delivery Service is bringing me a bunch of stuff I have to sign for."

"Okay, I'll call if I hear anything," said Judith, unlocking her car door. "For now, I'll continue on my round of good works. I think I'll check in on Father Tim."

"What for?" asked Renie, her disposition already back to normal. "He's got Mrs. Katzenheimer to look after him."

"True," agreed Judith. "It's just this crazy feeling I have that he's not exactly sick."

Renie lifted both eyebrows. "Sounds like a goofy theory, but at least it doesn't annoy the hell out of me, which is more than I can say for Kate Duffy." She started to get into the car, but bobbed up with a sly grin. "When are you and Joe going out to dinner?"

"Huh?" Judith goggled at Renie. Prevarication was useless. "How did you know?"

But Renie just shook her head. *"Coz."* She got behind the wheel and shut the door.

Judith watched Renie drive off onto Heraldsgate Avenue, still shaking her head and grinning.

Eddie La Plante was spraying the bushes in the small rose garden at the west end of the church. It was semienclosed, with a grotto where St. Bernadette knelt at the feet of Our Lady of Lourdes. The Dooley family had donated the shrine thirty years earlier when one of its members had been diagnosed as having a stomach tumor. Surgery had revealed that he'd swallowed a Ping-Pong ball during a particularly raucous St. Patrick's Day revel. The planned trip to Lourdes had been canceled, and the money set aside for the journey had gone into the grotto.

The minute Judith saw Eddie, she remembered that he was the person who had first mentioned Stella. Judith approached him gingerly, never sure of how he would receive an intruder in his floral domain.

"I see there are some buds coming out already," she said pleasantly. "Nice new growth, too. Did you prune all these yourself?"

"Who else?" retorted Eddie, still spraying away. "You think any of these snooty parishioners would lend a hand?"

Since most of the parishioners' hands were already callused, at least symbolically, from putting on bazaars, auctions, bake sales, carnivals, and endless other fund-raisers, Eddie's remark struck Judith as unfair. But Judith, determined to stay on his good side, assuming he had one, kept smiling.

"You've certainly done a good job here," she said, trying not to inhale Eddie's pest spray. "Did you work in the garden at your former parish?"

Eddie eyed her suspiciously from under the brim of his baseball cap. "*What* former parish? I hadn't been inside a church in forty years until I moved here."

"Oh." Judith mulled briefly. "It must be quite a change from . . . where you were before."

Eddie snorted. "Nope. One place is like another. A roof, three hots, and a cot. Big deal. Quince Street ain't Park Avenue."

Judith hoped Eddie didn't notice the flicker of surprise that crossed her face. "The rain doesn't bother you?"

"Nope." He polished off the last rose bush and set the spraying equipment aside. "It beats that wind in the Bay Area. The earthquakes aren't as bad, either, I hear. 'Course there hasn't been a real shaker since I came."

"Did the last big one down there scare you off?" Judith asked innocently.

Eddie took the baseball cap off and mopped his brow with a handkerchief that looked as if it had been borrowed from Phyliss Rackley. "Naw. It just rattled the dishes and made the lights blink. I was living down the Peninsula then. Moraga."

"You have family here?" she inquired in her most guile-less manner.

The suspicion in Eddie's eyes intensified. His weather-beaten face screwed up. "Why should I? What good is family?"

Judith thought of her own, flawed and sometimes aggra-vating, but nonetheless dear. "Oh—sometimes relatives are a trial, but they can be a comfort, too. I just wondered if you had anybody close up here, that's all."

Eddie gave her a baleful look and started to turn away. "Got to separate the bedding plants," he muttered.

"Eddie—who is Stella?" Judith's voice had risen, her tone implying command. She used it rarely, but it was well-honed from her days in the library and her nights at the bar.

Eddie jumped. "Stella? How should I know?" He was fumbling in his pocket, taking out his glasses case.

"You mentioned her to me the other day. Something about the Tresvant money. I thought you meant Sandy. Who is Stella?"

Clumsily, he withdrew his spectacles and put them on the end of his nose. "I don't know," he mumbled. "Some-body told me about her."

"Who told you?" persisted Judith.

His rheumatic fingers plied the case like a harmonica. "Can't recall."

"Does Stella have a last name?" Judith stared at the lit-tle case.

Eddie's old face scrunched up again. "I don't recollect. Oh—I think it's Maris."

"But you don't know who she is?" Judith was feeling frustrated.

"Nope." Eddie was cramming the glasses case back into his pocket. "Just a name, floating around out there. I for-get. Got to go. Where's my slug bait?"

Judith watched him shuffle off past the grotto. At least she had a last name. Perhaps, she thought with a gleam in her eye, she had more: Eddie's case for his spectacles was very unusual. Though obviously worn, it was hand-embroidered in an Oriental design, with butterflies. Judith wondered if it was the work of Eve Kramer.

ELEVEN

HILDE KATZENHEIMER HAD been the housekeeper at Our Lady, Star of the Sea, ever since she was middle-aged, which, it seemed to Judith, she'd reached at about twenty-five. Now, thirty years later, she looked virtually the same as when Judith had been a college student. Hilde had mousy brown hair hanging straight over her ears, a thin, pointed nose, a slit of a mouth, and lifeless gray eyes. She was almost as tall as Judith, but her figure had all the shape of a two-by-four. In her youth, she had married Mr. Katzenheimer, but had been widowed or deserted early on—no one knew for sure, even in a community where few secrets were kept for long. Childless and untrained, Hilde had found a job—and a home—in the parish rectory.

"He's starving to death," she said in her mournful voice. "Lent is one thing, Easter is another. Fasting is over."

"He hasn't eaten at all?" Judith asked as the two women stood in the parlor with its comfortable leather chairs and reproductions of the Italian Masters' Madonnas.

Hilde shook her head. "Not since Saturday. I heard him crying last night."

Alarmed, Judith considered. "Tell him I'm having a spiritual crisis."

"Won't matter. He refuses to come out."

"Try it," insisted Judith. "Young priests are always suckers for a spiritual crisis. Tell him I'm in a big void."

Hilde stared at Judith as if she actually expected to see her standing in a big void, then shrugged. "Hopeless," she concluded, but loped off in the direction of the rectory living quarters which had been designed for eight priests and now housed only two. Judith strolled around the parlor, admiring a Titian, a Raphael, and her favorite Botticelli, *The Madonna with Divine Child.*

Five minutes passed. Judith thumbed through a back issue of *Catholic Digest.* She studied an African crucified Christ clothed in tribal robes. She contemplated a photograph of the current archbishop, and felt her palms turn clammy. Was he even now making a decision that would change her life forever? Did he actually review the requests for annulment, or did they only pass through the hands of canon lawyers? Judith stared at the smiling, benevolent face and let out a little squeak when the parlor door opened.

"Mrs. McMonigle?" Tim Mills was pale, with dark circles under his eyes. He moved into the room with a tentative step.

"Father Tim! You startled me! How do you feel?"

Tim Mills gave Judith a hollow-eyed stare, then belatedly offered her a seat. "Sorry, I'm still a little . . . wobbly," he explained, easing himself opposite Judith. Under a red and white rugby shirt and blue jogging pants, his burly build looked less substantial than usual.

"Flu?" asked Judith blandly.

Tim put a hand to his blond crew cut. "Well . . . no. Sort of a stomach upset, though." His gray eyes roamed the parlor ceiling. Judith had the feeling he was arguing with himself. She wondered which side was winning. "Tell me, Mrs. McMonigle," he inquired, very serious, "what's troubling you?"

"You are," replied Judith bluntly. "I'm worried about your illness. I know I'm not one of the most active members of this parish, and I've been gone for several years. But something other than your stomach upset you Saturday. Do you want to talk about it?"

Without his clerical garb, Tim Mills looked younger than his twenty-five years. Judith observed his surprise, which was followed by a guarded expression. "Look, Mrs. McMonigle, I understood you were in deep despair. I got out of a sickbed to see you. Why are you grilling me like this?"

"I told you, I'm concerned." She leaned forward in the leather chair, hands clasped on her knees. "A terrible tragedy took place here three days ago. Sandy's murder was sufficient to disturb any sensitive soul. Sandy's masquerade was outrageous. You—and I, and everybody in the parish—have a right to be disturbed. But I think you're more distraught than most. Is this your first brush with real evil?"

Taken aback by Judith's forthright speech, Tim gnawed on his thumb and scowled. "Hardly. I've been hearing confessions for over a year."

Judith waved a hand. "I've only heard my own, but I'd guess that ninety-nine percent of them must be pretty tame. I'm talking about *real* evil. In this case, cold-blooded, premeditated murder."

"There have to be reasons for such things," said Tim. He was the picture of a contemporary man, grappling with age-old mysteries. "A chemical imbalance, abusive parents, a lack of self-esteem. Some perfectly normal-acting people suddenly go off the deep end. Often, their acts of aggression are triggered subconsciously, rooted in the past. They, too, are victims of an indifferent, callous society."

"Gee, Tim," said Judith with a wry expression, "whatever happened to *sin*?"

A hint of color spread over Tim's face. "Yes, of course, but we have to try to understand why people commit sin."

"Call me crazy, but I've got this nutty idea about free will," said Judith, with the notion that Bill Jones, Ph.D., would concur. "Sandy's killer made a conscious choice. I'm not excusing him—or her—on the grounds of a bad haircut at age nine. We're talking about good old-fashioned evil here." Judith paused, noting the change that came over Tim's face. He looked as if he were recognizing some new truth, and didn't much like it. "What bothers me where you're concerned," she went on in a less forceful tone, "is that I have this strange feeling you may know who the murderer is."

Tim's gray eyes widened. "Even if I did, let's say I'd heard it in confession, you know I couldn't tell anyone."

"Of course you couldn't. But I don't think that's how you might know." Judith sat back, waiting for Tim's reaction. She felt faintly cruel, but knew of no other way to get through to Tim. He was, she was certain, absolutely terrified.

"I have no idea who killed Sandy." Father Tim uttered the statement without inflection. His gaze was even. "Do you believe that?"

Judith hesitated. "Yes. At least I think *you* believe it. It's safer for you that way."

"Safer?" Tim's boyish features were perplexed.

Inwardly, Judith cursed herself for not being more clever. The fact was, she lacked confidence in her own deductions. The only thing she was sure of was that Tim Mills stood in a precarious position. "I understand you asked Sandy to help with the Easter decorations," said Judith, momentarily avoiding a direct response to Tim's remark.

"Oh—well, yes," replied Tim. "Sandy had called me a couple of times lately—questions about Emily's funeral, that sort of thing—so I thought maybe it would be appropriate to ask about some volunteer work. But John answered the phone. He felt I was demanding too much of Sandy." Tim's face was wooden.

"I heard John wasn't very pleasant about refusing," Judith noted.

Tim's expression turned ironic. "You could say that. Frankly, I was surprised. But Father Frank tells me that spouses—or should I say partners?—are often very touchy about too much volunteerism."

"True," conceded Judith, recalling that Dan had pitched a five-star fit any time she had offered her services to anybody who hadn't been him. On the other hand, it seemed to Judith that a lot of people got involved outside the home to avoid family responsibilities. Good works sometimes turned out badly.

Not wanting to wear out her welcome, Judith stood up and now addressed her earlier concern for Tim: "If I were you, I'd get well in a hurry. I don't think it's wise to call attention to yourself right now. Do you know what I'm saying?"

Tim had grown very solemn as he, too, got up. He looked like a college football player who had been chastened by his coach for missing a crucial block. "Yes," he said at last, "I do."

"Good." Judith proffered her hand. "You're sure you don't want to talk about anything else?"

Something flickered in Tim's eyes, then faded away. "No." He shook his head. "I can't."

Judith knew that was what he'd say. She was sorry. The archdiocese couldn't afford to lose another priest.

The sun had finally decided to come out from behind the clouds. Judith could have used her dark glasses as she pulled away from the church, but apparently had left them at home. Like most native Puget Sounders, she didn't consider sunglasses seasonal apparel, but necessary any time it wasn't completely cloudy. Bill Jones, born and raised in

Michigan, called it "the mole mentality." Judith and Renie called him insensitive to light.

It still wasn't noon. Judith drove away from Star of the Sea in a downcast mood. Across the street, the cherry trees had shed most of their blossoms, revealing wine-colored foliage swaying in the faint breeze. Daffodils, tulips, hyacinths, and narcissus preened in the sun. The early azaleas were in bloom, but others, along with the rhododendrons, wouldn't burst forth in all their glory until May, the most colorful month in the Pacific Northwest.

Judith was not cheered by pretty gardens and green lawns. She fervently wished that Sandy—or George Sanderson—had not been killed. But since he had, she wished that she didn't care who had killed him. If only, she thought, stopping at the arterial onto Heraldsgate Avenue, she could arm herself with the indifference that was typical of so many contemporary people. Murder, after all, was an everyday urban occurrence.

She was not entirely surprised to discover that she had not turned down the hill toward her home, but back up toward the business district. With a wry expression on her face, she felt as if she were letting the car drive itself. Past Chez Steve, Arlecchino's Costume Shop, the dry cleaners, and Falstaff's she went, pulling into a suddenly vacant spot across the street from Old As Eve Antiques.

Eve Kramer had converted a beauty parlor that couldn't compete with Chez Steve into a haven for elegance. At the moment, Eve was consulting with an older woman Judith didn't recognize, a tall dowager with upswept white hair, delicately rouged cheeks, and dangling diamond earrings. Judith discreetly withdrew to one side of the shop where she ostensibly admired some of Eve's needlework.

"I'll call the gallery in Dallas this afternoon about the lyre-back chair, Mrs. Woodson," promised a smiling Eve as her client made her stately way to the door. "They may have to get it from Paris, though."

Mrs. Woodson inclined her head, the earrings swinging above the collar of her cashmere coat. "You do that. I want the chair to complement the eighteenth-century porcelains on the marble mantel."

"Of course." Eve was still smiling. "As ever, your taste is impeccable." The door closed gently behind the departing Mrs. Woodson. "Old hag," snorted Eve. "She wouldn't know a Boulle marquetry desk from a brass spittoon. I hope she trips over her seven-hundred-dollar alligator shoes." Swinging around in Judith's direction, she all but pounced. "What do *you* want? Didn't Kurt tell you to knock it off?"

"What off?" Judith asked innocently. "Gosh, Eve, I had a nice visit with your husband. I thought we got everything squared away."

"What?" Eve simmered down slightly. "Oh, yes, Kurt came home waving a white flag, but that doesn't explain why you're here now." She fingered her full lower lip. "You make me nervous," she said at last, skewering Judith with a wary, dark-eyed gaze.

"I'm a bit nervous myself," Judith admitted. "You realize that one of us could be a murderer?"

Eve actually shivered under her blue silk wrap dress. "I didn't do it so that leaves you." She gave Judith an ironic look. "I ought to call the cops right now. Have you come here to steal my spare pair of embroidery scissors and do me in?"

Judith, in turn, studied Eve speculatively, concluding that despite Eve's earlier outburst, her bark did indeed outstrip her bite. So far. Judith tested the waters.

"Were those scissors really lethal?"

It was a question Eve had obviously already considered. "Yes, they could be. Especially to a thin person like Sandy. She—I mean he, I can't get over the fact Sandy was a man—God! Sandy used to come in here to meet John after work once in a while. Maybe I never really got a close look." She put a hand to her forehead. "Anyway, he didn't have much meat on his bones. My scissors came from Japan. Kurt got them for me when he went to Tokyo at the time Tresvant Timber was selling out. They're longer and sharper than the European or American versions."

"Have you any idea who took them out of your purse?"

Again, Eve had gone over all this territory before. "Not the foggiest. I left my bag on the counter in full view. I always do when I work up at SOTS. Let's face it, there's theft even at church, especially when you've got school kids around. I always figured my handbag was less likely to get pilfered if I kept it in plain sight." She slipped down onto a Louis XIV brocade-covered armchair and gestured for Judith to take its mate.

Gingerly, Judith sat. "Where were the scissors, exactly?"

Eve made a face. "That's the strange thing. I didn't think I'd brought them with me."

Judith's eyebrows shot up. "What?"

Eve had turned very earnest, a far cry from the volatile, hot-tempered virago Judith had grown accustomed to dealing with. "Kate Duffy brought that big box of rolls from Begelman's. She was so busy telling everyone how pious she is that she never put them out. I wanted to cut the string on the bakery box, so I went to get my scissors. I couldn't find them." Eve's wide-set dark eyes were filled with puzzlement.

"When did you last see them?" Judith asked.

"That morning. I was finishing off a piece for a wedding present. I could have sworn I put them in my bag. I almost always do." She fretted again at her lower lip. "The damned bag is so crammed, and Kurt is always yammering at me about cluttering it up because things fall out of it in the car. But he locked the Mercedes. He's very methodical."

"Could they have fallen on the ground in the parking lot?" Judith asked.

Eve shook her head. "I think I would have heard them. Except that Kurt was shooting his face off about my pasta salad. He wanted me to make one with fruit. The man can really bellow."

Eve's revelation about the missing scissors had sent Judith off in a new direction, though it was not one that totally surprised her. Indeed, it confirmed certain growing suspicions. Recognizing a dead end, Judith switched to a different, more hazardous topic: "You're from San Francisco, aren't you, Eve?"

Eve gave Judith a curious glance. "Right. Why do you ask?"

"Oh," Judith lied, "my Uncle Corky—mother's youngest brother—used to have an antiques store there, just off Geary. I thought you might have known him." Uncle Corky, in fact, had worked as the elevator operator in an old hotel at Geary and Mason during the Depression.

"What was the shop called?" Eve inquired, taking the bait.

"Uh—let me think." Judith did, wildly. "Corky's Collectibles ... no ... Unky's Junk ... um ... Corky and Porky? Gosh, Eve, I forget. Maybe it was before your time." She gave Eve Kramer a self-deprecating look. "You wouldn't have been in the business then anyway, right?"

Eve nodded. "I met Kurt there while I was in school at Cal-Berkeley. He'd had an urge to come West." The phone rang. Eve got up to answer it in her best business manner. Judith sat quietly while Eve discussed tapestries, both Flemish and her own. Five minutes passed before she resumed her seat across from Judith. "Where were we?" she asked her guest.

"In the Bay Area," replied Judith. She arched her neck, studying a wrought-iron candelabra with a grape-leaf design. "Is that where you met Eddie La Plante?"

Eve blanched. "Eddie!" Hastily, she did her best to recover herself. "You mean Eddie, the gardener?"

"The very one," replied Judith calmly. "That's quite a handsome spectacle case you made for him."

"I didn't make it for him," Eve said testily. "I gave it to him. It was an old one of Kurt's. Kurt wanted something in leather."

Judith trod very carefully on what was clearly shaky

ground. "Eddie treasures it," she said, figuring that the statement was at least possible. "It's probably one of the few nice things he has. Poor old guy."

"Eddie has everything he needs," huffed Eve. "He lives in a decent apartment at the bottom of the Hill, he loves to potter in the parish garden, he has plenty to eat. A guy like that could be homeless, out on the street, living under the freeway."

"True," agreed Judith. "But," she went on, skewering Eve with her black eyes, "you wouldn't let that happen to your father, would you?"

Eve gasped, a hand at her slim throat. "How did you know?"

Saying it was a wild guess wouldn't do. Judith merely shrugged. "It seems obvious. I assumed everybody knew. Your car is often parked outside his place on Quince Street." Judith felt the exaggeration wasn't out of line. At least it was nearer to the truth than the trumped-up story about Uncle Corky.

"Damn!" Eve's hands fell to her sides. Anger flared and died. For a long moment, she remained motionless, staring with unseeing eyes at one of her own beautifully stitched couch pillows. "I couldn't let him live in that shelter on Mission Street," she finally said. "After he got evicted from his place in Moraga, I couldn't track him down for six weeks. I still wouldn't know where he was if a friend of mine hadn't run into him outside a soup kitchen."

"I admire you for seeing after him," asserted Judith, getting up from the armchair. It was now well after noon. Gertrude would be seething. Eve wasn't the only one with filial obligations.

"The old fool should be under lock and key," Eve declared heatedly. "His brain is fried from too much booze and too many women. He wouldn't know anything about gardening if his last wife hadn't worked for a nursery."

"He's a widower?" Judith inquired as Eve walked her to the door.

Eve's expression turned furtive. "Well—yes, and no.

He's been both widowed and divorced. About five times. My mother died six years ago, but she left him when I was fourteen."

"Have you replaced John yet?" Judith asked with her hand on the crystal knob.

"No. It's going to be tough." Her piquant face puckered up with an emotion Judith couldn't quite read. "Oddly enough, I'll miss him."

The phone rang again. Eve excused herself. Judith went out into the spring sunshine, feeling no less depressed, but a lot more curious. Eve Kramer had been more amicable than she'd expected. But she'd also been less candid. Judith's concern for Father Tim was now matched by her growing anxiety for Eve.

"You know, Mother," said Judith, "you could open a can of soup yourself."

"I can't bend over to reach it, you dope," snarled Gertrude, shredding crackers into her cream of tomato. "If you'd organize this kitchen the way I used to have it, I could manage just fine. But oh, no, you had to redo it for your fancy-pants guests."

Judith's retort was cut off by the phone. Joe Flynn's smooth voice had an unusually businesslike edge: "I'm on my so-called lunch hour," said Joe, with the sound of masculine voices in the background. "I wanted to be sure of your time."

"I told you, the first week of May," said Judith, giving Gertrude a furtive glance. "I thought it was all pretty firm."

Joe chuckled. "It's firm, all right. What are you talking about?"

"Uh . . . dates?"

"What kind?" But Joe didn't wait for an answer. "Hey, I've got to make this quick. We've talked to all the people who were up at Star of the Sea about the time Sandy was killed. You fixed your conversation with him at approximately one-thirty, right?"

Embarrassed over her misinterpretation, Judith switched the phone from one ear to the other, as if the gesture might improve her hearing. "Right. Maybe a little later. It took me less than five minutes to get to Falstaff's. I was there before two." She paused, considering exactly how much time the short drive up Heraldsgate Avenue to the grocery store actually required. Though it was now only Tuesday, Holy Saturday seemed like a long time ago. "It could have been as late as one-forty," she amended.

"We got the call at one fifty-five p.m.," said Joe, "responding with patrol officers at two-oh-three, aid car at two-oh-nine, police back-up at two-fourteen, fire department at—"

"What? I can't hear you over Mother's soup."

"Never mind. The only people we could fix on the scene for sure were the two priests, John Frizzell, Kurt and Eve Kramer, Mark and Kate Duffy, and Wilbur and Norma Paine. Oh, and the gardener, Eddie Whazzisname."

"La Plante." Judith tried to ignore Gertrude's glare. "What about the housekeeper, Mrs. Katzenheimer?"

"Off buying her Easter bonnet, or something like that. She didn't show up until around four. Don't worry," said Joe, "we'll check out her alibi. She has obvious homicidal tendencies."

"That gives you less than fifteen minutes for the murder to have taken place, and for the body to be discovered."

"Right," agreed Joe, then apparently turned to whoever had been talking in the background and said something Judith couldn't hear. The voices died away, which was more than could be said for Gertrude's slurping. "Okay," Joe went on, "we've been trying to pin down everybody's movements during that critical fifteen minutes. Not that we're ruling out the proverbial unknown intruder, but after going over the layout, nobody could have entered the nursery without coming through the school hall. The other entrances were locked, and only the pastor and the principal have keys. All the nuns—all four of them—had already taken off for the weekend."

"So who have you talked to?" asked Judith.

"What's for dessert?" queried Gertrude.

"Arsenic," snapped Judith.

"What?" queried Joe.

"Skip it," said Judith.

"Got any of Auntie Vance's apple pie left?" interrupted Gertrude.

Judith shook her head. "So where were all of them?" she asked into the phone.

"What about the banana cream?" Gertrude was commencing to sulk.

Judith held up her thumb and forefinger, indicating the size of the remaining slice. Impatiently, she gestured at the refrigerator. Gertrude stayed put, lower lip thrust out, knife in one hand, fork in the other, looking for all the world like a convict about to start a prison riot.

"Let me see . . ." Joe was obviously referring to his notes. "Much coming and going at that point. Kurt Kramer was backstage, putting away some props the kiddies had hauled out. Eve went down the hall to a cupboard or closet to lock up supplies. Mark Duffy had to check on something in the boiler room—seems your janitor quit a couple of weeks ago and the parishioners are filling in until a replacement can be found. Father Hoyle was backstage, in the kitchen, the parking lot, the sports equipment room off the hall, and then went to see how Mark was doing with the furnace. Pastors are really busy guys, I see. Father Tim had been in the church, presumably going out the main entrance, and had returned just after you left, I gather. Get this—Wilbur Paine says he went to the car to wait for Norma, having taken off the rabbit suit and left it in the men's room."

"Why'd he do that?" inquired Judith, trying to avoid her mother's ominous glare.

"Says he thought it belonged to the school. The Santa suit he wore at Christmas did."

"That's possible," Judith conceded.

"Kate Duffy went to the dumpster which is located just

inside the rear door that leads from the back of the kitchen to that breezeway between the hall and the school itself. Norma insists she never left the church hall and kitchen area after the egg hunt, but with everybody else on the move, who can be sure?"

"What about John?"

"He doesn't remember seeing Norma at all, which, considering she looked like a mobile shrub, is hard to believe. Let's call him dazed."

"What about Eddie?" asked Judith, as Gertrude wrestled with the walker in an attempt to get up.

Joe sighed. "Eddie says he wasn't any place he shouldn't have been. If you ask me, Eddie lost the key to his roller skates a long time ago."

"I kind of feel that way about him, too. Though . . ." Judith saw Gertrude thumping angrily over to the refrigerator, making so much noise that the dishes rattled on the table. "Never mind just now. Joe, I've got a few things to tell you." She lowered her voice a notch. "Can you meet me at Toot Sweet in about an hour?"

Joe hesitated. "Maybe. I'll bring Woody. Get Renie to come along, and we can have a double date over hot fudge sundaes."

"I may do that. Hey—what about the rabbit suit?"

"As we supposed. The blood samples match Sandy's. Not much else—or rather, too much. Every little nipper at the church must have pawed Wilbur's paws. If we went by the fiber samples, the leading suspect would be a four-foot first-grader of Chinese-American descent."

Judith laughed in spite of Gertrude's thrashing about in the refrigerator. "Oh—did you talk to Norma Paine about why she ditched the costume?"

"Norma talked to *us*—lengthily and volubly," Joe replied. "She said she didn't realize Wilbur had left it in the rest room until later so she went back to retrieve it before somebody swiped it for their own Easter egg hunt. When she saw the bloodstains, she panicked. The dumpster was the first thing she thought of, since she knew that Falstaff's Market gets its trash collected every morning, Sunday or not."

The thought of Norma Paine in a state of panic almost overwhelmed Judith. "That makes sense—I guess." She glanced at Gertrude, who was sneering at a container of congealed tapioca pudding. "Around two, then?" Judith said, deciding she'd better hang up before her mother vandalized the refrigerator. "By the way, who found Sandy's body?"

"Tim Mills," replied Joe.

"I thought so," said Judith, and rang off.

Toot Sweet was Heraldsgate Hill's ice cream and confectionery parlor, located between Holiday's Drugstore and Nottingham's, the local florist. Wet Your Whistle and Shoot the Breeze was lettered in gold on the frosted glass door, along with the notation that the shop had been established in 1919.

Judith arrived on the dot of two. Renie had turned her down, succumbing to an unexpected spurt of artistic genius. Judith ordered a vanilla cream soda and sat sipping slowly for a quarter of an hour. Ginger came by, remarking favorably on her husband's handiwork with Judith's hair. Mrs. Dooley paused to report that though deep and savage, the bite on her youngest child's arm was healing nicely, thank you. Norma Paine entered Toot Sweet as stealthily as her ocelot-spotted nonjoggers' jogging suit would permit, and gave a little jump when she saw Judith.

"I just stopped by to look for a friend," she explained. "I'm not one for sweets, especially in the middle of the afternoon." Norma surveyed the score of customers with contempt. "At least," she noted condescendingly, "you're only having a soda."

"I'm using it to wash down a pint of lemon custard ice cream, rum cheesecake, three maple bars, and a dozen chocolate-covered peanut clusters." Judith smiled, wishing it were true.

"Judith!" cried Norma, apparently so overcome by such

a confession of decadence that she collapsed onto an empty chair.

"Actually," Judith began, feeling faintly remorseful, "I only ordered this . . ."

"Really, Judith," interrupted Norma, "I *cannot* get over this business with Sandy Frizzell! The nerve! As far as I'm concerned, they both should have been stabbed!"

"Huh?" Judith almost choked on her last swig of vanilla cream soda. "Isn't that a bit harsh?"

Norma's spotted bust jutted indignantly, almost knocking over a shaker of chocolate sprinkles. "Think of poor Emily! It's all a sham. She stipulated that John should be married in order to inherit. Well, he wasn't anything of the sort! Wilbur feels that he stands to lose the entire estate. It would serve John right."

"Hmmm," murmured Judith, marveling at Norma's lack of reticence regarding her husband's professional affairs. "Exactly how was the will worded?"

Norma blinked. "Let me see . . . It specified that John Casper Frizzell had to be an established family man with an unblemished reputation." She narrowed her eyes at Judith, then fluttered uncharacteristically as the waitress approached. "No, no, Shana, nothing for me! I'm watching my figure." Smiling politely, Shana started to walk away, but Norma's hiss summoned her back. Norma put a hand on the girl's ebony-skinned arm and lowered her voice: "That white chocolate torte with the orange filling and dark chocolate frosting—have you just the *teensiest* piece left, dear?"

Shana allowed that the existence of such an item was indeed possible, and scooted toward the counter. Norma gave Judith a vaguely shamefaced glance. "An indulgence, just to keep you company, Judith."

But Shana was back already, not with Norma's order, but with a message for Judith: "A Mr. Flynn called to say he and Mr. Price couldn't make it. Something came up." Shana's sculpted features turned mystified.

"Thanks, Shana," said Judith, outwardly unperturbed.

Inwardly, however, she was vexed by the cancellation. Typical, she thought.

"I've got to run," she announced. "I've got guests coming in about an hour. By the way," she added, getting to her feet, "if John doesn't get all that money, who would?"

Norma's attention was momentarily diverted by the arrival of her torte, which, Judith judged, probably weighed close to a pound. "Just the way you like it, Mrs. Paine," said Shana cheerfully, with a wink for Judith.

Torn between glaring at Shana and diving into the chocolate torte, Norma glanced up at Judith. "What? Oh, I don't know. That Stella, I suppose."

"Stella Maris?" asked Judith, picking up her purse and the bill for her soda.

Norma, her mouth already full, nodded.

"Who is she?" Judith inquired.

Norma shrugged her heavy shoulders. "Somb rewatib, no dowd."

"Oh." Judith gave Norma a halfhearted smile and walked over to the cash register. She was beginning to wonder if Norma and Wilbur Paine had a language all their own. Most of all, she was wondering about Stella Maris.

TWELVE

THE TWO COUPLES from Oregon arrived just before three-thirty. They were brothers named Nelson from Grants Pass and Medford, accompanied by their wives, all retired, and headed for the Canadian Rockies. Judith foresaw no problems.

The rest of the day passed uneventfully, except for Sweetums getting into a fight with the Ericsons' Dandy Dinmont and Gertrude getting into a fight with Auntie Vance over the phone about the allegedly measly number of pies her sister-in-law had provided for the Easter dinner.

"Next time bring *four*, you lazy old skinflint," snarled Gertrude as Judith walked into her bedroom later that evening. "How about lemon meringue for a change?" Judith paused as her mother's face turned red. "Don't you dare tell me to go pucker yourself!" Gertrude slammed down the phone, then gave her daughter a faintly guilty look. "Okay, okay, so I used your stupid phone. Vanessa is a real crab. She ought to keep a civil tongue in her head."

Judith suppressed a smile. Auntie Vance was the one person in the world who could get the better of Gertrude. Indeed, Auntie Vance could probably have gotten the better of international terrorists. She had, on an infamous Christmas past, even told Dan McMonigle where he could stick his figgy pudding. With a sprig of holly. Dan had never forgiven her. Auntie Vance didn't, as she'd so aptly put it, give a rat's fat ass.

The phone rang. Gertrude, sitting six inches away, refused to answer it. Sighing, Judith trudged across the room and picked up the receiver. To her surprise, the caller was John Frizzell.

"I just wanted to thank you again for your kindness today. And your cousin's, too," he went on in a lifeless voice. "I didn't have her number. It's hard to pick a Jones out of the phone book."

"They're unlisted," said Judith, "but I'll pass your message along. How are you feeling?"

"Rotten." The word sounded hollow. "I'm leaving for New York Friday. Would you mind checking out the house next week to make sure all the mail has been stopped? I don't know who else to ask."

"Oh—sure," Judith replied, responding to the bleakness of John's voice. How sad, she thought, that he was forced to ask a virtual stranger to help him out. "No problem. Who's the landlord?"

"Somebody over on the East Side," said John. "He owns a bunch of rentals. I imagine he'll try to get new tenants in here by the first of the month. I've leaving the place pretty tidy."

"I'm sure you are," Judith said consolingly. "If there's anything else I can do, John, let me know."

"Thank you." He sounded humble. "I guess everybody really does hate me. I've gotten a lot of crank calls and even a couple of letters today. Eve Kramer is furious, but at least I can understand her anger. I don't think it has much to do with me being . . . what I am."

Gertrude was tugging at Judith's slacks. "Who is it?" she hissed. "That fruitcake?"

"People can be terribly small-minded," Judith said, trying to escape from her mother's verbal clutches. "But you're right about Eve—she's mad because she's lost a fine assistant on short notice."

"Yes, I think so. Eve has her faults, but she's not narrow-minded." For the first time, John sounded faintly cheered. "I guess you could say I know All About Eve." He actually laughed. "God, I loved that movie! Bette Davis was divine!"

Judith concurred. "By the way, John, do you have some relative named Stella?"

There was a silence on the line. Then John's voice resurfaced, puzzled and devoid of cheer. "No. I haven't any relatives. Not since Aunt Emily died."

"Does the name mean anything to you?" Judith asked as Gertrude finally heaved herself off the bed and began to clump out of the room on her walker.

"It *does* sound familiar," John conceded. "Now where have I heard it. . .?" His voice trailed off.

"From Wilbur Paine?" hazarded Judith.

"Wilbur?" There was another, briefer silence. "I don't remember. Excuse me, Mrs. McMonigle, there's someone at the door. Maybe another casserole. Or a bomb threat." With a lame laugh, John Frizzell hung up.

Judith had barely replaced the phone when it rang again. This time it was Joe, full of apologies and, he confessed, a pastrami on rye. "It's almost nine o'clock and I'm just getting around to dinner. Chainsaw murder out in your old neighborhood. Somebody's bookie didn't pay up. Let's just say he went all to pieces."

"You ought to choke on your pastrami for that remark," said Judith, lying down on the bed and turning the three-way light to low.

"So what did you want to tell me?" inquired Joe. "How the touch of my hand at the base of your neck can send shivers up your spine?"

Since it was the utter truth, that was precisely what Judith would have liked to tell him. But she reined in her tongue and stuck to the facts. As concisely as possible, she related her visit with Father Tim, her interview with Eve Kramer, her exchange with Eddie La Plante, her accidental meeting with Norma Paine, and the phone call from John Frizzell.

"Are you really going to let him take off for New York?" she asked when she had finished her recital.

"Why not? We've no grounds to hold him," Joe replied. "Sure, I'd rather he stuck around, at least for questioning, but legally there's nothing we can do. Right now, I'm more interested in your concern over Father Tim."

Judith kicked off her shoes and straightened the pillow under her head. Outside it was dark, but the spring air was soft and fragrant. Through the open window, she could hear Arlene Rankers screeching at Carl to set out the recycling bin for the Wednesday morning pick-up.

"As a matter of fact," said Judith, "I'd rather not go into my theories about Tim right now. I just got an inspiration. I'll talk to you tomorrow." She was already sitting up, feeling for her shoes.

"Hey—what about this business of Eddie being Eve's dad?" asked Joe. "Why the big secret?"

"She's ashamed of him as far as I can tell," said Judith, leaning over the other side of the bed to push the window open another six inches. "I'll check back first thing in the morning, okay?"

Joe conceded that it had to be, and hung up. Judith shouted down to Arlene, who was standing in the driveway, haranguing her husband about pruning the laurel hedge some time in the near future.

"Have you got a minute?" Judith called.

Arlene looked up. "Of course!" Her smile was radiant. "Carl and I were just planning our summer garden. There's something so romantic about perennials. Shall I come up or do you want to come down? I can make cocoa."

"I've got guests," said Judith in a lower voice. "I'll meet you in the kitchen."

Two minutes later, Arlene was sitting at the dinette table, relating a horror story about how Kevin had gotten a speeding ticket racing to her rescue that morning, followed by the discovery that the spare tire was also flat, the tow truck had taken an hour and a half to arrive, and Arlene had gotten into a fight with Marvin Boggs, the service station owner.

"Marvin's a moron," declared Arlene, munching on a stale snickerdoodle. "I went to high school with him, and he was always getting suspended for wearing his clothes backward. He did it on purpose, you know."

Ordinarily Judith would have asked why, but she had more pressing matters on her mind. "Arlene, did you say that Mugs used to date Tim Mills?"

"Yes, in college." Arlene plucked a stray leaf out of her tousled red-gold hair. "It was just before he went into the seminary."

"Did Mugs ever meet his family?" Judith inquired, trying to keep her voice casual.

Arlene was digging about in the cookie jar. "Yes. In fact, she attended his parents' silver anniversary reception in Miles City. Lovely people."

The shadowy idea that had been forming in Judith's brain moved a couple of steps into the light. "Do you remember Tim's mother's name, by any chance?"

"Let me think," replied Arlene, removing her hand and taking a bite out of another cookie. "I hear Tim's feeling better today." She spoke in a musing tone. "Mrs. Mills . . . it's kind of an unusual name. It began with an 'S' . . ."

Judith held her breath. Perhaps the theory she'd been building wasn't so shaky after all. "An 'S'? What was it?"

Arlene was munching and thinking at the same time. The dual effort was apparently too much for her. She choked on the cookie and held the last uneaten bite out for Judith's inspection. "These aren't too fresh, Judith. I'm going to make a batch of my oatmeal crispies tomorrow. Shall I double it and bring you some?"

"Sure, sounds great." Trying to hide her impatience, Judith attempted to get Arlene back on track. "You said Mrs. Mills's first name was. . .?"

Arlene cleared her throat a couple of times before she spoke. "Squatting Frog." She paid no heed to Judith's look of dismay. "She's a full-blooded Sioux. They actually call her Sue, in fact. S-U-E." Arlene spelled it out for clarification.

Judith's theory, which had been built on the premise that Tim's mother had been named Stella, collapsed like a house of cards. Her disappointment made no dent in Arlene, who was now peering out the kitchen window, presumably in an effort to keep track of Carl's progress with the recycling bin. "Personally," said Arlene, giving up on trying to see her husband in the dark, "I think Indian names are fascinating. Carl used to play basketball in high school with Howling Cat Peterson."

"He did?" Judith remarked somewhat absently, but never doubted the fact for a minute. "Hey," she exclaimed, feeling a new brainstorm coming on, "Tim's mother is a Sioux? But he's very fair. Is his father blond?"

Arlene shrugged and, despite her criticism, ate the last snickerdoodle. "I've no idea. Why?" Her eyes were inquisitive buttons of blue.

Judith's answer was interrupted by the sound of the front door. "Excuse me," she said, getting up, "the Nelsons are back from dinner. Let me see if they need anything."

Five minutes later, the well-fed guests had trundled up to bed, content to make an early night of it since they planned to rise at six a.m. to get a head-start on their sightseeing and shopping.

"They are now Full Nelsons," Judith announced, resuming her place at the dinette table. "Arlene, I'm puzzled."

"About what?" Arlene was shaking cookie crumbs into

a little bowl. "If you save these, you can use them for ice cream topping."

"Good idea," said Judith vaguely. Household hints, of which Arlene Rankers had an invaluable store, were occasionally lost on Judith. "Well," she began, unwilling to divulge her real concerns over Tim Mills, lest her neighbor announce them on what Judith referred to as Arlene's Broadcasting System, or ABS for short, "I guess it's because Tim doesn't look the least like an Indian."

"Why should he?" Arlene noted Judith's blank expression. "Didn't I tell you? He was adopted."

Judith's theory, now somewhat altered and still unformed, began to rise from the ashes.

"But," asked Renie over the phone an hour later, "do you think Tim knows who his real parents are?"

"I didn't push it any further with Arlene," replied Judith. "She got off on his illness, and I didn't want to tell her my reaction to the cause, so I changed the subject to Eve Kramer."

"Any insights into the Prickly Pair?" quizzed Renie around a mouthful of popcorn. "Arlene knows Eve pretty well."

"Nothing much pertinent," responded Judith, wondering why all her relatives had to make so much noise when they ate. "Arlene scoffs at Norma's insinuations about Eve's roving eye, but I wonder if it's not out of loyalty. For all their spats, Arlene and Eve are good friends. So are Carl and Kurt. I did gather that Norma wasn't the only one who thought Eve had strayed upon occasion."

"She has some cause with Kurt roaring like a bull half the time," said Renie. "Gee, coz, do you suppose Eve had a thing for John Frizzell?"

"It's crossed my mind," Judith admitted, warning off Sweetums, who looked as if he was contemplating a spring onto the bed. "Ironic, huh? But it'd give Eve a more obvious motive than the will business, which still eludes me."

"It would give Kurt one, too," said Renie, making the kind of glugging sound that gave evidence to the washing down of popcorn with a can of cold Pepsi. "Let's see, who else have we got with apparent motives? Wilbur and Norma might have wanted to do in Sandy to keep the legal business here instead of in New York. Maybe they thought Sandy was the one who wanted to go back East."

"They were wrong. They should have killed John instead." Judith discouraged Sweetums with a rolled-up magazine. "Why do I keep thinking we've got the wrong victim?" She sighed, a wary eye on the cat. "There's still something odd about the Duffys. I don't believe Mark was going after the wheelbarrow. Where do you keep yours?"

"Out back, under the deck," said Renie, smacking her lips.

"Right. Mine's in the toolshed with Dan. Most people don't store a wheelbarrow in the house, especially not in a little bungalow like the Frizzell place. So why break in?"

"To get something else," reasoned Renie. "But what?"

Sweetums was hooking his claws in the yellow flounce that ran around the bottom of Judith's bed. She grabbed the animal by his flea collar. Sweetums yowled. Judith gave him a good shake. His grip on the flounce was firm. Grinding her teeth, she stared menacingly into his nasty little yellow eyes.

". . . letters, maybe, or a diary?" Renie was saying. Indeed, Renie had been saying a lot of things, none of which Judith had heard. "Hey, coz, speak up! Are you there?"

"Barely," snapped Judith, still trying in vain to unhook Sweetums. She twisted the flea collar, causing Sweetums's tongue to jut out and his eyes to pop like a pair of Tokay grapes. He released the chintz fabric. Judith released him. Sweetums gasped, wheezed, coiled into a ball, and flung his orange-and-white-striped body into Judith's lap. Judith shrieked.

"Coz!" Renie sounded frantic. "Say something!"

Judith was staring at Sweetums, who was nestling against her, a picture of purring contentment. He actually looked up and twitched his whiskers at her. Overcome by guilt, Judith stroked his ruffled fur.

"After invading my bedroom on a seek and destroy mission, my wretched nemesis has ceased taunting me and is actually displaying affection," Judith said in a clear, even voice. "I can't help but suspect this is not the real Sweetums."

"Oh," said Renie faintly. "I thought you were talking about your mother."

Filled with Swedish pancakes and lingonberry syrup, scrambled eggs, link sausage, orange juice, and endless cups of coffee, the four Nelsons ventured out into the city just after eight o'clock. Gertrude polished off the leftovers while Judith had a piece of toast and a bowl of cold cereal. By late afternoon, the four guest rooms would be full, with one couple arriving from Alaska for a three-night stay, and two single women coming in from California for the remainder of the week. The brief lull at Hillside Manor was over.

Phyliss Rackley showed up promptly at nine, full of complaints but brimming with energy. Judith decided to make a quick run up to Falstaff's to restock the larder. By chance, she ran into Kate Duffy, testing avocados in the produce department.

As ever, Kate was immaculately turned out, in a crisp white blouse and flaring lime-green skirt, her honey-colored curls in perfect array and her discreet makeup freshly applied. "I'm feeling blue," she said in a hushed voice, moving her expert hand to the early strawberries. "I think it's so sad that there won't be any kind of service here for Sandy. I don't care if she was a man, John should still have a memorial Mass."

"It'd probably be too hard on him," Judith said, filling a paper bag with plump oranges. No matter what the season, the produce section always smelled of damp, fresh earth and bountiful harvest. Judith was momentarily seduced by the colorful assortment of fruits and vegetables being sprayed at intervals by a gentle sprinkler system. "Going through the ceremony twice, I mean," Judith explained, getting herself back on track. "I suppose he's already shipped the, uh, body back."

Kate's fine gray eyes furtively scanned the bins, as if the produce were eavesdropping. Falstaff's was not yet crowded this early, and no other shoppers were close by. "This morning," she replied in her breathless voice. "He had to wait until the police released Sandy." A faint flush tinged her cheeks at the mention of such unpleasant realities. "Or so Norma told me. She's over in salad dressing."

Judith craned her neck, trying to see around the orderly rows of fresh spring vegetables. Salad dressing lay beyond coffee, tea, and beverages, and thus out of Judith's vision. "Norma ought to know," Judith remarked. "I suppose Wilbur had to make the arrangements."

Kate moved so close to Judith that she was practically nuzzling her shoulder. "She knows because he *didn't* make the arrangements," Kate whispered. "John insisted on doing it himself." The faintest hint of malice flickered in Kate's eyes, though whether it was for Wilbur or John, Judith couldn't be sure.

"Wilbur can't be pleased," Judith noted, making her tone confidential, but leaning away just enough to get at the grapefruit. "John's costing him a bundle. In fact," she continued, stuffing a dozen pink grapefruit into another paper bag, "John has caused a lot of trouble for a lot of people. Wilbur, Eve, Mark . . . Surely he'll drop the charges against Mark now that he's leaving town in a couple of days?"

Kate's color deepened. "I really don't know. You'd think so. It would be the charitable thing to do." She was all but muttering. "Truly, it was a very silly incident."

"And over such a silly thing," Judith said with a bland smile. "Why," she asked as guilelessly as possible, "did Mark want those scribblings in the first place?"

Kate didn't quite fall into the persimmons, but she definitely teetered on her sensible yet chic pumps. "Scribblings? *What* scribblings?" Her voice had risen, anything but breathless, and she caught herself with a hand at her throat.

Judith shrugged and picked up a tomato. "I'm sorry, I heard a rumor that Mark was looking for some . . ." She paused, apparently intent on the firmness of the beefsteak variety she was fondling. "I forget, was it letters?"

Kate's usually sweet face had tightened. Her gray eyes turned cold as steel. All signs of the soft, ethereal creature who seemed to float through life on a celestial cloud had vanished. In Judith's mind, an imaginary halo slipped over Kate Duffy's head and settled somewhere in the vicinity of her ears.

"It was *not* letters," Kate said through clenched teeth. "It was a *wheelbarrow*." She made as if to grab Judith by the arm, apparently thought better of it, and pressed her hands against the folds of her skirt. "Where did you hear this stupid rumor?"

Judith looked vague. "At Toot Sweet? Or Moonbeam's? Or was it the paperboy?"

Kate was crimson. "That Dooley!" She glanced around, taking in an old woman with a three-pronged cane, a young mother with a sleeping baby in a backpack, and the produce manager, who was busily sorting green and red peppers further down the aisle. "Ever since Dooley joined up with that ridiculous police auxiliary, he's been a dreadful little snoop. I wouldn't put it past him if he did it just to become a common window peeper!"

Thinking that Gertrude would probably agree, but feeling the need to defend Dooley since she had implicated him, Judith scooped up two more tomatoes and shook her head. "Now, Kate, Dooley's a terrific kid. He's got an inquiring mind, that's all. He even reads books. Anyway, I'm not sure where I heard the story about Mark looking for something other than the wheelbarrow. You know how rumors run amok on the Hill."

Kate's rage had dwindled into a severe pout. "I certainly do. It's outrageous." Her eyes flashed at Judith. "I swear to you on the Holy Bible that Mark wasn't looking for any *scribblings*."

Judith inclined her head. "I believe you," she said. But she wondered what in fact Mark *had* been looking for. The reaction she'd wheedled out of Kate certainly indicated that it was *not* a wheelbarrow.

THIRTEEN

HAVING LOST KATE in dairy products, and missed Norma at the checkout stand, Judith headed for Holiday's Drugstore to get Gertrude some corn plasters and Tums. It was ten o'clock, and the store was just opening. Judith crossed the threshold in front of Carl Rankers and behind the Episcopal rector of St. Alban's.

"You're getting a late start for work," Judith commented to Carl as they both headed for medicinal aids. "Is somebody sick?"

Carl's blue eyes twinkled in his tanned, craggy face. "Arlene has tennis elbow. She hit me with Kevin's racquet."

Judith grinned, not knowing whether to take Carl seriously. "I thought she was making oatmeal crispies this morning."

Carl perused the liniment section. "She is. She's one of those rare women who can bake hurt." He moved a step closer to Judith and lowered his voice. "Actually, I've got a touch of bursitis. But that's not why I'm running late." The twinkle had faded, and his expression had turned uncharacteristically serious. "I stopped by SOTS to see how Father Tim was doing and if he needed any help with the liturgy. He's much better, but he can't locate Eddie La Plante."

Judith stared across the bunion display. "Eddie? Maybe he just wandered off. He's kind of strange."

"Oh, sure," Carl agreed, picking up a small box that contained a tube of rubbing ointment, "but reliable. He was supposed to be up at church by eight o'clock when a load of bedding plants were to be delivered from Nottingham's. He never showed."

A vague alarm was going off in Judith's head. "Did Father Tim call him?"

"Eddie doesn't have a phone," replied Carl. "I drove down to his place on Quince Street at the bottom of the Hill, and there was no sign of him."

"Has anybody seen him?" Judith asked.

Carl shook his head. "I nosed around a bit, but could only find an old lady who said she'd seen him coming home late yesterday afternoon. I figured her for the type who sits by the window and passes the time watching the neighbors."

"Maybe he had a stroke or a heart attack," Judith said. "Do you think we should call 911?"

"I suggested that to Tim, but he said to wait. I have a feeling he thinks Eddie may have gone off on a bender. Somebody said he used to be quite a boozer."

Judith's unseeing gaze roamed over the shelves filled with vitamins, headache remedies, stomach medications, and dental hygiene products. "I've heard that myself," she murmured, but her mind was already racing ahead.

Carl tapped her shoulder in a friendly manner. "I've got to run. We're doing a big presentation this afternoon for WestBank. I'm going to show how our leading-edge agency can bring them new investment business by giving away gerbils."

"How about cats?" Judith retorted, but Carl, with the

twinkle back in his eyes, was already moving down the aisle.

Spurred by the news about Eddie, Judith quickly made her purchases and headed home. She ignored Gertrude's grumblings over the wrong kind of corn plasters and went straight to the phone. Eve Kramer was not at the antiques shop yet, but on the second call, Judith caught her at home.

"What do you mean that old fool is missing?" snapped Eve. "Oh, damn! If he's gone off the wagon again, I'll kill him!" Apparently she considered her words in the context of recent events, and simmered down to a mere rolling boil. "I'll swing by his place on my way to the shop," Eve said. "I've got a key. Thanks, Judith. And thank Carl for me, too." She hung up without further ado.

Reassuring herself that there was nothing more to be done in the matter of the missing Eddie La Plante, Judith poured herself a cup of coffee and sat down to pay some bills. It occurred to Judith, not for the first time in the past five days, that she was being foolish to think she could help solve Sandy Frizzell's murder. She'd let Renie talk her into getting involved. Ever since they were kids, Renie had been able to con Judith into all sorts of mischief and adventures. But this was real life, and she had no resources, other than her knack for getting people to open up. She had no reason to become involved except that the crime had taken place in her own church. And that Joe Flynn happened to be the homicide detective assigned to the case. Judith glanced down at the last check she'd written, to Scooter's Delivery Service. She'd signed it "Judith G. Flynn." Annoyed with herself, she tore it into bits and wrote out a replacement.

Phyliss passed through the kitchen with the dirty linen from breakfast and a grievance about her sinus drainage, or the lack of it. A call came through from Manitoba, asking for a reservation in late June. Sweetums appeared on the outside windowsill above the sink, preened a bit, and dove into the rhododendron bushes. Apparently he'd given and received all the affection he could stand for a while.

Shortly after eleven, the phone rang again. It was Eve Kramer, sounding less angry and more disturbed. "There's no trace of him," she said, the usual bite in her voice replaced by anxiety. "His dinner dishes were still in the sink, but there's no sign that he had breakfast. I can't tell if he slept in his bed or not, because he never makes it." She paused, and Judith heard her suck in her breath. "Do you think I should notify the police?"

Judith considered. She realized that it was possible Eddie was sleeping off a mighty drunk in a back alley at the bottom of the Hill. Such a revelation would cost Eve dearly. Judith also knew that Eve must be pretty desperate to confide in her. But then Judith was one of the few people who knew that Eddie La Plante was Eve's father.

"I would," Judith said at last. "Has he ever suffered from amnesia?"

"Amnesia or Alzheimer's?" Eve's tone had resumed its cutting edge. "Actually, neither. He just gets fogged in sometimes from all those years of drinking. But to my knowledge," she added on a softer note, "he hasn't touched a drop since he came up here from California."

"Has he ever gone off like this before?" Judith asked as Phyliss trudged through the kitchen again, this time armed with a cedar mop and a dust pan.

"I saw the Lord in your basement," she announced, and kept right on walking.

"Good, Phyliss," said Judith in an aside, accustomed to her cleaning woman's frequent visitations from On High. "Excuse me, Eve, I didn't quite catch that."

"I said, he hasn't gone off like this since he moved here." It was Eve's turn to speak away from the phone, apparently to a customer. Judith gathered she was now calling from the shop. "I've got to run, Judith," said Eve in a hushed voice. "Someone's here to interview for John's job."

Judith hung up and wrote out the last of the checks for

her current bills, noting that her balance was teetering on the edge. At least she had begun to accumulate a bit of savings for the first time since before she'd gotten married. She was about to make a transfer via phone when Renie banged on the front door.

"I was out running errands and thought I'd bring back the plastic containers I borrowed Sunday for the leftovers," she said, breezing in through the entry hall in a disreputable-looking Stanford University sweatshirt and baggy pants that were worn out at one knee. Judith recognized that Renie had only two kinds of clothes: haute couture and really crummy. Judith had never quite understood her cousin's extremist approach to dressing, but Renie herself probably didn't, either.

"Thanks," said Judith, taking the items from Renie and putting them into a kitchen drawer. "Have you heard about Eddie La Plante?"

Renie hadn't. She sat at Judith's dinette table and listened to the brief account. "Do you think there's any connection between Eddie and the murder?" Renie asked, removing the lid from Judith's cookie jar.

"Not that I know of," replied Judith. "Unless Eddie saw something Saturday."

"Maybe he did." Renie gave Judith a disappointed look over the rim of the cookie jar. "This sucker's empty."

"I know," said Judith. "Arlene is bringing over oatmeal crispies."

"When?" asked Renie in a sunken voice.

"Soon, coz, soon. Relax."

Renie did, or at least appeared to, though Judith noted her cousin's eyes darting in the direction of the Rankers's house. "Maybe Eddie is just out doing some errands," Renie suggested.

"It's possible," agreed Judith, tensing as she heard Gertrude thumping around somewhere on the second floor. "We may be alarming ourselves for nothing."

"I never guessed Eddie was Eve's father until you told me on the phone last night," said Renie, pulling a frayed thread off the sleeve of her sweatshirt. "I remember when she and Kurt moved here. It wasn't long after we did, and the Rankers gave a party to welcome all of us. The Duffys, too. Gosh, that was twenty years ago!" Her brown eyes widened at the thought of so much time passing so swiftly.

"Mike got toilet-trained just about then. Finally," remarked Judith with a little grimace. "You and Bill had just moved back from Port Diablo."

"Right," said Renie, half rising out of her chair. "Here comes Arlene. Does she know Eddie is Eve's dad?"

"I don't know." Judith got up to open the back door. "She would if anyone did. I'll try pumping her."

"Get the crispies first," Renie called.

Arlene settled in at the table while Judith put on her fourth pot of coffee of the morning. Renie was already smacking her lips over the oatmeal crispies while Arlene regaled the cousins about the missing Eddie La Plante.

"I suspected foul play as soon as Carl told me," she said with a dark look. "Once these things start, they don't stop. Any one of us could be next."

"True," said Renie, gobbling up another crispie. "Hey, coz, I could use some milk. You got enough?"

Judith did. Renie poured it herself while Judith tried to think of a discreet opening to find out how much Arlene knew about Eve and Eddie. As it turned out, Arlene volunteered the information.

"Poor old darling," she lamented, "with no relatives around and probably not a lot of friends. I always wondered why he moved to the Hill. I think he came here from Florida."

"California, actually," corrected Judith, figuring she wasn't giving much away with the revelation. "Eve Kramer thought we should call the police."

Arlene looked only mildly interested. "Did she? So did Carl, but Tim wanted to wait awhile."

Taking her cue from Judith, Renie posed an indirect

question: "I think it's nice of Eve to be concerned. Sometimes she strikes me as a bit self-absorbed."

"That's armor for Eve," Arlene replied as Judith poured coffee into three unmatched mugs. "It defends her from Kurt's verbal abuse. Not," she went on, holding up a hand, "that Eve can't dish it out, too. But Kurt can be a real grouch. If Carl criticized me the way Kurt does Eve, he'd have been wearing his ears around his elbows years ago."

Neither cousin doubted Arlene's word for an instant. Judith presented sugar for Renie and cream for Arlene, then sat back down at the table. "Maybe Eve came from a family where there was a lot of, uh, bickering. She might have been used to it."

The theory cut no ice with Arlene. "Eve was an only child. Her parents were divorced. She used to visit her mother in . . . let me think . . . San Rafael, as I recall, but she died a few years ago. Eve never talked about her father."

"She looks French," said Judith. "What was her maiden name?"

Arlene still seemed oblivious to the cousins' probing. She sipped her coffee and furrowed her brow. "I don't know," she said in some surprise. "I guess I never asked." Arlene set the mug down on the table and rested her chin on her hand. "She *does* look French, but somehow I don't think she is. All I do know is that her family name began with an 'F.' A long time ago, she embroidered her initials on an evening bag. They were 'EFK.' It was lovely, all in tiny seed pearls."

"Sounds elegant," remarked Judith with a sharp, swift kick under the table for Renie.

"Sure does," agreed Renie, wincing. "Remember that party you gave for us and the Kramers and the Duffys?"

Arlene put on her most nostalgic expression. "Of course I do, sweetie. You were all so cute. The Kramers had only been married a year or two, and the rest of you still had that newlywed glow."

"We did?" Renie was obviously trying to dig back

through the sands of time to her dewy status as a near-bride. "As I remember, I wasn't speaking to Bill because he objected to my magenta tights with the chartreuse miniskirt and purple vinyl boots."

"You were adorable," Arlene assured Renie. "And Kate wore the dearest frock, all eyelet and sweet peas. She'd bought it in Los Angeles before she and Mark moved up here."

"The Duffys came from L.A.?" Judith asked.

Arlene nodded once. "That's right. Well, not really. Mark's from Wisconsin and Kate's from the Dakotas. But they met in Los Angeles."

Renie was frowning in puzzlement. "Los Angeles? Or Chicago? I thought Mark went to Northwestern."

"He did." Arlene had turned a trifle vague. "Let me think . . . No, it was definitely L.A. Mark had some notion about being a moviemaker, or whatever they call them in Hollywood. Kate was . . ." Arlene suddenly went blank. "You know, I'm not sure what she was doing down there. Going to college, maybe. Or working in Disneyland."

Visions of Kate Duffy sitting in on a seminar with Goofy and Pluto flitted through Judith's mind. But Arlene was finishing off her coffee and getting up from the table.

"I must run. I'm going to meet Quinn McCaffrey and his family at the airport." Arlene retrieved the dish she'd used to transport the oatmeal cookies. "They've been in Denver, visiting her parents."

Renie stopped eating crispies long enough to make a face. "Quinn! The man's an ass! With any luck, some Mormon terrorists will take him hostage, and the school will be spared his ineptitude."

Arlene raised her eyebrows. "I like Quinn. I think he's doing a good job as principal. You sound like your husband. Bill's too much of an intellectual," she huffed, heading for the back door. "He doesn't think much of anybody who doesn't have an I.Q. over 3.0."

"That's so," said Renie in a baffled tone as Arlene departed the house. She turned a puzzled face to Judith. "What did she mean?"

"Never mind." Judith poured them each more coffee. "The word for the day is 'flummoxed.' Coz, what do you suppose that 'F' stood for in Eve's initials?"

"For flummoxed?"

Judith gave Renie a baleful glance. "Don't be dim. I wonder how much background work Joe is putting into this investigation?"

"What kind?" asked Renie as Gertrude's walker banged down the backstairs. It was approaching noon, and Gertrude was approaching the kitchen.

"Like digging around into these people's pasts. Now I know it's possible that Eve took a stepfather's name, assuming she had one, but it's more likely that La Plante isn't really Eddie's last name. In fact, it's sort of a joke— you know, because he's a gardener."

Renie wrinkled her small nose. "That's a joke?"

"The only joke around here is you two jokers," said Gertrude from the little hallway that led into the kitchen. "Get off your butts and put some lunch on the table. It's two minutes to twelve."

Renie got up to greet her aunt, bestowing a large, noisy kiss on the older woman's wrinkled cheek. "Hi, goat-breath, where's your broom?"

Gertrude surveyed her niece with blatant disapproval. "Look at you, a middle-aged matron, running around in college clothes like some lamebrained coed! Why don't you grow up and get yourself a decent housedress, Serena?"

"Like yours?" Renie gestured at Gertrude's red-yellow-and-green-striped coffee coat. "Not me, I don't want to look like a stoplight. Come to think of it, most of your clothes would stop traffic, you old coot."

Judith ignored the banter between her mother and her cousin and proceeded to start lunch. "You staying?" she called to Renie.

But Renie declined. She had to meet a photographer in

less than an hour. "I've got to go home and change into my ripped-up jeans and skimpy halter top," she said with a leer for Gertrude and a wink at Judith. "See you."

Judith watched the clock while her mother filled up on an egg salad sandwich, potato chips, a dish of stewed prunes, and four of Arlene's oatmeal crispies. It seemed to take Gertrude forever to eat lunch. Judith could have used the upstairs phone to call Joe, but didn't want to leave the main floor in case Phyliss needed her.

At last, Gertrude trundled off on her walker to watch her favorite soap opera. Judith dialed Joe's direct number in the homicide division and was only mildly surprised to find him out of the office. Woody Price was able to come to the phone, however.

"Woody," Judith began, "are you and Joe doing any research on our favorite suspects?"

"Research?" Woody sounded faintly puzzled. "What do you mean, Mrs. McMonigle?"

"On their backgrounds," said Judith, making undecipherable notes on the back of an old envelope that had brought her the plumber's latest bill. "You know—where they came from; went to college; if they did; previous marriages, if any; all that stuff."

"We only run them through the computer to see if they have any priors," replied Woody. "That is, criminal records. None of them do, although I probably shouldn't tell you that. The most we came up with were some parking and speeding tickets." His rich baritone took on a teasing note. "I see you were picked up five years ago for doing fifty in a thirty-five-mile zone."

"Dan sent me out for a case of Twinkies," Judith said with some asperity. "Hey, wait a minute—are you including *me* as a suspect?"

Woody's voice took a turn toward remorse. "Well, not really, of course, but you *were* the last person we know of who saw Sandy Frizzell alive. It's just procedure, you understand. It'd look odd if we didn't include you."

Judith made a face into the phone. "Gee, thanks. I'd sure hate to be left out. Hey, where *is* Joe, by the way?"

"He's officially on his lunch hour," Woody said, "but actually, he went up to . . ." Woody paused, apparently consulting his notes. "It's one of your Catholic terms. I'm a Methodist, you know," he added apologetically. "Lieutenant Flynn may be doing some work on this case. He went to the chancery."

"Oh!" The word was a little gasp. "I see. Thanks, Woody."

Judith stood with her hand on the phone, momentarily distracted from the homicide investigation. Woody might be right about Joe's visit to the archdiocesan chancery office; perhaps the trip was connected with the murder case. But Judith had a feeling that something else was happening that had nothing to do with Sandy Frizzell. She realized that the kitchen floor seemed to be heaving before her eyes, and took a deep breath.

"God works in wondrous ways," announced Phyliss Rackley, trudging in from the pantry.

"I hope so," breathed Judith.

"You bet he does. Not that I'm a wagering woman, gambling being a sin that sends many a soul to damnation. But," Phyliss rattled on, oblivious to her employer's disturbed countenance, "there I was, putting on the last wash, and I hit my elbow on the dryer and spilled detergent all over and it made me sneeze and now my sinuses are draining like crazy. What do you think of that?" asked Phyliss, triumphantly waving a crumpled Kleenex.

"I think that's . . . miraculous," said Judith, regaining her grip on reality. "You'll have to give a testimonial at your church on Sunday."

"Witness," said Phyliss. "We witness. You're right, I will." She blew her nose like Gabriel's horn, then headed for the living room.

Judith was restless. There was always plenty to do at the B&B, but she felt at loose ends on this Easter Wednesday.

A glance at the calender told her that there were only ten more days until Joe would get the decision about the annulment. Maybe he already had it; maybe that was why he was up at the chancery office. If the verdict went against him, if his marriage to Herself was declared valid, then what? Judith couldn't imagine getting married outside the Church. Indeed, she couldn't imagine getting married again at all. Not even to Joe.

For the first time since Dan died, Judith realized that it wasn't just being freed from a miserable marriage that felt so good, but freedom itself. The thought was new and made her faintly light-headed. As a widow, she could go where she wanted, do as she pleased, kick up her heels, and suit herself.

Yet she had done almost none of those things in the four years since Dan's death. She'd worked her tail off to get her affairs in order, to start up the B&B, to keep Mike in college, and to make herself financially and emotionally independent. The result was that she had become a slave to her commercial venture. But at least she was her own mistress. There was no one else to whom she was accountable.

Except Gertrude. Maybe, Judith thought, freedom was only an illusion. Coming home to Mother had its definite drawbacks. She could not imagine Gertrude and Joe living under the same roof. Until now, Judith had not addressed the problem. Her innate sense of logic told her it would not go away.

It was, Judith realized, easier to try to solve the murder case than her personal dilemma. Pouring out the last cup of coffee from the pot she'd made for Renie and Arlene, Judith sat down at the dinette table and tried to put some of the pieces of the puzzle together. Ten minutes later, she was on the phone to Renie.

"I need you as a sounding board," declared Judith. "Can you come over? I can't leave because of the guests."

"I've got Torchy Plebuck here, going over about a hundred proof sheets," protested Renie. "I can't walk out on him to play Dr. Watson."

"How long?" queried Judith.

Renie sighed. "At least another forty-five minutes." She hesitated. "I'll get there by three-thirty, okay?"

"Fine," said Judith. For the next hour she forced herself to work on Hillside Manor's books, bid farewell to a temporarily rejuvenated Phyliss Rackley, and call Aunt Deb to pick her old but agile brain. If Joe and Woody weren't doing any background research on the SOTS suspects, Judith would.

When it came to people, Renie's mother was a far better source than her sister-in-law, Gertrude. Although Deborah Grover was a great talker, she was also a sympathetic listener. Like Judith, she genuinely enjoyed people and had a talent for getting them to spill their troubles. Gertrude, of course, didn't give a damn.

"Let me see, dear," mused Aunt Deb, "Kate Duffy isn't a local girl." To Aunt Deb, "girls" were defined as any female under seventy. "Fargo, I think, a feed merchant's daughter. A very large family, though I don't recall any of them visiting her. Odd, isn't it?"

It was the sort of remark that usually required no answer. Yet when Aunt Deb made such a seemingly casual statement, it didn't come off the top of her head, but from some deep place in her mind where she had examined the matter and come to a conclusion based on her knowledge of human nature.

"You're right," said Judith. "I wonder why not."

"Offhand, I'd say money, in the beginning," said Aunt Deb, "but later, after Mark got established with his film production company, he could have paid their way. At least for her parents. But I don't know if they're still living. I certainly don't remember Kate going back to see them."

Judith could picture Aunt Deb in her wheelchair, with the phone plastered against her ear and her open, sympathetic face turned toward the apartment window. The comings and goings of her neighbors were a source of constant entertainment for Deborah Grover. Much better than TV, she insisted, and Judith wished her aunt had been keeping her eagle eye on Eddie La Plante.

"Do you think there was a rift?" asked Judith.

"Well, I don't know. Kate is such a sweet girl. I can't imagine her quarreling with anyone. Yet if she got her back up, I think she'd be very hard to budge."

"She met Mark in Los Angeles," Judith noted. "Did she go to college?"

Aunt Deb uttered a plaintive little sigh of apology. "I don't know that, either. She worked at Donner & Blitzen in better dresses before she and Mark had their first baby. Mark's parents came out from Wisconsin to give them a hand when Christopher was born. I met them up at church. I must say his father had rather shifty eyes. Mrs. Duffy was nice enough, though somewhat flashy for my taste. But then I've always been a bit of a prude. Or so your Auntie Vance tells me."

"Auntie Vance tells us all more than we need to know," remarked Judith, "but she means well. I think. What about the Kramers?"

"Well." Aunt Deb's tone was judicious. She rarely criticized others, and was obviously trying to be fair. "Eve is a California girl, which no doubt accounts for a lot. People *will* talk. I've nothing against her, of course, but one hears things. It's probably just common gossip."

"About her being . . . *fast*?" asked Judith, employing a term from Aunt Deb's own lexicon.

"Well, yes, but she's a pretty little thing in her way, and that always gives rise to gossip. Kurt used to travel quite a bit for Tresvant Timber. He's from California, too, but not the sort I think of as a Californian. If you know what I mean."

Judith did. The local consensus on Californians was that they were all glib, suntanned wheeler-dealers with no morals and a conversational bent toward litigation. Kurt definitely did not fit the mold.

"Do you know anything about their families?" queried Judith as Gertrude thumped into the kitchen and opened the refrigerator.

"No, I don't," admitted Aunt Deb. "I'm woefully uninformed about this younger generation. When I was still able, I'd hear things through Altar Society. But now I only pick up snatches of parish news at bridge club. Most of those people are elderly, like your poor old auntie and your mother."

Judith's mother was even now tearing apart a box of chocolate-covered bunnies that Tess, Uncle Al's lady friend, had brought on Easter. Gertrude glared at Judith. "These things get smaller every year. What does Tess do, shrink 'em?"

"The Paines are natives, right?" said Judith into the phone.

"Oh, yes," said Aunt Deb with an undertone of endorsement. "Norma was a Blodgett before she married Wilbur. The Blodgetts owned a tug and barge company. Your Uncle Cliff worked for them for a while after the war. Wilbur's father was an attorney in the old Phipps Building at Third and Douglas. I spent six weeks in that office, filling in. It was after Renie got her own apartment, and I was feeling adrift."

"Really?" Her native city, Judith reflected briefly, was still a small town in many ways. And Heraldsgate Hill was not unlike a country village, surrounded though it was by the greater metropolis. "I thought you always worked part-time for Mr. Whiffel."

"I did," said Aunt Deb, "but that was the summer he had his prostate surgery. The Paine firm needed extra help, and Mr. Whiffel didn't. And as I said, I felt lost with Renie almost a mile away. I guess I'm just an old fool."

"You talking to that old fool, Deb?" growled Gertrude, devouring two bunnies at once. "Tell her to put a sock in it."

Judith put a hand over the mouthpiece of the telephone and made a warning face at her mother. At the other end,

Aunt Deb, failing to elicit a sympathetic response from her niece, resumed speaking. "Wilbur was just out of law school. His father was very hard on him. I helped Wilbur with his first case. He was very grateful, but of course I wanted to see him do well. He's a nice boy, if a bit timorous."

"Norma doesn't give him much encouragement to be a real tiger," Judith remarked, removing her shielding hand from the receiver.

"She's a strong woman," asserted Aunt Deb. "Is that my dear sister-in-law in the background?"

"Uh, yes, she's having a little snack," said Judith with a wary glance at Gertrude, who had now gulped down half of the dozen bunnies.

"How nice," sighed Aunt Deb. "I wish I were as able-bodied as she is. Then I could gorge myself on sweets like a *greedy pig,* too." The sudden bite in Aunt Deb's voice carried all the more force because it was so unusual. It seemed to Judith that Aunt Deb's darker side could only be aroused by criticism of Renie, bad manners, braggarts, Richard Nixon—and Gertrude.

"I've got to run," said Judith. "Guests are coming soon. So is Renie." A quick look at the schoolhouse clock told her that it was three twenty-five. Renie should be along at any moment.

"Give Renie my love. I miss her so," lamented Aunt Deb, at her most forlorn. "Call and let me know how she looks."

"Huh?" Judith cocked her head. "When did you see her last?"

"At breakfast. She made me a Belgian waffle. I do wish she had more time for her old mother, but I know she has to work. Tell her not to forget my aspirin when she comes by before dinner."

Judith rolled her eyes. The only thing comparable to living with Gertrude was waiting on Aunt Deb. Renie had her own cross to bear. Judith started to sign off, but as usual, Aunt Deb wanted to prolong the conversation:

"Remind your mother that I'm having bridge Friday. Tell her not to forget her sandwich."

"Sure, Aunt Deb, I'll talk to you later." Judith made the second pass at hanging up.

"Oh, and ask Renie to pick up a birthday card for Cousin Mabel Frable when she stops to get the aspirin at Holiday's."

"Okay, I'll tell her. Take care." Judith gritted her teeth, fingers clenched around the receiver.

"I forgot to tell you something . . . now what was it?"

Accustomed to her aunt's favorite ploy for staying on the line, Judith decided to be firm. "I've got to run, Aunt Deb. Renie's just pulling up." It was true: The door to the Jones sedan had just slammed in the driveway.

"Oh." Aunt Deb sounded pitiful. "I guess I'll have to let you go then, dear. I'm sorry. I'll tell you about the adoption some other time."

"Adoption?" Judith frowned into the phone. "What adoption?"

"That's what I meant to say," said Aunt Deb complacently. "It was Wilbur's first case."

"Oh, I see." Judith gestured for her mother to get the door. Gertrude remained planted on her walker in the middle of the kitchen. "Yes, I'll call you back real soon."

"You do that," said Aunt Deb, with a hint of command in her wistful voice. "It's such a coincidence that the child turned out to be Father Mills. Goodbye, dear."

Judith froze. "Hold it!" Renie was banging on the front door. Gertrude's eyes gleamed mulishly as she stood rooted to the spot. "Do you mean," Judith said to her aunt, "that Tim Mills was adopted through Wilbur Paine's law office?"

"His *father's* law office, dear. Why, yes," Aunt Deb continued somewhat smugly, "I did the papers myself. To help out young Wilbur, you know."

"But I thought Tim's folks were from Montana." Judith waved wildly at Gertrude as Renie's pounding increased in ferocity.

"They were," said Aunt Deb. "But his real parents' relatives lived here. At least his mother's did."

Judith was torn between letting Renie in herself, giving her mother a swift kick, and—irony of ironies—keeping Aunt Deb on the line. "Who were his real parents?" she asked in an eager tone.

Aunt Deb emitted her pleasant little chuckle. "Oh, dear Judith, you know I can't tell you that! It's quite confidential. I couldn't breach professional ethics, you know."

"But Aunt Deb, this is *me,* your niece! This is a murder case! You know I wouldn't tell a soul!" Judith had turned desperate. Gertrude had sat down, munching away at more bunnies. Renie's pounding had stopped.

"Oh, I know you have the best of intentions," soothed Aunt Deb, "but I still couldn't tell you. Why, I wouldn't even tell Renie. It's been wonderful chatting with you, but Mrs. Parker is at my door. We'll talk again soon, dear. Give my love to Gertrude." Aunt Deb hung up.

"What the hell is going on?" demanded Renie, hurtling through the back door. "The front's locked and you two stoops are lolling around the kitchen while I get bruised knuckles. I thought you'd been murdered, too!"

"Keep your fractured fingers off my bunnies," Gertrude snarled. She gave her niece a sidelong glance. "I have to admit you don't look so scruffy this afternoon. I'll bet that rig set you back at least forty bucks."

Since Renie was wearing a taupe designer suit and coffee-colored blouse that had probably run close to a grand, Judith felt it was just as well that Gertrude still thought in terms of Depression-era prices. "I was on the phone with your mother," said Judith.

The explanation was sufficient for Renie. She sank onto a chair across from Gertrude. "So what else does she want at the drugstore?"

Judith told her. Gertrude finished the bunnies and excused herself to go watch her favorite afternoon talk show. "A hot topic today. Pervert clowns," she informed her daughter and niece. "You'd be surprised how many of 'em are running around with red noses and big feet. Can't trust 'em with the kiddies. Those baggy pants cover up more than you could guess."

"I'll bet," murmured Judith as her mother exited the kitchen. Judith's shoulders slumped as she collapsed into the chair vacated by Gertrude. "I need to thrash all this stuff out with you, coz. I feel like I'm shadow boxing."

"Go ahead," urged Renie. "Frankly, I don't think you've got much to go on."

Judith acknowledged Renie's assessment with a faint nod. "What I've got is more of an impression. I can't put it into words, not even to you. I know who didn't kill Sandy. But I'm not a hundred percent sure who did."

"Tell me who didn't then," said Renie, disappointment crossing her face as she shook out the empty wrappers Gertrude had left from the box of bunnies.

But Judith shook her head. "I don't think I should. Yet. In case I'm wrong, it could be a dangerous mistake. I have the horrible feeling that the killer is totally without a conscience. There may already be another murder."

Renie's eyebrows lifted. "Eddie? Oh, no!"

A noise at the front door indicated that the Nelsons were back from their day of fun, ready to rest up before dinner. Guests at Hillside Manor had their own keys, but Judith went out to the entry hall to play her part as the solicitous hostess. The waterfront had been wonderful; the public market had been a treat; the downtown stores had offered too many temptations. Both male Nelsons gave evidence of the last statement, being burdened with frazzled expressions and large shopping bags from Donner & Blitzen, Nordquist's, E. Motion's and Le Belle Epoch. Amid good-natured jibes, the quartet headed upstairs, letting Judith know they'd be in the living room for sherry and hors d'oeuvres at six p.m. The ritual was standard operating procedure for Hillside Manor, with rum punch substituting for sherry during the summer months. She was starting back for the kitchen when the couple from Alaska arrived. For the next ten minutes, Judith explained the amenities of the house to them, showed them around the main floor, and then escorted them to their bedroom upstairs. They were a taciturn pair, fiftyish, stout, and noticeably wary of anything that went on in the Lower Forty-eight. Judith left them to their own devices, hoping they were inoffensive ones, and hurried down the back stairs.

In the kitchen, Renie was still quivering over the suggestion that Eddie La Plante might be the second victim in the SOTS murder case. "Coz," ventured Renie as Judith sat down again, "if La Plante isn't Eddie's real name, what is it? And why change it?" The gaze she gave Judith was quizzical, yet canny. "Are you thinking what I'm thinking?"

"I suppose so," said Judith in a tone of resignation. "Those initials on Eve's bag, right?" The implications were too dreadful, but Judith had to give them voice. "It may be a longshot, but it's certainly possible. The 'EFK' could stand for Eve Frizzell Kramer. And Eddie may very well be not only Eve's father, but John's."

"That," said Renie with a grim face, "is what I was afraid of."

"Me, too," agreed Judith. "In fact, it scares me to death."

FOURTEEN

"WE'VE GOT TO talk to John," said Renie, galvanized into action. "Or Eve. Let's go."

Judith glanced at the schoolhouse clock. "It's after four. I shouldn't leave. Although," she temporized, "the California contingent said they'd have dinner on the way. I guess they're driving up."

Even as Judith mulled, the phone rang. Renie, already on her feet, answered in her best boardroom voice, but quickly shifted gears: "What? When? How is she?" Renie's eyes were enormous, her face suddenly pale.

Judith stood up, balancing storklike on one foot. "What is it?" she breathed, afraid to find out.

Renie put the phone down. "Arlene says Kate Duffy tried to commit suicide."

"What?" Judith reeled against the table. "Is she okay?"

"Satisfactory condition at All Souls Hospital. She drank nail polish remover." Renie's round face was etched with contempt. "Why, coz? If anybody seems innocent, it's Kate Duffy, if only because she's got the brains of a bug."

"You don't like Kate much, do you?" Judith remarked in an oddly toneless voice.

Renie considered. "I don't *dis*like her. She irks me with all that sanctimonious crap. I think she wants attention." Renie made a sharp gesture with one hand. "Like this stunt. Who'd drink nail polish remover to commit suicide? All she'd do is get sick. Or drunk. The stuff's loaded with alcohol."

"The question is," puzzled Judith, "why do it at all? *Now*?" She gave Renie a keen look. "Where's Mark?"

"Arlene said he and the kids are with her at the hospital."

While Judith felt Renie was being a bit hard on Kate, the situation stymied her. "I suppose she drank the stuff of her own free will."

"Huh?" Renie made a face. "Well, sure. How else would you get anybody—even a nincompoop like Kate—to drink enough nail polish remover to put them in the hospital?"

"I don't get it." Judith was at the refrigerator, taking out a package of frozen pastry puffs. "If Eve and John are half-sister and half-brother, and Eddie La Plante is really Edgar Frizzell, at least the part about the will makes sense. Eve might have felt that some of Emily's money should have gone to Eddie, and thus, to her."

"But even if Eddie is Edgar, he and Lucille would have been divorced years ago, before Eve was born," protested Renie. "He and Eve wouldn't be any blood relation to Emily."

Judith turned on both the oven and a front burner on the stove. "Conscience money, maybe. Or some sort of divorce settlement that was never paid off. Had Lucille lived, she and Emily would have split the estate between them. If John had never shown up to hold poor old Emily's hand, the Kramers would have gotten a big piece through Kurt's connection with Tresvant Timber. Let's say

Kurt and Eve knew that Sandy was really George Sanderson, then they would have a motive for exposing him, and in the process maybe breaking Emily's will. But I'm not sure either of them would go as far as killing Sandy to bring out the truth."

"Both the Kramers have tempers," Renie noted. "And they're the two people who just might have had the embroidery scissors with them. Still, it would have made more sense to kill John. He's the heir."

"True," agreed Judith, selecting a long-handled wooden spoon from a ceramic container on the kitchen counter. "But that would be too obvious. The Kramers aren't stupid." She paused, thrashing about in her kettle cupboard. "As for Wilbur and Norma's motive, what have you picked up from your downtown grapevine about the Borings?"

Renie sighed. "With a prominent family like that, there's practically a rumor of the week. They're changing ad agencies, they're selling out, they're moving the entire aerospace division to Moose Jaw, Saskatchewan. But there is a bit of a buzz that at least two major law firms, one of which has heavy-hitting D.C. connections, are wooing the Borings. Plus, a couple of the Paine junior partners are big on pro bono work, all of which could upset the financial apple cart with the Tresvant family business going down the drain."

"Or back to New York," remarked Judith. "By the way," she noted, eyeing Renie curiously, "you never told me your mother worked in the Paine law office."

Renie's eyes widened. "She did? Oh—you're right, but it was only for a month or two, right after I got my apartment on Hawthorne Place. I forgot all about it. You must have known it at the time, too." She caught the glint in Judith's gaze and cocked her head. "Don't tell me Mother possesses some vital scrap of information."

Pointing a saucepan at her cousin, Judith nodded. "You got it. The elder Paine's office handled Tim Mills's adoption. Didn't your mom ever mention that pertinent fact?"

"Jeez!" Renie stared at Judith. "If she did, it went right by me. You know Mother, she *does* run on. I suppose she may have said something when Tim was assigned to the parish, but it didn't register at the time."

"She won't tell me who his real parents were," said Judith, melting butter and stirring flour into the pan. "Could you worm it out of her?"

Renie looked dubious. "Mother has always taken her duties as a legal secretary very seriously. She can be a real clam if she thinks she's morally bound to keep a secret."

"Too many people are keeping secrets," Judith said, adding chicken broth and milk to her mixture. "The Paines, the Kramers, Eddie, even Father Tim. I can come up with motives for Eve and Kurt and Norma and Wilbur and maybe even Eddie. But not the Duffys. This suicide attempt of Kate's . . ."

The phone interrupted Judith's conjecture, and to her surprise, it was Joe. She took a deep breath, avoided Renie's gaze, and waited for him to mention his visit to the chancery. But, by coincidence, it was the Duffys he was calling about.

"I hear you've been badgering Woody and accusing us of not doing our duty," Joe said in that pleasant voice that rarely failed to unsettle Judith. "Back off, Jude-girl. Remember when I was in vice?"

"Sure," replied Judith, keeping her tone light. Joe Flynn had been assigned to the vice squad as a rookie when Judith had first met him.

"I called in my chips with Les Lowenstein in L.A.," said Joe. "I worked with him before he moved to California to get some smog."

Les Lowenstein's name echoed from out of the past. He and his future wife had double-dated occasionally with Joe and Judith. "Good old Les," said Judith a bit numbly.

"He's way up in the LAPD now," Joe went on without missing a beat. "I got him to check out our suspects, and guess whose names came leaping out of the computer?"

"Who?" Judith exchanged glances with a mystified Renie.

"George Sanderson and Mark Duffy." Joe sounded smug.

"What?" Judith pressed the phone closer and waved at Renie to keep quiet.

"Porno flicks, back in the early sixties," said Joe. "George—Sandy—acted in them, and Mark was the cinematographer, though that's a fancy name for a guy grinding a camera at people grinding."

"They couldn't show *that* then," Judith countered, but knew her quibble was beside the point. So Mark knew who Sandy really was. "Wait, how did that come up in the police records?"

"They got arrested for a wild party on the set. Drug traffic, mainly. But Sandy and Mark weren't charged. Hang on, Woody's just handing me something . . ."

Judith took advantage of the interruption to relay an abbreviated version of his information to a startled Renie. A moment later, he was back on the line: "Okay, this bulletin just in, as they say on the six o'clock news . . . The flick they were working on was called *Bottoms Up,* starring Big Boy Bob Bedloe, Stormy Day, Sandy Dandy, and Kitty Cabrini. What do you bet this is our Sandy AKA George? The director was Ernest True—I'll bet—and the . . . never mind, no sign of John Frizzell here, at least as far as I can tell, but then he might have been Big Boy Bob. Huh?" He had turned away from the phone, apparently talking to Woody Price. "Oh, no, Woody says this Big Boy's real name was Robert E. Lee, but he changed it for obvious reasons. At least one that I can think of."

"Joe," Judith interjected, "did you hear about Kate Duffy?" He hadn't; Judith told him. "This could be the reason Mark tried to break into John and Sandy's house. Maybe Sandy was blackmailing Mark with some evidence, and with Sandy dead, Mark thought he could get it back. And maybe it's why Kate drank nail polish remover.

She may be ashamed that the truth about Mark will come out."

"That's pretty feeble," Joe said dubiously. "The suicide part, I mean. I was going to talk to Mark about this soft-core porno stuff, but I'd better wait until tomorrow. It sounds as if he's got enough problems."

"But she's okay, I gather," protested Judith. "Joe," she continued, on a rising note of urgency, "I don't think you should hold off too long. Eddie's missing, and John's about to leave town, and I have this feeling that . . ."

"Yeah, right, right," Joe broke in impatiently. "Calm down, Jude-girl, we've got the situation under control. Old Eddie is probably down under the public market sharing a nice jug of kerosene with some other social dropouts. Hey, I've got a date with a chainsaw killer. Catch you later."

Judith's heart wasn't in her velouté sauce. She added and stirred and blended and simmered, but the latest news from Joe had set her off on a new tangent. "Maybe," she told Renie, "this is where the Duffys fit in. But would Mark kill Sandy to keep his porno past a secret?"

Renie shook her head slowly. "In my opinion, Mark couldn't kill anybody. Oh, he can get mad, but he's not your basic homicidal type. I hope," she breathed. "Are we still going to talk to Eve and John?"

Judith gave the sauce a final stir with the wooden spoon and chewed on her lower lip. "Well . . . no." She turned off both the stove and the oven. "We can do that later. I've got a better idea." Her black eyes danced at Renie. "Let's go break and enter."

"Huh?"

"If I race like mad when I get back and chloroform Mother, I can get everything done on time for the hors d'oeuvres hour," said Judith, hurrying to get her sweater from its peg in the back hallway. "Let's go."

"Where?" queried a mystified Renie.

Judith paused at the bottom of the back stairs, en route to inform Gertrude of their imminent departure. "The Duffys are all at the hospital, right?" She didn't wait for Renie to answer. "That means their house is empty. They've already been broken into once this week. Let's see if lightning can strike twice."

The Duffy house was seven blocks away, a Tudor brick on a tree-lined street with a panoramic view of downtown to the south and the mountains to the east. The cousins approached boldly, in full late afternoon sunlight, disguising themselves as good Christian women who had come to aid the Duffys in their time of need.

"Let's hope they haven't gotten a burglar alarm system installed since the last break-in," said Judith as they marched up the front walk with its neat border of tulips and hyacinths.

"They probably haven't had time," replied Renie, unable to refrain from guilty glances at the adjacent houses. "Do we go through a window like any other do-gooders, or are you going to resurrect your old skills at picking locks?"

But Judith was already turning the doorknob. "I'm going to walk right in," she told a startled Renie. "We got lucky. But I figured that in all that panic over Kate, the door might not have gotten locked."

Inside, the house was very quiet. Except for an overturned planter at the foot of the stairs in the entry hall, there was no sign of turmoil. The furnishings were traditional, tasteful, and moderately expensive. Kate's care for her home was evident in its tidiness, its personal touches, its comfort. Judith felt like a cheap spy.

"She probably drank the stuff upstairs," Renie said in a whisper. "The ambulance guys or the medics may have knocked over this planter getting her out."

"I told you in the car that's not what we're here for," Judith asserted, but climbed the stairs all the same.

"So we're fixing dinner for the Duffys in the bathroom? How do we explain that if we're caught?" asked Renie.

"We screwed up and had to throw it down the toilet," Judith replied impatiently. "Which way to the master bedroom? I've only been in this house once before, and just downstairs."

"Over there," said Renie, pointing to the right. "Their room faces the mountains."

The bedroom was spacious, with its own fireplace and a small deck. A queen-sized bed was covered with a handsome, if slightly rumpled, wedding ring quilt. Judith wondered if that was where Kate had collapsed after drinking the nail polish remover. She made no comment, however, and went straight to a two-drawer oak filing cabinet in the far corner.

"You take the top, I'll do the bottom," Judith told Renie.

"What the hell are we looking for?" asked Renie. "Dirty movies?"

"Among other things," said Judith. "Maybe a birth certificate, even a marriage license or divorce papers."

Twenty minutes later, they had found none of those things. The cabinet was crammed with insurance papers, investment data, some of Mark's business contracts, and household files. It was all quite innocent. Judith felt discouraged.

"Maybe they've got a safety deposit box," suggested Renie.

"Then they'd store their investment stuff in it instead of here," Judith pointed out. "They must have their personal records somewhere else." She went to the walk-in closet. The Duffys kept their belongings divided, with Mark's clothes on the left and Kate's on the right. On a shelf sat a half-dozen shoeboxes, two folded blankets, three photo albums, and a can of mothballs. Judith also spied a covered carton on the floor at the far end of the closet, wedged in behind a set of matched luggage. With Renie's help, she eased the box out into the bedroom and removed the lid.

"Ah," she cried in a hushed voice, "this may be it." On top was an invitation to the Duffys' twenty-fifth wedding anniversary, celebrated the previous fall. Next was a newspaper clipping of their daughter's wedding. The cousins kept digging.

"Dim though I may be," said Renie, glancing at Mark's diploma from Northwestern University, "I presume your brilliant idea is that Kate, the Do-Good Queen of SOTS, enjoyed a flaming youth, and is actually Tim's mother?"

"It could be her, it could be Eve," admitted Judith, sorting through souvenirs of the Duffy children's high school years. "It could even be Norma Paine. But Kate's the only one of the three to try to kill herself this week."

They were almost three-quarters of the way through the box. Judith slipped open a black photograph folder, then stared in disbelief.

"What is it?" demanded Renie. "Kate's wedding picture with the Mysterious Stranger?"

"See for yourself," said Judith in a strained voice, handing the photo to Renie. "Kate's got on a white veil and a long dress, but she's not a bride—she's posing in the chapel of the Missionary Sisters of the Sacred Heart in Tioga, North Dakota, and she's a nun."

A noise from downstairs paralyzed both cousins. Judith gestured at Renie to put everything back but the photo. Tiptoeing out to the hall, Judith warily looked down the stairwell. Mark Duffy was passing through, apparently on his way to the kitchen. Judith stood motionless, calculating their chances of escaping unnoticed.

The kitchen was through the entry hall on their left. If they could get past the door without being seen, they might get out of the house undetected. Judith darted a glance into the kitchen. Mark's broad back, still clad in his dark business suit, was turned as he did something at the sink. Judith and Renie slipped across the hall.

So intent were the cousins on stealth that Renie didn't see the overturned planter. She tripped, suppressing a curse and almost falling into Judith. Startled, Judith grabbed Renie's arm. They raced for the front door just as Mark wheeled into the hallway.

"Who's there?" His voice was sharp.

Judith threw herself and Renie against the door. "Mark," said Judith in as calm a voice as she could muster, "you *are* here. Renie and I came by to see if we could do anything for you."

Bewilderment crossed Mark's handsome face. "How'd you get in?" he asked.

"The door was open," Judith said truthfully enough. "We knocked, but you didn't hear us," she added, not so truthfully. The hands behind her back fiddled with the lock. "How's Kate?" she asked with a concern that wasn't totally feigned.

Mark was eyeing the door as if it, rather than the cousins, had betrayed him. "That's odd, I could have sworn I clicked the lock on the way in."

Judith turned the knob. It moved freely. "No—see?" She paused as Mark's confusion deepened, then continued in a brisk voice: "We saw your car parked outside and we knew you were home. But you didn't come to the door, so we walked in and here you are." She offered Mark a bright smile.

But Mark's expression had turned strangely bland. "You saw my car?" His hazel eyes shifted from Judith to Renie. "You saw it, too?"

"Sure," said Renie. "I've always liked your Volvo. Nice color."

Mark advanced on the cousins, his tall, broad-shouldered figure faintly threatening. Judith and Renie felt their backs up against the door. "Actually," said Mark, in an even, yet ominous tone, "my car is parked in a garage downtown. I was at a meeting on the East Side when they notified me about Kate. One of my clients kindly offered to drive me to the hospital. My son, Greg, brought me home. Now," he went on, his voice rising, "what the hell is all this?"

Judith had never seen Mark angry before. His eyes flashed, his bronzed skin darkened, and he was almost shaking. She swiftly decided that the best defense was a good offense. "Look, Mark, you've been covering up. This isn't a game. Not only is there a killer out there, but your wife is so afraid of something that she tried to commit suicide. Isn't it time you stopped lying?"

Mark still looked livid, but the contortions of his face indicated he was at least thinking about Judith's words. Somewhat to her surprise, Renie broke in:

"Hey, it's okay." She actually took a step forward and put a hand on Mark's arm. "Whatever it is, it's not worth Kate drinking nail polish remover and puking like a wino."

"Serena!" Mark glared at Renie, but he didn't pull away. "Watch your mouth! You've got a hell of a lot of nerve talking about Kate that way!"

Renie was unmoved by Mark's wrath. "Well, it's true. Kate's grandstanding. Or else she made a stupid mistake."

To Judith's surprise, Mark's rage fizzled like a wet sky rocket. He stepped back, grasping at the balustrade. "She thought it was paint thinner."

Renie ran a hand through her short chestnut curls. "Jeez!"

"Well, she did." Mark's expression was pugnacious. "She was distraught. She made a mistake. I'm glad she did, or otherwise it could have been fatal."

"Of course you're glad," soothed Judith. "So are we." She edged forward, trying to gain some physical or at least psychological advantage. "But why was she so upset?"

For all of Mark's usually outgoing manner, he was basically a very private man. His face closed down; his heels seemed to dig into the tiled floor. "She didn't kill Sandy. Neither did I."

"And you didn't break into Sandy and John's house to get your wheelbarrow," countered Judith. "What were you after that was so incriminating? *Bottoms Up?*"

Mark wilted inside his well-tailored suit. "God!" His gaze skidded off Judith like an out-of-control car off a lamppost. "What are you talking about?" he asked thickly.

Judith sighed, wishing she hadn't put herself in the position of upsetting so many people. "It's a matter of record. You were the cinematographer. Sandy was in the movie. To keep anyone up here from discovering your background, you went to the Frizzell house and tried to steal the evidence."

Still clutching the balustrade, Mark rocked slightly on his heel. "I didn't steel anything. I never got the chance." His face had turned ashen.

"Is that why Kate tried to kill herself?" asked Judith.

But Mark's lips clamped shut. He was staring up into the stairwell as if he expected someone to come down and rescue him. "Maybe," he said at last, then turned back to the cousins. "Yes," he went on a bit too hastily, "that's what set her off. She did it for my sake. She was embarrassed over my connection with smut."

The explanation was a little too pat for Judith. She deliberated on how far she could—or wanted to—push Mark Duffy. After all, his wife had caused him a great deal of pain in the last few hours. Porno flicks or not, he was a decent man. Judith decided against mentioning the photo of Kate in her nun's habit.

"Was John in skin flicks, too?" asked Judith, trying to keep her tone one of polite inquiry rather than that of a relentless interrogator.

"What?" Mark seemed lost in thought. "No. I think he was a set decorator at Paramount or Metro. And Sandy only acted in a couple of those X-rated films. I don't blame him, he was just a kid at the time, trying to feed himself."

A portrait of Sandy was emerging in Judith's mind: an orphan, a runaway, a lonely, unskilled youngster in L.A. falling victim to God-only-knew what perverted benefactors. That he should have ended up making skin flicks wasn't too surprising; that he had survived the experience was. And yet the trail that had led him to John Frizzell had also brought Sandy to an untimely death in the school nursery at Our Lady, Star of the Sea. The portrait was done in mixed media, and it gave Judith genuine pain.

Renie posed the next question: "Did you know all along that it was Sandy?"

Mark frowned at her. "No, of course not! He was George back then, though he probably called himself something else in the credits. Most of the cast did. I never saw anything but the rough cut." His long mouth twisted with irony. "It was *very* rough—and raw."

Renie pressed on: "When did you figure out who Sandy really was?"

Mark didn't need to reflect. "Not until I went into the nursery after Father Tim raised the alarm. It was a terrible shock. You know how you look at people, but you don't really *see* them?" Mark passed an unsteady hand over his forehead. "For the first time, I saw the real Sandy—in death, she—he—looked quite different." Mark paused, and Judith imagined that the lifeless, bloodless face was swimming before his eyes. "The impersonation was over," Mark continued with an anguished expression. "Sandy was a corpse with long blond hair and bad makeup. I recognized George, and I damned near had a heart attack."

"So he wasn't blackmailing you, but you thought he might have one of the movies he'd acted in where you'd been the cameraman?" queried Judith.

A faint smile touched Mark's mouth. "I only did the one." He had relaxed a little, one hand in his trouser pocket, the other fingering his long chin. "I don't know what I thought, really. Maybe that if Sandy had prints of the film, John might get nasty. I guess I panicked. The whole situation with Sandy posing as John's wife and then getting murdered was so bizarre that I figured anything could happen next. I suppose I behaved stupidly."

It occurred to Judith that Mark hadn't acted any more foolishly—or criminally—than she and Renie had done in invading the Duffy house. Judith rationalized that the cousins had a better motive. Maybe.

"Did you ever find out if, uh, *Bottoms Up* was actually there?" Renie asked.

"No." Mark loosened his tie and undid the top button of

his shirt. "John never gave me a chance to explain. Once I calmed down, I realized it probably wasn't. Kate said they brought almost nothing with them from the East. It's not likely they'd haul along a couple of old X-rated movies."

"Come on," said Renie, starting for the door. It took Judith a moment to realize her cousin was talking not to her, but to Mark. "Have dinner with Bill and me and the kids. You never did know your way around a stove."

Mark started to protest, then grinned. "Let me make sure I'm not starting a fire, okay?"

It was ten minutes before Mark finished checking out the kitchen and changing clothes. The cousins waited in the living room, speaking of neutral topics in normal voices, and airing their conjectures about the Duffys in a whisper.

"Kate didn't drink nail polish remover for Mark's sake," Renie murmured.

"Right," agreed Judith, frowning at a wood carving of Mother Cabrini with her arms around three orphans. "I wonder if she even knows exactly what Mark did in L.A."

"She's too naive," responded Renie. "John must have met Sandy in L.A. But I gather Mark didn't know John from his movie days. Speaking of pictures, have you got Kate's?"

Judith patted her purse. "It isn't a full-fledged nun's habit, certainly not the kind they wore thirty years ago before they started dressing from L. L. Bean. A novice, maybe. She probably dropped out before the final vows." She gazed at Mother Cabrini in her artfully crafted flowing veils and billowing skirts. "Holy cats!" exclaimed Judith so loudly that she immediately put a hand over her mouth.

"What's wrong?" asked Renie, alarmed.

Judith was still staring at the small statue. "You didn't hear Joe say it, but one of the other actors in *Bottoms Up* was a Kitty Cabrini. Quick, what order did St. Frances Xavier Cabrini start? They run Columbus Hospital, on Hospital Hill."

"Oh, sure, I designed their PR program when they put up that new addition about five years ago," replied Renie. "They're the Missionary Sisters of the Sacred Heart. Oh!" It was Renie's turn to look astonished. "Oh, *no!*"

Cocking her head to make sure Mark hadn't yet come back downstairs, Judith folded her arms across her breast. "Now *there's* a reason for Kate to drink nail polish remover. Imagine what would happen if it got out that *she* was cavorting in the buff in skin flicks?"

Renie's grin practically split her face. "I want the video! I'll show it at the next Parish Council meeting. I'll send a copy to the Pope!"

"You're cruel," reprimanded Judith, but she couldn't help smiling at her cousin. "Unfortunately, you're also typical. Every single SOT would just love to get their mitts on a print of that film and see Kate Duffy make a fool of herself. No wonder she hasn't had much to do with her family, between leaving the convent and making dirty movies. It would be bad enough for any self-respecting wife and mother, but for the saintly Kate, cavorting around as Kitty Cabrini would be positively fatal."

"*And* funny." Renie was still grinning. "Kate has no chest. Better it should be Norma Paine."

"Knock it off," commanded Judith in a whisper, then raised her voice as she heard Mark's tread on the stairs. "On the other hand, it could have been a box turtle. Oh, hi, Mark," she said, looking up in feigned surprise. "Do you know anything about reptiles?"

Mark's grin was a bit off-center. "No," he replied, gazing at each of the cousins in turn. "But I know a couple of snakes in the grass when I see them."

Judith and Renie had the grace to blush.

FIFTEEN

THE ONLY UNHAPPY customer that night at the B&B was Gertrude. Her supper was over an hour late, the scalloped potatoes were half raw, and her tapioca pudding had curdled. If Judith didn't stop gadding all over town instead of tending to business, the focal point of which was her aged and infirm mother, there was going to be Big Trouble.

"Shut up and peg out," ordered Judith, pushing the cribbage board at Gertrude. It was almost eight p.m., with the California guests having arrived dead tired at seven-thirty, the four Nelsons off to dinner, and the Alaskan couple ordering pizza in their room, apparently distrustful of any restaurant that didn't feature muskrat. Or so Judith had decided, often finding visitors from the forty-ninth state a bit eccentric.

Gertrude moved a red peg eight holes along the crib board, in a manner similar to her clumping guidance of the walker. Her beady eyes glistened at Judith. "Ha! I got His Nibs! That's one more—I'm out!" She yanked at the last peg and gave her daughter a triumphant look.

"Waxed you again, dopey. You're not much of a card player. How about a little rummy?"

"*You're* a little rummy," murmured Judith as the buzzer rang in the third-floor bedroom to alert them that someone was at the front door. "Drat, one of the guests must have forgotten the key."

Judith was wrong. Joe Flynn stood in the twilight, holding a huge bouquet of spring flowers. "Give these to the old bat and get on something elegant. We're going to Bayshore's for drinks."

"Joe!" Judith grabbed the proffered bouquet, taking in the heady fragrance of the flowers and Joe's presence on her doorstep. He was dressed in a charcoal suit instead of his usual sports coat, and he looked extremely dashing.

"Go," ordered Joe before Judith could protest. "I'll have you home by ten."

Judith went. She put the flowers in a vase in the kitchen, lied to Gertrude about her sudden departure, and hastily donned a raspberry-red cotton knit dress with a wide black woven belt. In less than ten minutes, she was back downstairs. Joe was on the sofa, reading the evening paper.

"Homicide Detective Joe *Blynn*? Can't these reporters ever get it right? I've been Finn, Lynn, Quinn, everything but Rin Tin Tin. Hell, I've been on the force for almost thirty years!" He scrunched up the paper and angrily tossed it in the direction of the fireplace.

"Is that a story on the Frizzell investigation?" asked Judith. "I haven't seen the paper tonight." She gave the crumpled first section a wistful look.

"No, it's the chainsaw murder. Sandy's old news. Hey," he said, brightening as he gazed up at Judith. "You look terrific."

"Oh—thanks." Judith hoped she wasn't blushing. It would be a ridiculous reaction for a woman of her age. "Renie talked me into this when we went shopping last month."

"It's great," said Joe, getting to his feet. "Let's go dazzle 'em."

Bayshore's was located in the curve of land that swept from Heraldsgate Hill to the downtown area. The restaurant was built on a small bluff that overlooked not only the bay, but the naval depot, the ferry docks, and the string of high-rises that rimmed the water. Judith hadn't been inside since she'd gotten married to Dan. She was bemused by the altered decor, with the plush velvet upholstery exchanged for sleek leather, and the flocked wallpaper stripped down to the original pine paneling. Only the magnificent view and the excellent service remained unchanged.

"Garth," said Joe in greeting to the bartender. "Send us over a couple of Anthurium Sprues."

Garth, half-Filipino, half-Norwegian, and all first-class mixologist, made magic behind the bar. Joe and Judith sat down on a dark leather couch by the window. He lighted a cigar; she sighed with pleasure.

"I shouldn't be here, you know," Judith said.

"Pretend we're looking for Eddie La Plante," said Joe, leaning back with one leg resting on the other knee.

"Any trace of him?" Judith asked, suddenly dragged down to reality.

"No. But that may not mean anything sinister."

Judith shivered. "I think it does. Joe," she said, turning on the couch to look at his profile, "I've got some more stuff to tell you. I called today, but Woody said you were up at the chancery office." The statement had the nuance of a question.

Joe swiveled as Garth brought their drinks, two tall glasses with an exotic flower in each and a crimson liquid that struck Judith as a lot more lethal than nail polish remover. "Thanks, Garth. Run us a tab." Joe cocked his head at Judith, the cigar perched on his shoulder like a parrot. "Yeah, I went to see Father Gonzales. He used to be pastor at St. Henry Emperor's when I lived out there. I wanted to check out Hoyle and Mills. They seem okay.

It's too bad Frank Hoyle took off for the week. He might have been some help."

Judith's panic ebbed, replaced by disappointment. "Oh," she said somewhat faintly. "Yes, yes, Father Hoyle could have provided us with some information," she went on rather hastily. "He might even have known who Stella Maris is."

"Whoever she is, she'll be rich if anything happens to John. According to Wilbur, if Emily died without heirs, the entire estate went to Stella." He raised a red eyebrow at Judith. "If I were John, I'd be nervous."

"If John had been Sandy, it would all make sense." Judith sipped experimentally at her drink and was relieved to discover it wasn't as potent as it looked. "I gather you've had no luck trying to track Stella down?"

"You gather right. The only Maris I ever heard of was Roger. I doubt that Stella played for the Yankees. We found some S. Marises around the country, but they were all Steves, Sheldons, or Sams. Only one was a woman, and her name was Sheila."

"Maybe Stella lives in Canada, or abroad," suggested Judith, watching the last purple light fade behind the mountains. "How come nobody's ever heard of her?"

Joe shrugged and puffed at his cigar. "Beats me. She may have a different married name."

"I guess it doesn't matter since she doesn't get anything with John alive and kicking. Are you really going to let him take off for New York the day after tomorrow?" Judith inquired.

"Why not? I've nothing to detain him for. As far as I can tell, he's the one person in the school hall who couldn't have done it. According to you, Sandy was still alive when he got there. Father Hoyle saw John pull into the parking lot."

"True." Judith gave a brief nod. Halfway into her Anthurium Sprue, she was feeling very relaxed. Maybe it packed more of a punch than she thought it did. "Joe," she began, suddenly disinterested in murder, "what's going to happen to us?"

Joe slipped his arm around her shoulders. "I don't know. What do you want to happen?"

Judith allowed herself to let her head rest against Joe's arm. "I'm not sure. Sometimes I feel as if the last twenty-three years hadn't happened. We could be sitting here back in the sixties, watching the same sun disappear behind the same mountains and wondering what Lyndon Johnson was going to do about Vietnam instead of who killed Sandy Frizzell. Back then, I knew what I wanted. I thought you did, too." Her tone held a faint note of reproach.

Joe chuckled and gave her a little squeeze. "Not me. I didn't think at all. That was the problem."

Judith angled about in his embrace so that she could see his face. The soft light from the lantern on the low table in front of them caught the gold flecks in his eyes and added contours to his round face. Judith refrained from tracing his jawline with her finger.

"What happened?" she asked in a breathless voice. "You never told me the whole story."

Joe let out a deep sigh. "It's a short story, really. I'd met Herself at MacArthur's Bar by headquarters one night after work. She was singing and playing the piano. I got to hanging out there with the other guys once in a while, especially when you were working evenings at the downtown library. Then, after a really ugly narcotics O.D., I got looped to help me forget what it's like to see fourteen-year-old kids being put in bodybags. Herself had just gotten her latest divorce. She was celebrating. The next thing I knew, we'd celebrated all the way to Vegas. I woke up at Caesar's Palace a married man." He made a wry face at Judith. "What could I do, claim I'd been abducted and raped? I was a big boy. I figured you were better off without somebody that dumb."

"Callous," said Judith. "That's what I called it." Her black eyes narrowed, then softened. "All these years, I never knew you'd called from Vegas until it came out last

Thanksgiving. I didn't know who to strangle—you, for flying off in the first place, or my mother, for not telling me you phoned. It occurred to me that maybe I'd been a bit unfair. I spent the better part of two decades picturing you with horns and a pitchfork." She gave Joe a vaguely contrite look.

He was looking equally penitent. "I did have a Weedeater," he acknowledged, "but no pitchfork. I wondered why you never tried to reach me. After a while, it dawned on me that Gertrude hadn't delivered the message." He gave a rueful shake of his head. "Then it was too late. You'd signed on with Dan."

Silence, surprisingly comfortable and reassuringly empathetic, fell between them. Judith was the first to break it, with her head tipped to one side and her black eyes fixed on Joe's round face. "Okay, so why did you stay with Herself for so long?"

"Well, we *were* married," said Joe with a touch of sarcasm. "I could ask you the same question about Dan."

Judith had to acknowledge the truth of his statement. But she still wasn't ready to excuse Joe's irresponsible behavior. Phone call or not, his desertion had cost her eighteen years of misery. On the other hand, it must have cost him, too.

"So why did it go sour?" she asked, hesitantly putting her hand on his.

"Herself never stopped celebrating. Oh, she'd quit drinking for a time, like when she had our daughter, or her other two kids were graduating from something, but she'd always go back. A couple of years ago, she got a DWI, and damned near ran down a whole day care center on their way to the zoo. Thank God she hit a telephone booth instead. I tried to get her to go to AA—I'd been attending Al Anon for a while—but she could never admit she had a problem. I gave her an ultimatum—me or Jack Daniels. She backed Jack and told Joe to go." He shrugged again. "That was it. Let's face it, she's ten years older than I am, and she's going to drink herself into the grave. I see enough stiffs on the job without having to watch one at home. It was no marriage, it was a living hell. She can't even put a coherent sentence together anymore."

To her horror, Judith found herself feeling sorry for Herself. Vivian Flynn had gotten exactly what Judith had wanted: Joe Flynn. And he hadn't made her happy. She'd had to fill up the holes in her life with alcohol. Renie was right—you had to be half nuts to survive in this crazy world.

"Where *is* Herself?" Judith asked as Garth brought a dish of nachos.

"In a Florida condo, on the Gulf. It was part of the settlement from her second husband." He fed Judith a nacho and took one for himself. "She's spent a lot of time there over the years. I hated it. Too hot, too many crawly things. But it gives her an excuse to drink because there's nothing else to do."

A group of people at a table in the far corner erupted into laughter. A pair of young lovers on the next couch looked as if they were having trouble staying in a vertical position. Two middle-aged men, one black, one white, were going over a set of blueprints, nibbling on Tempura prawns, and drinking vodka martinis. Judith wondered if any of them was facing a decision as critical as her own.

Joe signaled to Garth to bring another round, then silenced Judith's feeble protest with a finger on her lips. "It's only nine o'clock. Relax. If your guests have a problem, let your mother handle it. It'd be good for her."

The idea of Gertrude coping with any sort of crisis that didn't involve her digestion or a deck of cards proved beyond Judith's grasp. But she didn't argue with Joe. She was too happy to be with him, too awash in the past, too removed from her usual routine to allow the world to intrude.

"I'm glad you wouldn't let me wait until May to see you," Judith confessed, lifting her face to his.

"Me, too," said Joe. He hesitated, then brushed her lips with his. "Hell, Jude-girl," he murmured, pressing her knee, "we've waited most of a lifetime. We're both nuts, you know."

"Right." Judith slid her arm around his neck. "Did any two people ever have such a weird romance?"

"Two Sprues coming up," announced Garth cheerfully, then stopped in his tracks. "Excuse me, Lieutenant, I didn't know you were busy."

Joe turned slightly. "Yeah, well, we're engaged."

Garth broke into a grin. "Congratulations! When did that happen?"

Joe looked at Judith, a wry smile on his face. "Oh, about twenty-five years ago. We're sort of slow movers."

"Doesn't look like it to me," said Garth, with a faint leer. "How about some champagne?"

Joe's beeper went off. He swore softly and broke away from Judith. "I'd better call in. Be right back." With less spring than he would have exhibited twenty-five years earlier, Joe got up from the couch. Judith took a sip from her second drink and ate another nacho. She felt slightly giddy, and not just from the drinks. The idea of being engaged overwhelmed her. And yet, in some strange, illogical way, she had never really *not* been engaged to Joe Flynn. Their marriages to other people had technically put aside their plans to marry each other. But deep down, Judith had never belonged to anyone but Joe. And now, she realized with a sense of awe, it seemed he felt the same way. All the emotions she had experienced during those years apart washed over her like May rain: the terrible hurt, the sense of rejection, the anger, the jealousy of Herself, the need to strike back by marrying Dan . . . Yet Judith had never really let go of Joe. Maybe he'd never let go of her, either. She took a bigger swallow from her glass and ate three nachos.

"Murderers are a pain in the butt," declared Joe, returning to the couch but not sitting down again. "They've caught a suspect in that harpoon killing. Hell," he grumbled, picking up his glass and drinking deeply, "the son of a bitch did it, no doubt about it, we've got two eyewitnesses. But I still have to go back downtown."

With some alarm, Judith noted that Joe had almost drained his drink. "You shouldn't drive when you've had two of those. Do you want to get arrested?"

Joe was already taking Judith's arm to lead her out of the bar. "I'll arrest myself after I get there." He gave her his devilish grin. "'Actually, I'm as sober as a judge. Just don't ask which one, some of them being inclined to tipple in chambers before they administer justice. It has the same effect as being blindfolded."

Resignedly, Judith let Joe escort her out to the parking lot and into his car. She had to admit that his driving was unaffected, which, in Joe's case, meant that he broke the speed limit by at least ten miles, darted in and out of traffic, and took most corners on two wheels. She supposed he knew what he was doing, and tried to relax.

As he drove her home, she also tried to tell him what information she'd gleaned during the last twenty-four hours. Joe listened attentively, like a sponge absorbing water. When she had finished, he seemed most intrigued by Judith's assumption that Kate Duffy was actually Kitty Cabrini.

"That's good," he said, careening into the cul-de-sac that sheltered Hillside Manor. "We can check it out, I imagine. I'll call Les Lowenstein. I wonder if it's enough of a motive for Kate—or Mark—to kill Sandy?"

"I wonder, too," admitted Judith. "By the way, that photograph of Kate in her nun's outfit was taken at Tioga, North Dakota." She gave Joe a sidelong look to see if the location registered.

It did, but not precisely in the way Judith had expected: "Are you implying a connection between Kate Duffy and Father Tim's adopted family?"

"It's a thought," said Judith as Joe pulled into the driveway behind a small, sporty car with California plates.

"Right idea, wrong state," said Joe, glancing up at the house to see if Gertrude was peering out from behind the curtains. He turned the key to Park and swung around in the seat, one arm draped over the steering wheel. "I'll go you one better. Some twenty-four years ago, a young mother who had been deserted by her husband died at Holy Innocents Convent in Deer Hoof, Montana. She left a year-old boy behind. His name was Timothy Joseph Sanderson."

SIXTEEN

"So," SAID RENIE over the phone, "Joe *has* been doing his homework. Now why couldn't Tim's real mother's name have been Stella instead of Linda Lou?"

"That would have been convenient," admitted Judith, lying on the bed in her bathrobe and still tasting nachos. "Except, of course, that she's dead. Linda Lou Sanderson, I mean. I'm going to talk to Tim tomorrow, first thing. It's all coming together now."

"It is?" Renie sounded skeptical. "What I don't get, is how Sandy—George Sanderson, I mean—and his wife ended up in Montana."

"One of the nuns who was there at the time told Woody Price that they were driving through, en route from L.A. to Canada," explained Judith. "She couldn't remember why, thought possibly Sandy was taking Linda over the border to get cheaper medical care, or something, but along the way, the Sandersons had a big blow-up. Maybe Sandy decided to come out of the closet. Anyway, he ended up dumping Linda Lou and the baby at the convent. He took off, and Linda Lou died in the infirmary there about a month later of some blood disease. The Millses heard about the orphaned baby and offered to adopt. With the father still living, but his whereabouts unknown, the situation got complicated, legally. Linda Lou had a sister here, and the Millses contacted her. She put them in touch with Wilbur Paine's father's law firm, and eventually, they worked out the adoption. The Millses took little Timmy back to Montana, and they all lived happily ever after. Until now."

"Hmmm." Renie had turned meditative. "Any connection between that convent and the one where Kate Duffy was a novice?"

"Nope. They're run by different orders. The one in Montana is Dominican."

"Bill has this theory," said Renie, suddenly sounding eager. "He thinks that when Kate couldn't hack it as a nun, she took off for L.A. and went into porno movies to purify herself. She used the name of Cabrini because St. Frances founded the order Kate had flunked out of, so it was some sort of mockery. Except Bill isn't sure if Kate intended to mock Mother Cabrini or herself. He figures she was probably a virgin sacrifice, eaten by vampire bats."

"You wish," replied Judith, but for once, Bill's idea didn't sound so weird. Somehow it suited the mentality of a woman who would drink nail polish remover to commit suicide. "What else does Bill think?"

"Huh?" said Renie, sounding surprised at her cousin's unexpected show of interest. "Oh, he just wishes Quinn McCaffrey had co-starred." She paused as Bill made some derogatory comment about the school principal in the background. "So what the hell does all this mean?" asked Renie.

"Joe and I didn't have time to draw a lot of conclusions—we just exchanged data, and he took off." Judith rolled over onto her stomach, wishing the nachos would come to terms with the Sprues. "There are at least two major things going on here—Sandy—or George Philip

Sanderson—is Father Tim's dad. Whether Tim knows that or not, I can't be sure, but I'm guessing that if Tim ever saw a picture of his real father, he may have recognized Sandy in the church hall the other day. If he did, it must have been a horrible shock. He certainly acted as if something had gone awry when he was talking to him—or her, depending on your point of view. I'd had a feeling that Tim recognized Sandy, but I couldn't be sure in what guise. For all I really knew, Sandy could be an ex-priest who had taught Tim philosophy in the seminary. But I think now that Tim realized he was standing there, making plans about Emily's money, with his very own father. That was why he got sick. It was shock."

"But did Sandy recognize Tim?" asked Renie.

"I don't see how he could have," said Judith. "He hadn't seen Tim since he was a baby. Kids change, but adults don't, even in disguise. Oh, sure, Sandy fooled Mark, but I suspect there's a big difference between recognizing one's own father and a casual acquaintance. On some deep, visceral level, a child must know its own parent. The real question is, did Sandy recognize Kate or Mark from their L.A. days?"

"Kate had her clothes on," put in Renie, impishly. "Okay, okay," she said quickly before Judith could upbraid her, "I'll be fair. Just once. Kate's changed quite a bit since she was first married—improved, actually. Her hair's lighter and a different style, she dresses better. But she's still Kate, and Mark has merely gotten to be an older version of himself. But even if Sandy did recognize them, he couldn't say so without giving away his own disguise."

"Exactly. It's no wonder Sandy and John wouldn't have dinner with the Duffys. I suspect they were both very anxious to get out of town before it dawned on Kate or Mark who Sandy really was," said Judith, stifling a yawn. "I take it you didn't press Mark about Kitty Cabrini while he was at your house for dinner."

"Nope, he and Bill got off onto fishing and sports and movies. I decided to give Mark a break. Anyway, he left about seven-thirty to go back to the hospital and hold Kate's fragile hand. I'd have taken along one of those buzzer things. That would have given her a jolt."

Judith decided it was hopeless trying to reform Renie's attitude toward Kate Duffy. Besides, Judith was tired. It had been a long, eventful day. "I'm going to sleep now," she said.

"Oh." Renie sounded disappointed. "Well, I'm going to work," she declared, her voice brightening. "Thanks to Kate Duffy, I just got an amazing idea for the City Arts Council's Oktoberfest symbol. It's an angel riding a broom. Get it?"

"No," said Judith, and let Renie roll along on her burst of boundless late-night energy.

But if Judith's own energies were depleted, her mind wouldn't allow her to rest easy. Setting the phone down and switching off the night light, she succumbed to the images that were gnawing at the edges of her brain: Sandy being Tim's father, Kate hiding not only a failed religious vocation but possibly a stint in skin flicks, Mark ashamed of his excursion into pornography, Eve concealing her father's identity. It was no wonder, Judith realized, that Eve had given John a job. He was, after all, her half-brother. The bitterness Eve had shown over his abrupt resignation was easier to understand. So, perhaps, was her outrage over the will, if for no other reason than he had come into so much money through deception. If only, Judith thought, Eve's real name was Stella, everything would make more sense. But Eve wasn't Stella, and nobody else involved in the case was, either.

Judith's mind drifted from the school hall to the Duffys' house to Bayshore's and back again. Who *was* Stella Maris? Where was Eddie La Plante? Why wouldn't the final pieces of the puzzle come together? Judith felt as if she'd set out a jigsaw picture of an autumn landscape and had come up with segments of splashing ocean surf. She tossed and turned, then lay very still. Her left thumb rubbed at her ring finger. It was an old habit, born out of the years of her marriage, when she'd check to make sure she hadn't lost her wedding ring. The finger was bare, and for a brief instant, Judith panicked. She should be wearing a ring, not the plain gold band that Dan had given her, but Joe's baguette diamond set in platinum. Judith let out a deep sigh. In the first year of their marriage, Dan had pawned Joe's ring for a primitive home computer that blew up six weeks later. Judith turned over one more time and finally went to sleep.

Judith was late to morning Mass. The Nelsons had headed north and the Alaskans south, but the Californians had lingered over coffee. Judith didn't get up to church until just before Holy Communion. She rarely attended Mass during the week, and felt vaguely guilty that her motives were temporal, rather than spiritual. In consequence, she prayed all the more earnestly, and even avoided taking stock of her fellow worshippers until Father Tim gave the last blessing.

As usual on weekdays, attendance was sparse: a dozen senior citizens, all women except for one man; a couple of young mothers with babies and toddlers attached; Mrs. Dooley, wearing a new raincoat she'd probably bought for Easter; Mr. and Mrs. Ringo, Gertrude's favorite pair of old saps; the bank president, rendering unto God before he did likewise unto Caesar; the head butcher from Falstaff's, apparently aware that man did not live by bread and beef alone; and a young refugee couple from Cambodia, no doubt not yet converted to the notion that from Monday through Friday American Catholics succumbed as earnestly to the Protestant work ethic as did their separated brethren. Kurt Kramer and Norma Paine rounded out the small congregation, with Wilbur serving as the acolyte. He looked like an aging choirboy in his black cassock and white surplice as he trooped off the altar behind Tim Mills.

"Judith!" cried Norma, catching up with her prey in the south vestibule. "I've heard the most horrid rumors! Kate Duffy tried to hang herself from their upstairs deck, Mr.

La Plante has been kidnapped by the Japanese owners of Tresvant Timber, and John Frizzell is going to use all of his inheritance to open a hospice for AIDS victims in Greenwich Village! Isn't it awful?"

"Two out of three would be, if they were true," said Judith more curtly than she'd intended. Norma was interfering with her goal of catching Tim Mills before he took off on his appointed rounds. Norma, however, could prove useful. "Tell me something, Norma—you're the sort of spouse who takes a deep, intelligent interest in your husband's work. How would an heir in a will be tracked down?"

Norma's expression, which had initially been smug, switched to wary. "Are you referring to that Stella person?"

"Yes. I'm curious," Judith admitted. "I gather Wilbur didn't have an address of any kind."

Norma shrugged her heavy shoulders. "Maybe not. I suppose he'd make a search—advertise, you know."

Norma seemed too vague for Judith's taste. "I've heard of missing heirs. Though of course," Judith allowed, "Stella isn't the heir. And John will no doubt now make a will of his own."

"In New York." Norma's face turned sullen. "Really, it's so crass of him to take the Tresvant money out of the city. It's been here for almost a hundred years."

"Now, now," said Wilbur mildly, looking more like himself in his dark brown business suit, "we mustn't be bitter, my dear."

Norma grunted, splashing holy water on herself as if it were bug repellent. "He's nothing but an opportunist! I have to have my say, Wilbur, I don't think he's entitled to a penny! He was *not* a family man. Deceitful, that's what he was. Not the least bit of good will come out of all this!"

"It hasn't already," Judith pointed out, wincing at her garbled syntax. "I mean, Sandy's dead."

Norma dismissed Sandy's demise with a wave of her

hand. "Oh! Well, I can hardly count a person like that! It would be different if it had been one of *us*."

"A pity it wasn't," snapped Kurt Kramer, who had apparently lingered in the church proper to pray alone. His blue eyes iced over as he regarded Norma with distaste. "It still could be, the way our fellow parishioners have already begun to wrangle over Emily's million-dollar bequest. Quinn McCaffrey wants to send out a questionnaire. Good God!"

Fending off trouble, Judith intervened, moving between Kurt and Norma to address Wilbur: "Tell me, if John didn't get the money for some reason, how would you go about finding Stella Maris?"

At her elbow, Judith could have sworn she heard Kurt snicker. But Wilbur was pulling on his short upper lip and looking judicious. "There are formal procedures. We'd exercise all the means at our disposal, and meanwhile appoint a caretaker for the estate." He looked at Judith over the rims of his spectacles, an almost shy gaze. "It wasn't very considerate of Emily to be so secretive about Stella. Ordinarily, we insist on getting a current address for a potential heir. But Emily was very coy."

"Naturally," Norma butted in, "Wilbur couldn't coerce Emily. She was a very important client. Not to mention stubborn as a mule."

"Did you point out to Emily that there might be a problem?" Judith asked.

Wilbur shuffled a bit in his brown oxfords. "Well, yes. But Emily was adamant. She just gave me an odd little smile and said, 'Don't worry about Stella Maris. She won't be hard to find if you take the trouble to look for her.'"

This time, Judith was sure that Kurt Kramer snickered.

When Judith finally reached the rectory, Tim Mills was involved in a lengthy phone call. Mrs. Katzenheimer provided pale coffee and a litany of complaints about the problems that always cropped up during the pastor's absence.

"Six couples want their babies baptized, two older parishioners are at death's door, three marriages have to be performed over the weekend, the Parish Council meeting was postponed, the Altar Society president broke her hip, and the principal's locked himself out of the school. The next thing I know, the archbishop will make one of his surprise visits. Overwhelming."

Judith made sympathetic noises, then sat down at the desk usually reserved for the parish secretary, Kitty Duggan, who was spending Easter in the Holy Land. "Did Father Tim go to see Kate Duffy in the hospital?"

"Oh, he did, last night after one of the wedding rehearsals. Poor little Mrs. Duffy, she was a mess! It's *him*, I suppose, chasing other women. Men are enough to drive any woman to suicide! Disgusting!" Hilde Katzenheimer made an angry pass with her dustcloth at the glass-fronted bookcase.

"Mark?" Judith gave the housekeeper a skeptical look. "Do you really think so?"

Mrs. Katzenheimer straightened a picture of St. Mary Magdalene praying over a rock in the desert. Her thin body twitched indignantly. "Well, don't you? He's a handsome devil, with enough charm to coax a kitten out of a tree. I've seen the way those silly women in the parish give him the eye. If I had to guess who the Other Woman is, I wouldn't have to look far, would I? Obvious!"

Judith considered dumping her weak coffee into the Boston fern that stood next to the desk. "Really?"

Mrs. Katzenheimer was looking very self-righteous, her pale blue eyes narrowing and her mouth fixed in a tight line. "You ought to know," she said pointedly.

Startled, Judith was about to ask why, when Father Tim appeared, full of apologies. "'Tis the season for fallen away Catholics to get an attack of conscience. It happens the week after Easter and the week after Christmas, I'm told. I'd rather they poured out their guilty consciences in the confessional than over the phone, though." He gave Judith a diffident smile. "Let's go in the parlor, okay?"

Judith got up to follow his lead. At the door, Mrs. Katzenheimer plucked at Judith's sleeve. "She ought to be ashamed of herself," she murmured.

"Who?" Judith whispered back.

"The hussy." Mrs. Katzenheimer drew herself up to her full, yet unimposing height. "Who else? Arlene Rankers."

Having thought for some time that she'd heard everything, Judith realized she hadn't. Until now.

Judith waited quietly while Tim Mills got a grip on his emotions There had been no other way to confront the issue of his parentage than to come right out with the facts. Judith was not happy with the role she'd been forced to play, but she'd acted it out with a minimum of words and a maximum of tact. Nevertheless, Tim Mills was visibly upset.

"The one thing I had were some pictures," he said when he'd finally wiped at his eyes and had gotten his voice under control. "My aunt—my real mother's sister—gave them to my adopted parents. I only knew their first names, George and Linda Lou. There was just one picture of my dad." He paused, leaning back in the armchair and staring off in the direction of the Botticelli Madonna. "It had been taken at Easter, with me on his lap. He was holding a yellow rabbit and looking sort of startled. Maybe it was the flash from the camera. But it was the same expression I saw on Sandy's face when I was talking about the money for the church. I'd stared at that picture a thousand times when I was a kid. I couldn't forget that face." He gave a sad shake of his head, clenching and unclenching his fists. "I'd never seen Sandy up close until then. I just couldn't believe my eyes. It was such a shock. I thought she—I mean, I was still thinking of Sandy as a woman—must be some relative, like my dad's sister. Only later, when I found the body, I knew the truth. I couldn't believe it." His chin sagged on his broad chest; his hands fell limply at his sides.

Judith gave him a moment to collect himself again. "So you knew before the police did that Sandy was a man? Is that why you went to the nursery, to talk to Sandy?"

Tim's mouth worked in vain, but at last the words straggled out. "I went to see Sandy alone because I thought she—he—was my aunt, or some other relative. But then—when I found the body—I knew . . . I mean, I couldn't believe it . . . Yet it *had* to be. But it was so fantastic! How would you like to discover that one of your parents was some sort of . . . *aberration*?"

"You get used to it," replied Judith, thinking of Gertrude, and immediately regretted her flippancy. "That is, Sandy wasn't exactly an aberration. He was just pretending to be someone—something—he wasn't."

"Maybe." Tim lifted one broad shoulder in a pathetic manner. "But it really screwed me up. The more I thought about it, the worse it got. All the emotions I'd never dealt with came to the surface. Rage, rejection, even hate. It was pretty horrible."

"But understandable," noted Judith. It crossed her mind that those were the same emotions she'd experienced when Joe had dumped her. And jealousy, of course. Whether lovers or spouses or even children, human beings reacted in the same basic ways.

"The strange thing was," Tim went on as if Judith hadn't spoken, "Sandy had called the rectory two or three times in the past couple of weeks asking for me. By chance, I was never around. Mrs. Katzenheimer finally made an appointment for Sandy to see me Monday afternoon. I thought it was about the money."

"Do you still think so?" Judith wished she had a cup of real coffee. The parlor smelled faintly musty. The morning was very still and overcast. Earthquake weather, Judith realized, and felt uneasy.

"I don't know," replied Tim, his flushed cheeks returning to their normal color. "He wouldn't have recognized me, would he? There's been absolutely no contact with my family in Montana."

"I don't see how he could," Judith admitted. "Though he might have tracked you down through your mother's sister."

Tim dispelled that notion. "I never knew her. She felt it was best to keep out of my new life. If it came to that, I doubt she'd know who I was. Besides," he added, as if he'd just thought of it, "I don't imagine my aunt would have had much time for the man who'd abandoned her nephew and sister."

"There was never any question of her adopting you, I take it?"

Tim gave Judith the ghost of a grin. "The reason I got those pictures was because she traveled light. My aunt was a flower child, my mom—my adopted mom—once said." The grin died; he gnawed at his lower lip. "Despite all this, my parents are Mr. and Mrs. Mills. I don't want to lose sight of that. They're terrific people."

"So I've heard," said Judith. Her mind flitted over a portfolio of topics. There were several questions she wanted to ask Tim, but knew he was anxious to head off for his weekly visit to Vintage Village, the old folks' home at the bottom of the Hill. Nonetheless, there was something at the back of her brain that nettled. She grimaced, trying to recall what it was, but had no luck. Instead, she asked after Kate Duffy.

"She'll be fine," Tim said, seeing Judith to the door. "Physically, I mean. I still can't get over her taking that stuff. Mark said it was all a mistake."

"Then it probably was," Judith said evenly. Whether Kate had drunk nail polish remover to expiate her ancient guilt for leaving the convent, or if she'd done it merely to get Mark's attention as Renie had surmised, the result was the same: Her husband was dancing attendance, and would no doubt be very solicitous of his wife for a long time to come. There would be no more flirtations, if indeed there ever had been, Arlene Rankers or any other more likely candidate notwithstanding.

In the parking lot, Judith noticed Arlene's car parked next to her own. A moment later, Arlene came through the cloister, wearing her gardening gear and carrying a trowel and a spade. Even at her grubbiest, Arlene was sufficiently attractive to entice somebody else's husband. And if a good heart was a prerequisite for seduction, half the men on Heraldsgate Hill would be swooning at her feet. But Judith knew Arlene, and completely dismissed Mrs. Katzenheimer's wild accusation. On the other hand, she wasn't going to denounce the rumor publicly. It might be good for Arlene's ego.

"What are you doing?" Judith asked, aware of the obvious.

Arlene bristled with the exercise of a duty well discharged. "If old Eddie's gone off on a toot, somebody has to put in those bedding plants before they wilt. Honestly, some people are completely unreliable." Her blue eyes fixed Judith with a sudden flash of fear. "Do you think he's dead?"

"I don't know." Judith and Arlene exchanged appalled glances. "This is getting to be a scary place."

Arlene shuddered. "It's awful. I've been looking over my shoulder the whole time I worked. If anybody had come near me, I'd have whacked them with this." She swung the spade in one hand, leaving no doubt as to her lethal intentions.

"Say, Arlene," said Judith as a van bearing the inscription Lenny's Locks pulled into the parking lot, "did the Duffys ever get any of their loot back?"

"No, not a single thing." Arlene's face took on a tragic expression. "I think that's what drove poor Kate to take her life. She missed her pearls."

"That seems a little extreme to me," remarked Judith. It also seemed odd that though marked, none of the Duffys' stolen goods had turned up in five days.

The locksmith was getting out of the van. Arlene turned to greet him. Clearly, they were old acquaintances from Arlene's previous lapses in locking herself out of the house, the car, and everything but her local polling place. "Hi, Lenny, Quinn McCaffrey asked me to show you the door. This way." Still armed with her trowel and spade, Arlene led the locksmith out of the parking lot toward the main entrance to the school.

Transfixed, Judith stood alone next to her car for a few moments. One of the elusive puzzle pieces had just fallen into place: Only the principal and the pastor had keys to the school. Quinn McCaffrey had lost his, or so he thought. Father Hoyle was out of town. Presumably, so were his keys.

Judith had a feeling that Quinn McCaffrey was mistaken. She had to hurry home and call Joe. She also had to ask Quinn a vital question. And Eve Kramer, too.

Joe wasn't in. He was testifying at a hearing involving one of his subordinates who had been accused of malfeasance. Woody was at the hearing as well, the bloodless voice informed Judith. They would probably be gone all morning.

The call to Eve also proved fruitless. One of her children answered the phone at the shop and told Judith that Mrs. Kramer was at the dentist's. Quinn McCaffrey's wife said that her husband had taken their kids to the aquarium. Even Renie wasn't home.

Frustrated, Judith hurled herself into the running of Hillside Manor. She had a pair of retired schoolteachers arriving for the night from Idaho. On Friday and Saturday, the B&B would be full with the Californians, newlyweds from across the state, and four bicyclists from British Columbia. Friday night, she had to provide a buffet supper for a group of realtors at a million-dollar condo over on the Bluff. On Saturday, she was set to cater one of the upcoming wedding receptions at the school hall. She hoped and prayed that the event would go more smoothly than the

Easter egg hunt. Life went on, however, she realized with
an unaccustomed sense of gloom. Some people got married, others were buried. It was all part of humanity's endless tapestry. A corpse could be hauled out of the nursery
one Saturday, and on the next, a bride would use the nursery to change into her going-away outfit. Tears of sorrow
and tears of joy looked much the same to the casual ob-
server.

After fixing Gertrude's lunch, Judith went to work on
the food for the realtors' buffet. The task would take most
of the afternoon, and if history repeated itself, would re-
quire at least one trip to Falstaff's to pick up something
she'd forgotten on her earlier forays. As she kneaded
dough and filled salad molds and stirred sauces, Judith
went over the murder case in her mind. Not one of the suspects who had been on hand at the school hall had an iron-
clad alibi. Any one of them could have slipped into the
nursery and killed Sandy. All of them had a motive, however obscure.

But not everyone had access to Eve's embroidery scis-
sors. In Judith's mind, there were only three people who
could have used those scissors—Eve, Kurt, and the killer.
Perhaps it was precipitous to rule out either of the
Kramers. Yet Judith's theories were growing more viable.
The puzzle was complete, except for one glaring gap. It
wasn't crucial, but for her logical mind, it was necessary.
Judith was almost certain she knew who had stabbed
Sandy, she was less sure how it had been accomplished,
but ever since she had spoken with Father Tim earlier in
the day, she was convinced of the motive. Strange, she
mused, whipping up a batch of sour cream frosting, that
human beings could be so different, but their emotions so
similar. In the case of Sandy's killer, Judith understood all
too well.

The teachers arrived, gray-haired and jolly, headed
eventually for the ocean. One was tall and stout, the other
small and spare. They were both classic examples of a
dying breed, the spinster schoolteacher who had given her

life to education. The world was not going to be the same without their dedication, thought Judith, and offered them an early glass of sherry.

By late afternoon, Gertrude was complaining about the weather feeling "too close," Sweetums dragged in a dead bird, the Californians brought back two bewildered young men in jogging suits, and Judith had to remind her guests that they had paid only for their own stay. Extras weren't included.

Joe had not called by suppertime. Judith stuffed Gertrude with baked beans and ham, along with some of the fruit salad she'd made for the buffet. "Don't forget my sandwich to take to Deb's tomorrow," Gertrude reminded Judith. "I'd like tongue."

Heading out across the Hill with three hampers of food, Judith felt her uneasiness grow. She had to talk with Joe. She wished she'd been able to get in touch with Quinn McCaffrey and Eve Kramer, but neither of them had returned her calls so far. Now she would be gone for at least three hours, possibly returning too late to contact anybody until morning.

By then, it might be too late. Judith turned the car toward the Promenade that faced the bay and ringed the Bluff. The old-fashioned globe streetlights on their granite pedestals were not yet turned on. Across the bay, the mountains were obscured by dull, gray clouds. The flowering plum trees that bordered the far side of the Promenade had lost their blossoms and were now filling out with deep red leaves. Somehow, they looked somber against the evening sky, with no wind to give them life. Judith signaled to go right, heading up a side street where the dazzling glass and concrete four-story condominium rose haughtily atop the Bluff.

A million bucks, mused Judith. It was a lot of money to pay for a view, no matter how spectacular. Was it, she wondered, enough to kill for?

Judith thought not. Despite what Joe had said, money wasn't the only eternal motive.

SEVENTEEN

THE BUFFET SUPPER had not gone well. Perhaps it was the weather, oppressive and unnatural. Perhaps it was the makeup of the gathering, a highly competitive, overly energetic, relentlessly optimistic group. Perhaps it was Judith herself, whose distraction with the murder case caused her to forget the teriyaki chicken wings, drop the Viennese torte, and leave a spoon in one of the molded salads. Although the event's organizer graciously told her everything had been wonderful, Judith knew better. She had driven home in an utter funk, and was cheered only slightly by the fact that all her phone calls had been returned, including the one to Renie.

But Joe was not at home or at work when she rang him back. Since it was going on ten p.m., Judith fretted. Fifteen minutes later, she recalled that he and Woody and a couple of other police officers were going to the baseball game. Judith was relieved.

Eve, thankfully, was in. Judith asked after Eddie, who, Eve replied plaintively, had not yet been found.

Judith then asked Eve another, seemingly less painful, question. The answer satisfied Judith.

Quinn McCaffrey sounded sleepy, as if his vacation had been undone by the trek to the aquarium with his children. Again, Judith's inquiry was simple. Quinn's reply confirmed her suspicions. With a sense of growing triumph, Judith called Renie.

Bill, who hated the telephone almost as much as Gertrude did, answered. His wife, he reported in an aggrieved voice, was out at some half-baked dinner meeting for half-witted graphic designers who didn't know enough to stay home where they belonged. He was on his way to bed, which, his tone implied, was where any sensible person ought to be at such a late hour.

Judith had to agree. Taking a chance that the game had been a short pitcher's duel, she tried Joe's number again, but had no luck. Worn out by her exertions, she went to sleep with the light still on.

Joe called while Judith was cleaning up from breakfast. Not wanting to be overheard, Judith said she'd call him right back from the private phone on the third floor. When she'd finished her recital, there was a long pause before Joe spoke.

"That's pretty shrewd guesswork, Jude-girl," he finally allowed. "But it's all circumstantial. And you still haven't answered one of your own questions."

Judith gave the phone an impatient shake. "That's immaterial at this point. The important thing is you have to make an arrest. *Now.*"

"I can't." Joe's voice conveyed helplessness. "Be reasonable. I need real evidence."

"Okay." Judith took a deep breath. "Get a search warrant."

"For what?"

Judith told him. Joe balked. "It's outside my jurisdiction. They'll think I'm nuts."

But Judith was adamant. "Not when they find Eddie La

Plante's body, they won't. Just do it." She hung up the phone with a bang.

Convinced that Joe would follow through no matter how much he protested, Judith went about her business for the rest of the morning. Phyliss Rackley showed up with various gastric complaints and a new hymn.

"It's an inspiring piece," Phyliss enthused, rattling the Xeroxed sheet music at Judith. "Want to hear it? It's called 'As the Deer Longs.' "

"I've heard it," Judith replied, trying to lure Phyliss away from the antique rosewood spinet at the far corner of the living room.

"You couldn't have," insisted Phyliss. "It's all original. Pastor Polhamus wrote it himself. Listen to these notes of praise, you'll be uplifted. You could use it. Frankly, you're looking kind of peaky."

As a concession to domestic tranquility, Judith allowed Phyliss to advance on the piano. Squatting on the stool, with her sausage curls bouncing, she began to play and sing:

> *As the deer longs for the harvest stores,*
> *and the tortoise crawls along on all fours . . .*

"Somebody kill that cat!" yelled Gertrude from the dining room. "He's howling like a demon!"

"Mother!" Judith tried to shush Gertrude.

"Well, now!" Gertrude was smirking as she stumped into the living room on her walker. "It's Phyliss, pitching a fit. Why don't we shoot her and put her out of her misery?"

Oblivious to Gertrude's gibes, Phyliss was already into the third verse. Judith waited as patiently as possible, then rifled through a stack of music books atop the piano.

"Isn't that something?" asked a blissful Phyliss when she'd finally wound down.

"It sure is," responded Judith. "But I like this version better. Here," she said, thrusting a yellowed hymnal at her cleaning woman. "That passage has been used by several different composers. This one was done by Sister Mari-anne Misetich in 1973. It's a Roman Catholic hymn."

Phyliss blanched as she squinted at the open music book. "No! It's a trick! What kind of popery is this?"

"*Poopery,* the way you sing it," cackled Gertrude. "Wise up, Rackley, the next thing you know you'll be wearing a St. Christopher medal around that goiter of yours."

Judith wasn't in the mood for the usual quarrel between her mother and Phyliss. Nor did she have time for it, since she was due to drive Gertrude to Aunt Deb's for the Fri-day bridge session. "It doesn't matter, Phyliss," Judith soothed. "Pastor Polhamus may have done a new arrange-ment. Maybe you didn't hear him quite right."

Phyliss was looking thoughtful as well as deflated. "Maybe. My ears plug up something fierce with all this spring pollen." She was still staring at the book. "At least he doesn't have us singing mumbo-jumbo like this foreign stuff on the opposite page. What's that anyway, an incan-tation?"

Judith glanced at the hymnal. "No, it's just a Latin translation, the way we used to sing it. See, here's the new version, 'Queen of Heaven, Ocean Star'."

"It was better in Latin," grumbled Gertrude. "You didn't have to know what it meant. All you had to do was sing the blasted thing."

Judith was now staring at the music book as intently as Phyliss had done. The English and Latin words leaped out at her:

> *Mother of Christ, Star of the Sea,*
> *Pray for the wanderer, pray for me . . .*
> *Mater Christi, Stella Maris . . .*

"Good grief!" Judith gasped, "Emily was right! Stella Maris has been under our noses all along! It's not a per-son, it's the Latin name for Star of the Sea!"

Gertrude's beady eyes glittered at her daughter. "Of course it is, you lamebrain. Why didn't you ask me? Some of us still think the old ways were best."

Judith gave her mother a shaky smile. "So," she said in a breathless voice, "did Emily."

After completing the arduous task of getting Gertrude, tongue sandwich, walker, and all, up to Aunt Deb's apartment, Judith headed for church. With Eddie still missing, and no new janitor on the scene, she would have to set up for the reception herself. It would be better to complete that job now and save the morning for preparing the food. Judith reasoned that if she weren't so rushed, she might avoid leaving various cooking utensils in the refreshments.

Her mission didn't take very long, requiring only a half-dozen tables and twice as many chairs for servers and pourers. The Altar Society would provide the reception decorations, assuming they could function without their laid-up president. Judith took one last look around the church hall. It seemed so benign, with its colorful banners and velvet stage curtains and racks of folding chairs. Come Monday, it would be filled again with lively, raucous students, easing the horror of last week with youthful innocence or childish heartlessness, depending on one's point of view.

Giving herself a good shake, Judith headed for the parking lot. A faint breeze stirred the shrubbery and nudged at the gray clouds overhead. Judith was relieved. She hated April's darker moods.

A Nottingham's truck was pulling away, apparently having completed the job of decorating the church for the first of the three weekend weddings. A scattering of white petals was left in a trail behind the truck as evidence of the delivery.

Halfway to her car, Judith came to a dead halt. The petals were evidence of something else, she realized—the missing piece she hadn't been able to find until now. Everything fit. A bit frantically, she wondered if Joe had carried out her instructions. Shifting her weight from one foot to another, she contemplated calling him from the rectory. But Father Tim's car was gone, and Mrs. Katzenheimer hadn't been around when Judith had arrived. She would have to call Joe from home. He would laugh his head off when she told him about Stella Maris. How like that old traditionalist, Emily Tresvant, to revert to the Latin. She must be laughing somewhere, pleased with her little joke on contemporary Catholics. Kurt Kramer had known, Judith was sure of that now. He, too, was an arch-conservative in many ways, and his snickers of the previous day indicated he knew the truth about Stella Maris. But it was Emily who had had the last laugh.

Belatedly, it occurred to Judith that Emily Tresvant was the forgotten soul in all the events that had transpired over the past week. It was Emily, after all, whose death had triggered so much mystery, confusion, and speculation. Judith decided to slip into church and offer a prayer for the old girl's soul.

During the day, only the south entrance was kept unlocked. Security was a problem in any urban parish, even without murderers lurking in the nursery. Judith crossed herself, went through the vestibule, and entered the church.

In the wan April light, the masses of flowers in the sanctuary looked subdued, as if they were waiting for the Wedding March as their cue to burst into dazzling color. Judith admired the freesia, iris, tulips, and narcissus with their background of bridal wreath. The stately Easter lilies had already been shunted off to the side altars. Kneeling at the communion rail, Judith wondered if someday soon she and Joe would be joined in Holy Matrimony in this very church. The thought sent a shiver down her spine.

So did the sound which emanated from the other side of the altar. Judith hadn't seen anyone in the church when she had entered, but the enormous floral arrangements blocked her view of the north transept. Briefly, she attempted to pray, asking for the repose of Emily Tresvant's soul. She had gotten halfway through her second Hail Mary when she heard another noise, this time of soft footsteps on the carpeted floor. Out of the corner of her eye, Judith tried to glimpse her co-worshipper. She could see nothing but a dark figure, partially obscured by a spray of lilacs.

Judith rattled off another *Ave* in her head, anxious to be gone. The other person's presence made her nervous, though she wasn't sure why.

Before she could get to her feet, the figure approached with a quick, light tread. John Frizzell knelt next to her and offered a tentative greeting.

"I thought you were leaving for New York today," Judith whispered.

"I am. I've got a four-thirty flight," replied John, also in a whisper. "I came to see Father Mills about establishing a memorial to Sandy. But he's not in. I saw your car in the parking lot."

"Right," said Judith, managing to get up, though her legs were suddenly unsteady. "Good luck, John. I'll check on the house." She offered him an uncertain smile.

John was also standing again. "What do you think about the Star of the Sea altar?" He'd stopped whispering, but his voice was very soft. He gestured to the other side of the sanctuary where he'd apparently been praying. "I know of a seventeenth-century Italian Madonna at a shop where I worked in New York. I'd like to donate it in Sandy's name to replace the present statue. It's a bit chipped, you know."

"It sounds lovely," Judith said. "I'm sure the parish would be grateful." The statement wasn't entirely convincing, for Judith wasn't sure she believed it herself.

John put a hand on Judith's arm. "Here, take a look. The Madonna I have in mind is taller by at least four inches. See what you think about the proportion. They might have to replace the velvet hanging behind it, get a longer one."

Reluctantly, Judith let John guide her over to the side altar with its representation of a blue-and-white-clad Blessed Virgin with stars in her halo and ocean waves at her feet. "Eve could help choose something appropriate," Judith remarked. "She has excellent taste."

"She has a big mouth," said John, so softly that Judith almost didn't catch the words. He'd stepped to one side, and was reaching down to pick up an object from the floor between the small altar and the entrance to the sacristy. Judith's eyes widened as she saw the shovel Arlene had been wielding the previous morning. John's refined features were strangely twisted, all semblance of constraint evaporated. "Did Eve tell you about Eddie?" he demanded, his voice now rising. "She didn't tell *me*. She even refused to admit we were related because she wanted Eddie kept such a deep, dark secret!"

"Hey, John, she gave you a job," Judith asserted, wondering how fast she could run on her shaky legs. "She's helped support Eddie for some time. If she'd told people about Eddie, Emily would have been outraged. She despised him, she would have raised an awful ruckus. Eve's done her best. What more can you expect of a half-sister?"

John was advancing with the shovel in his hands, carrying it like a Highland warrior wielding a claymore. "It's not what I expect from her, but what she expected from me! I was glad for the job at the time, but I wasn't about to let her move into my personal life. She and that eagle-eyed husband of hers might have figured out the truth about Sandy."

Judith tried to keep calm, but it was no mean feat, with John's breathing growing more irregular and his entire body taut with strained nerves. "Okay, it seems as if it served both your purposes to keep your family ties a secret. That was fair enough. So what more did you want from Eve?"

"I didn't want her at all," John said in a sullen voice. "She wanted me to take on Eddie's care, just because I came into money! But she wouldn't even tell me who he was until I inherited! Then she wanted Kurt's share, out of the old will. She's a bitch!"

Judith made a faint gesture with one hand as she tried to backpedal toward the main altar. The wedding flowers' heady scent reached her nose, an oddly discordant sensation. John and Sandy had made a mockery of marriage, all for the sake of a fortune. Sandy would never benefit, and John's crimes had repealed his rights. Judith's frenzied brain tried to compose a coherent response. "Eve's waspish, I'll grant you that. I tell you what, let's drive over and talk to her. Maybe the two of you need an intermediary, okay?"

John's thin face split into a rictuslike grin. "I intend to give her what she needs." He gave the spade a lethal swing, narrowly missing the statue of Our Lady behind him. "And you, as well, for you infernal meddling!" He came at Judith, still grinning. She let out a little squeal of fear, then whirled around and ran toward the entrance to the south vestibule. But John was too quick for her, hurtling over a row of pews and beating her to the door. The grin was gone as he stood before Judith, barring her way.

"The police came this morning," he said, his voice once again soft. "They asked a lot of questions. There were only two people who could have seen those cartons in the hallway—you and your cousin. Neither of you were home. I came up here and noticed your car. You weren't in the hall, so you had to be in church. Which one of you told that Irishman about the boxes?"

"Well," said Judith, trying to keep calm and play for time, which was her only possible ally, "Kate Duffy said you didn't bring much out West with you, so I couldn't imagine what you were sending back. Unless," she added pointedly, "it was the Duffys' stolen goods. Nobody would look for them in New York. What was it you really wanted, Mark's camcorder?"

John's face fell. "Yes. But there was nothing of interest on the tape. Just a bunch of silly kids chasing eggs."

"But Eddie saw you, right?" Judith was having trouble staying on her feet. She desperately wanted to collapse into the nearest pew. "When? While you were using the key you stole from Quinn McCaffrey to get into the entrance of the school by the dumpster?"

John's eyes flickered, though whether from astonishment or anger, Judith couldn't tell. "Yes," he said on a hostile note. "I'd taken the key when I went to see him last Friday about a donation to the school."

"And you took Eve's scissors when you went to pick up your final paycheck from her at home last Saturday. Why pick on Eve, John? Because she wanted your help with Eddie?"

"Because she *demanded* it," John replied, a nerve twitching by his eye. "She was green with envy because I ended up with all the money. But she and Kurt didn't deserve a dime. The bitch was even serious about trying to break the will!" John's thin lips quivered with indignation. "Kurt would rather have seen the parish get all the money instead of me!"

"So you parked your car across the street and sneaked into the school hall," said Judith, wondering wildly who might be due to show up in the church. The organist, perhaps, or someone from the Altar Society. "I noticed the petals on your Peugeot when I saw it parked in the lot. It didn't dawn on me until just now that they wouldn't be there unless you'd parked somewhere else first—and you had, across the street and down the block under those plum trees. Nobody left working in the school hall could see you from there. Sandy was already dead when I talked to you." Judith gulped at the horror that had taken place while she and the others had gone about their innocent, ordinary business. "That was the part I couldn't figure out—where the car had been before you pulled into the lot in plain sight of Father Hoyle. Then you must have gone into the men's room to wait. You found Wilbur's rabbit suit and put it on. That must have come as a pleasant surprise."

A faint smile touched John's mouth. "It did. It was perfect. Then you saw me in the rabbit suit, and from the start, I was worried. You weren't as big a fool as most of them. But nothing happened, and I assumed I'd fooled you, too. And what a nice touch it was to implicate that pompous little ass, Wilbur Paine! He thought he was going to be a big shot, playing executor of Emily's estate! I fixed him—and that fat old witch, Norma, too."

"You fixed a lot of people, John," said Judith mildly. "Including Eddie. Your father."

John's sallow skin turned even more pale. "That was an accident," he murmured. "He came to see me and insisted I give him money, too! We quarreled. He still fancied himself a macho man." John snorted with contempt. "I defended myself. Unfortunately, he struck his head on the kitchen counter. He was dead before he hit the floor."

"Yes," Judith said softly. "I suspect he came to your house while you were talking to me on the phone the other night." She saw the confirmation in the set of John's jaw. "So you packaged him up and shipped him to New York along with the Duffys' belongings." Sadly, Judith shook her head. "You caused your own father's death—and murdered the one person you loved. Why, John?" Judith knew she was on dangerous ground, but her prospects were looking grimmer by the minute anyway. She could only stall John for so long.

His haunted brown eyes had a hypnotic quality that Judith had to force herself to shake off. "Why?" John echoed. "You're so smart, why do you think?"

Judith's shoulders slumped. "Okay, I'll tell you why. Everybody thought Sandy's murder had something to do with the money. I don't think so. I figure it was an even more basic emotion than greed. You were jealous. Sandy was falling in love with Tim Mills."

John's head jerked up, and for one hopeful second, Judith thought his grip on the shovel had loosened. But his fingers tightened around the stout wooden handle, the knuckles as white as his face. "That's a lie," he breathed. "Sandy *didn't* love Tim Mills. Sandy only pretended to be attracted to that young priest because he knew it would drive me wild! He thought if I was jealous, I wouldn't leave him and take off with all the money. He *used* Tim Mills, he toyed with my feelings! Imagine! After all these years!" John looked genuinely shocked.

"But would you have left Sandy now that you were rich?" Judith asked, her tongue feeling like lead.

John's eyes darted away, then back to Judith. "I . . . No, no, I wouldn't have. But sometimes, I said things . . . It was just lately." He swallowed hard, his Adam's apple bobbing above his shirt collar. "You straight people probably don't believe we can have mid-life crises, too."

"Oh, yes, I do," Judith said faintly. "That's the whole heart of the matter, I'd guess. I've been jealous in my time, too." *I'd like to kill Herself.* Judith had thought as much many times over the years. The difference was, if put to the test, she wouldn't have done it. But John Frizzell hadn't possessed Judith's moral principles. "Jealousy is a powerful, consuming emotion. There couldn't be any other motive where Sandy was concerned. You two had been together for years. In your mind, you *were* a family man—Sandy was your family, your whole life. And then he seemed to be straying, drawn to a younger man. You couldn't stand the idea of losing him. Even the money didn't seem so important. You're a collector, John. You saw only one way to keep Sandy yours for all time. And that was to kill him." Judith's mouth had gone completely dry, and her head fell toward her breast. Human feelings were so primitive, so fragile. Sexual persuasion was of no importance when it came to matters of the heart. All people really were created equal.

Tears glinted in John's eyes. "For the last two weeks, all Sandy could talk about was that young priest. He didn't even seem to care that it devastated me. He let on that he was besotted. It wasn't like him. In all the years we'd been together, I'd never known him to look at another man."

Judith tried to gauge how far John's defenses had fallen. He was still barring the door and gripping the shovel, but his concentration was elsewhere. She took a desperate gamble:

"What irony!" she exclaimed. "It was such a useless killing! Sandy would never have left you, even if Tim had been willing, which I'm sure he wasn't. A celibate is most certainly not a homosexual, John. You know that."

John's eyes, dulled with pain, stared at Judith. "You can't be sure. Nobody ever can be. And you didn't know Sandy."

"But I know Tim Mills," said Judith in a quiet voice. "I also know that if Sandy had been attracted to Tim, it couldn't have led to sex. Sandy may not have realized that, but eventually he would have had to. I don't doubt that Tim stirred great emotions in Sandy." Judith licked at her dry lips. "But those feelings were paternal. Sandy was Tim's father."

If Judith had hoped to break John with her revelation, she was mistaken. Although he stood as if paralyzed for a long moment, his subsequent reaction was not passive, but violent. John swung the spade again, slashing the air with a sharp sound that stung Judith's ears.

"No! No! No! You're lying!" He advanced on Judith, breathing heavily, with beads of perspiration on his forehead and upper lip. "For that, you die!" He lifted the shovel just as Judith ducked. The shovel glanced off the pew, but John struck again. Judith screamed. She was trapped between the pews. Her foot caught on the kneeler, sending her tumbling onto her knees. John lifted the shovel once more. Judith closed her eyes tight and tried to pray.

The door to the vestibule opened. Judith heard it, rather than saw it, and held her breath. An arm lashed out, connecting with John Frizzell's head. He crumpled like a broken doll, and thudded to the floor. Judith dared to open her eyes, but slowly.

"So that's where my shovel went," said Arlene Rankers, dusting off her trowel. "Why can't people leave things alone?"

EIGHTEEN

JUDITH AND ARLENE were sitting in the rectory parlor with Joe Flynn and Woody Price. The women were imbibing freely from Father Hoyle's best bottle of scotch, and the policemen were shuffling a lot of papers. Pope Urban IV was curled up on his favorite pillow next to a small statue of St. Francis of Assisi. The cat looked as if he were contemplating making a meal out of the plaster birds St. Francis was holding.

"Exactly how much did you hear?" Joe asked Arlene, not without a glint of admiration.

"Enough," said Arlene, now faintly dazed in the wake of the afternoon's drama. John had been knocked unconscious by her blow with the trowel. Judith had run out of the church to get help, luckily finding Father Tim pulling up in his car. After unlocking the rectory, he had gone to Arlene's aid to keep John Frizzell secure. Judith had called the police, who had sent a patrol car within three minutes. To everyone's relief, John had submitted to his arrest without a struggle. Joe and

241

Woody, trying to keep their astonishment to themselves, had arrived after John had been handcuffed.

"I came along just when John was ranting about Sandy's infatuation with poor Father Tim," recalled Arlene, with a sad shake of her head. "I got so interested, I decided not to intrude. I mean, I felt like an eavesdropper. That is, I hated to interrupt. I'm not the sort to butt in, but I couldn't very well leave." Confusing herself with her own contradictions for once, Arlene wiggled in the armchair. "Then it dawned on me that John must have killed Sandy. And Judith must be in trouble. So I whacked him." She shrugged. "Will he be all right?"

Joe was at his most bemused. "He'll have a hell of a headache for a while, but where he's going, he won't need to think a lot. If I were him, I wouldn't want to."

Judith was eyeing Arlene with gratitude. "I'll never be able to thank you enough. You saved my life."

Arlene looked unaffected. "I've always felt that a good sock in the head gets most people's attention. It's the least I could do." Her expression softened slightly. "After all, you *are* my favorite neighbor."

"And vice versa," murmured Judith. "Even if *you* are a hussy."

"Huh?" Arlene's blue eyes widened over the rim of her glass.

Judith leaned back in the chair and sighed deeply. "Never mind. I'll save that for later. Like the next time you get a bad perm. Okay?"

Somehow, Arlene kept a curb on her usually rampant curiosity. It was, after all, not a typical day. She turned to Woody. "Where's my shovel?"

Woody Price wore his customary stoic expression. "I'm afraid we'll have to impound it as evidence, Mrs. Rankers. John Frizzell did try to kill Mrs. McMonigle with it."

"What!" Arlene sprang out of the armchair, almost spilling her scotch. "Now just a minute, young man! Isn't it enough that I worked my tail off to get in those bedding plants for the church? How do you expect me to plant my own annuals without that shovel?"

Woody's features remained unchanged. "I don't think that's a serious problem, Mrs. Rankers. You seem to do as well with a trowel as most people do with a shovel. Just ask John Frizzell."

At the Manhattan Grill, the lights were low and the steaks were rare, just as Joe had promised. Judith, however, ordered the barbecued ribs. It was the first day of May, and she was wearing green silk and an anxious expression. She had not had the time or the inclination to get a permanent as she'd originally planned. The sleeker look became her, she'd decided, almost as much as did the company of Joe Flynn.

"You are semi-amazing," Joe said over his thick New York cut. "The Port Authority cops at Kennedy couldn't believe it when they opened that crate and poor old Eddie fell out."

"He had to be somewhere," Judith remarked. "I think John was really conscience-stricken about killing Eddie. He not only wanted to get rid of the body, but he probably intended to give the old guy a decent burial. You know, to make amends for not having taken care of him in life."

Joe looked skeptical as the waiter refilled their glasses with a vintage cabernet sauvignon. "You give people too much credit," he said, not without a hint of admiration. "He probably just figured it was easier and safer than trying to get Eddie out of the house and into the bay."

"Well maybe," Judith allowed. Now that more than a week had passed since her brush with death and John Frizzell's arrest, Judith's interest in the case had diminished. She was all but foaming at the mouth to hear Joe's report on the annulment proceedings.

"By the way," said Joe with a twinkle, "don't tell Renie, but Kate was indeed Kitty Cabrini. According to Les, who swears he saw *Bottoms Up* four times at the old Green

Parrot Theatre, she played a nurse who donates her body to medical science."

Judith rolled her eyes. "Great. You're right, I won't tell Renie. There's no need for anyone to know. I also hear the Borings are going to stick with Wilbur Paine's firm. For now."

"And the Duffys got all their stuff back," remarked Joe, polishing off the last bite of steak. "As for Our Lady, Star of the Sea, your parish may end up with Emily's vast fortune after all."

Judith wiped barbecue sauce off her fingers with a linen napkin. The restaurant was busy, its darkly polished booths full of contented diners. Brass fixtures gleamed everywhere, with oak-framed mirrors giving the illusion of space without taking away the sense of intimacy. "But that will happen only if John says so, right?" queried Judith.

Joe sipped at his wine. "I suppose. But he's been talking to Father Hoyle. Whether or not John gets the death penalty—and I doubt that he will, given this state's record on such crimes—he seems genuinely repentant. Hoyle figures he'll donate the bulk of his fortune to the church to make amends. I doubt that the Kramers would fight it now. It was, after all, what Emily wanted."

Judith allowed the waiter to offer her a warm, damp towel and a finger bowl. "Emily was the sort who always got what she wanted. Except for my mother." Judith laughed softly to herself at the recollection of Gertrude and Emily going head to head so many years ago.

"What do you mean?" asked Joe, lighting up a cigar.

"Oh—it had to do with my wedding to Dan. And Lucille's funeral." Judith shrugged. "Mother won."

"Did she now?" Joe sat back in the booth and eyed Judith curiously. "She doesn't always, though. Or at least she shouldn't."

Judith put the last rib back on her plate. "What do you mean?"

"I mean," said Joe, quite seriously, "that your mother would rather shoot herself in the foot than let me marry you. But that's not her choice. What do you say, Jude-girl?"

"I don't understand what you're talking about. You haven't even told me what's going on with the annulment." Judith sounded slightly cross.

Exhaling on his cigar, Joe grimaced. "There is no annulment," he said flatly.

Judith's heart skipped a beat. "What?" The word came out in a gasp. "You mean it's been . . . denied?"

Slowly, Joe shook his head. "There never was one. I didn't need it. Herself had been married the first time in the Church, then by Protestant ministers the second and third times around. And she and I went to a justice of the peace in Vegas. Our marriage was never valid to begin with. I found that out over a year ago." The green eyes slid away from Judith's face, his expression suddenly hidden in another cloud of cigar smoke.

Judith stared at him, her mouth gaping. "You mean . . . you knew all along . . ." She virtually pounced on the small table. "But why? Why didn't you tell me, Joe?"

The smoke dissipated. Joe's round face was engagingly boyish. "Because you weren't ready to hear it. Maybe you still aren't." He gave a little self-deprecating laugh that was a far cry from his usual sanguine style. "Maybe I'm just your favorite fantasy."

For a long time, Judith stared at him. For over twenty years, she had kept the memory of his love alive. It had sustained her during her marriage to Dan. No matter how miserable her husband had made her, she could always remind herself that no woman who had been loved by Joe Flynn was a total washout. "I don't think it's all been fantasizing," she said at last, wringing the towel with her agitated hands. "But I'm not sure I want to get married again. It wasn't my most cherished experience."

Soberly, Joe considered her words. "Or mine, if it comes to that." He put the cigar down in the glass ashtray, his forehead creasing. "Okay, I too can wait. I still have a civil divorce decree to pick up. Meanwhile," he added

with the gold flecks glittering in the green eyes and turning Judith's will to mush, "how about a lot of one-night
stands, starting about now?"

Judith lowered her gaze to the towel which she still held
in her nervous fingers. "I don't know . . . How would I explain it to Mother . . . What would Mike think . . . I ought
to ask Renie . . ." Her head jerked up. "Joe, are you sure
about this marriage thing? Are you really free in the eyes
of the Church? Who have you consulted about it?"

Joe put down his cigar and reached across the table to
take Judith's chin in his hand. "Believe me, it's true about
the annulment regulations. I got it from your very own
pastor. It's strictly according to Hoyle. Want to come home
with me or challenge Gertrude to a hot game of cribbage?"

Judith gazed into the depths of Joe Flynn's green Irish
eyes. In her mind, fragments of memory joined glimpses
of what was yet to come. *If* she wanted it enough.

With a confident smile, Judith threw in the towel.

Murder Is on the Menu at the Hillside Manor Inn

Bed-and-Breakfast Mysteries by
MARY DAHEIM
featuring Judith McMonigle

JUST DESSERTS
76295-1/ $3.50 US/ $4.25 Can

FOWL PREY
76296-X/ 4.99 US/ $5.99 Can

HOLY TERRORS
76297-8/ $4.99 US/ $5.99 Can

DUNE TO DEATH
76933-6/ $4.99 US/ $5.99 Can

Buy these books at your local bookstore or use this coupon for ordering:

Mail to: Avon Books, Dept BP, Box 767, Rte 2, Dresden, TN 38225   C
Please send me the book(s) I have checked above.
❏ My check or money order— no cash or CODs please— for $_____is enclosed
(please add $1.50 to cover postage and handling for each book ordered— Canadian residents
add 7% GST).
❏ Charge my VISA/MC Acct#_____Exp Date_____
Minimum credit card order is two books or $6.00 (please add postage and handling charge of
$1.50 per book — Canadian residents add 7% GST). For faster service. call
1-800-762-0779. Residents of Tennessee. please call 1-800-633-1607 Prices and numbers
are subject to change without notice. Please allow six to eight weeks for delivery.

Name_____
Address_____
City_____State/Zip_____
Telephone No._____   DAH 0593

TAUT, SUSPENSEFUL THRILLERS BY EDGAR AWARD-WINNING AUTHOR

PATRICIA D. CORNWELL

Featuring Kay Scarpetta, M.E.

BODY OF EVIDENCE

71701-8/$5.99 US/$6.99 Can

"Nerve jangling...verve and brilliance...high drama...
Ms. Cornwell fabricates intricate plots and paces the action
at an ankle-turning clip."
The New York Times Book Review

POSTMORTEM

71021-8/$5.99 US/$6.99 Can

"Taut, riveting—whatever your favorite strong adjective,
you'll use it about this book!"
Sara Paretsky

ALL THAT REMAINS

71833-2/$5.99 US/$6.99 Can

"Riveting...compelling...original..."
Cosmopolitan

Buy these books at your local bookstore or use this coupon for ordering:

Mail to: Avon Books. Dept BP. Box 767. Rte 2. Dresden. TN 38225   C
Please send me the book(s) I have checked above.
❏ My check or money order— no cash or CODs please— for $_____is enclosed
(please add $1.50 to cover postage and handling for each book ordered— Canadian residents
add 7°₀ GST).
❏ Charge my VISA/MC Acct#_____Exp Date_____
Minimum credit card order is two books or $6.00 (please add postage and handling charge of
$1.50 per book — Canadian residents add 7°₀ GST). For faster service, call
1-800-762-0779. Residents of Tennessee, please call 1-800-633-1607. Prices and numbers
are subject to change without notice. Please allow six to eight weeks for delivery.

Name_____
Address_____
City_____State/Zip_____
Telephone No._____   PDC 0793

Meet Peggy O'Neill
A Campus Cop With a Ph.D. in Murder

"A 'Must Read' for fans of Sue Grafton"
Alfred Hitchcock Mystery Magazine

Exciting Mysteries by M.D. Lake

AMENDS FOR MURDER 75865-2/$4.50 US/$5.50 Can
When a distinguished professor is found murdered, campus security officer Peggy O'Neill's investigation uncovers a murderous mix of faculty orgies, poetry readings, and some very devoted female teaching assistants.

COLD COMFORT 76032-0/$4.50 US/$5.50 Can
After he was jilted by Swedish sexpot Ann-Marie Ekdahl, computer whiz Mike Parrish's death was ruled a suicide by police. But campus cop Peggy O'Neill isn't so sure and launches her own investigation.

POISONED IVY 76573-X/$3.99 US/$4.99 Can

A GIFT FOR MURDER 76855-0/$4.50 US/$5.50 Can

And Coming Soon
MURDER BY MAIL 76856-9/$4.99 US/$5.99 Can

Buy these books at your local bookstore or use this coupon for ordering:

Mail to: Avon Books. Dept BP. Box 767, Rte 2. Dresden, TN 38225   C
Please send me the book(s) I have checked above.
❏ My check or money order— no cash or CODs please— for $_____is enclosed
(please add $1.50 to cover postage and handling for each book ordered— Canadian residents add 7% GST).
❏ Charge my VISA/MC Acct#_____Exp Date_____
Minimum credit card order is two books or $6.00 (please add postage and handling charge of $1.50 per book — Canadian residents add 7% GST). For faster service, call 1-800-762-0779. Residents of Tennessee, please call 1-800-633-1607. Prices and numbers are subject to change without notice. Please allow six to eight weeks for delivery.

Name_____
Address_____
City_____State/Zip_____
Telephone No._____

MDL 0993

FOLLOW IN THE FOOTSTEPS OF
DETECTIVE J.P. BEAUMONT
WITH FAST-PACED MYSTERIES
BY J.A. JANCE

UNTIL PROVEN GUILTY   89638-9/$4.99 US/$5.99 CAN

INJUSTICE FOR ALL   89641-9/$4.50 US/$5.50 CAN

TRIAL BY FURY   75138-0/$4.99 US/$5.99 CAN

TAKING THE FIFTH   75139-9/$4.99 US/$5.99 CAN

IMPROBABLE CAUSE   75412-6/$4.99 US/$5.99 CAN

A MORE PERFECT UNION   75413-4/$4.50 US/$5.50 CAN

DISMISSED WITH PREJUDICE

      75547-5/$4.99 US/$5.99 CAN

MINOR IN POSSESSION   75546-7/$4.99 US/$5.99 CAN

PAYMENT IN KIND   75836-9/$4.99 US/$5.99 CAN

WITHOUT DUE PROCESS   75837-7/$4.99 US/$5.99 CAN

And also by J.A. Jance

HOUR OF THE HUNTER   71107-9/$4.99 US/$5.99 CAN

DESERT HEAT   76545-4/$4.99 US/$5.99 CAN

Buy these books at your local bookstore or use this coupon for ordering.

Mail to Avon Books Dept BP Box 767 Rte 2 Dresden TN 38225   C
Please send me the book(s) I have checked above
❏ My check or money order— no cash or CODs please— for $_____ is enclosed
(please add $1 50 to cover postage and handling for each book ordered— Canadian residents
add 7°₀ GST)
❏ Charge my VISA MC Acct#_____Exp Date_____
Minimum credit card order is two books or $6 00 (please add postage and handling charge of
$1 50 per book — Canadian residents add 7°₀ GST)   For faster service call
1-800-762-0779   Residents of Tennessee please call 1-800-633-1607   Prices and numbers
are subject to change without notice   Please allow six to eight weeks for delivery

Name_____
Address_____
City_____State/Zip_____
Telephone No _____

                                        JAN 0993